The RANGELAND AVENGER

ALSO BY MAX BRAND

Trouble in Timberline
Three on the Trail
Rogue Mustang
Lawless Land
The Trail to San Triste
The Making of a Gunman
Thunder Moon Strikes
Thunder Moon's Challenge
Gunmen's Feud
Wild Freedom
The Man from the Wilderness
Six-Gun Country
Galloping Danger
Gunfighter's Return
Storm on the Range
Way of the Lawless
Rider of the High Hills
Man from Savage Creek
Shotgun Law
Gunman's Reckoning
Rawhide Justice
The Last Showdown
The Long, Long Trail
The Outlaw of Buffalo Flat
Frontier Feud
War Party
Drifter's Vengeance
Cheyenne Gold
Ambush at Torture Canyon
Trouble Kid
Thunder Moon

The RANGELAND AVENGER

Max Brand

DODD, MEAD & COMPANY
NEW YORK

Originally published in 1922 in *Western Story Magazine* under the title of THREE WHO PAID, written under the pseudonym of George Owen Baxter, and subsequently in book form under the title THE RANGELAND AVENGER in 1924.

Published by Dodd, Mead & Company, Inc.
79 Madison Avenue, New York, N.Y. 10016
Distributed in Canada by
McClelland and Stewart Limited, Toronto
Manufactured in the United States of America
First Edition

Library of Congress Cataloging in Publication Data

Brand, Max, 1892–1944.
The rangeland avenger.

(Silver Star western)
I. Title. II. Series.
PS3511.A87R26 1985 813′.52 84-24641
ISBN 0-396-08562-8

The RANGELAND AVENGER

1

Of the four men, Hal Sinclair was the vital spirit. In the actual labor of mining, the mighty arms and tireless back of Quade had been a treasure. For knowledge of camping, hunting, cooking, and all the lore of the trail, Lowrie stood as a valuable resource; and Sandersen was the dreamy, resolute spirit, who had hoped for gold in those mountains until he came to believe his hope. He had gathered these three stalwarts to help him to his purpose, and if he lived he would lead yet others to failure.

Hope never died in this tall, gaunt man, with a pale-blue eye the color of the horizon dusted with the first morning mist. He was the very spirit of lost causes, full of apprehensions, forebodings, superstitions. A hunch might make him journey five hundred miles; a snort of his horse could make him give up the trail and turn back.

But Hal Sinclair was the antidote for Sandersen. He was still a boy at thirty—big, handsome, thoughtless, with a heart as clean as new snow. His throat was so parched by that day's ride that he dared not open his lips to sing, as he usually did. He compromised by humming songs new and old, and when his companions cursed his noise, he contented himself with talking softly to his horse, amply rewarded when the pony occasionally lifted a tired ear to the familiar voice.

Failure and fear were the blight on the spirit of the rest. They had found no gold worth looking at twice, and, lingering too long in the search, they had rashly turned back on a shortcut across the desert. Two days before, the blow had fallen. They found Sawyer's water hole nearly dry, just a little pool in the center, with caked, dead mud all around it. They drained that water dry and struck on. Since then the water famine had gained a hold on them; another water hole had not a drop in it. Now they could only aim at the cool, blue mockery of the mountains before them, praying that the ponies would last to the foothills.

Still Hal Sinclair could sing softly to his horse and to himself; and, though his companions cursed his singing, they blessed him for it in their hearts. Otherwise the white, listening silence of the desert would have crushed them; otherwise the lure of the mountains would have maddened them and made them push on until the horses would have died within five miles of the labor; otherwise the pain in their slowly swelling throats would have taken their reason. For thirst in the desert carries the pangs of several deaths—death from fire, suffocation, and insanity.

No wonder the three scowled at Hal Sinclair when he drew his revolver.

"My horse is gun-shy," he said, "but I'll bet the rest of you I can drill a horn off that skull before you do."

Of course it was a foolish challenge. Lowrie was the gun expert of the party. Indeed he had reached that dangerous point of efficiency with firearms where a man is apt to reach for his gun to decide an argument. Now Lowrie followed the direction of Sinclair's gesture. It was the skull of a steer, with enormous branching horns. The rest of the skeleton was sinking into the sands.

"Don't talk fool talk," said Lowrie. "Save your wind and your ammunition. You may need 'em for yourself, son!"

That grim suggestion made Sandersen and Quade shudder. But a grin spread on the broad, ugly face of Lowrie, and Sinclair merely shrugged his shoulders.

"I'll try you for a dollar."

"Nope."

"Five dollars?"

"Nope."

"You're afraid to try, Lowrie!"

It was a smiling challenge, but Lowrie flushed. He had a childish pride in his skill with weapons.

"All right, kid. Get ready!"

He brought a Colt smoothly into his hand and balanced it dexterously, swinging it back and forth between his eyes and the target to make ready for a snap shot.

"Ready!" cried Hal Sinclair excitedly.

Lowrie's gun spoke first, and it was the only one that was fired, for Sinclair's horse was gun-shy indeed. At the explosion he pitched straight into the air with a squeal of mustang fright and came down bucking. The others forgot to look for the results of Lowrie's shot. They reined their horses away from the pitching broncho disgustedly. Sinclair was a fool to use up the last of his mustang's strength in this manner. But Hal Sinclair had forgotten the journey ahead. He was rioting in the new excitement cheering the broncho to new exertions. And it was in the midst of that flurry of action that the great blow fell. The horse stuck his right forefoot into a hole.

To the eyes of the others it seemed to happen slowly. The mustang was halted in the midst of a leap, tugged at a leg that seemed glued to the ground, and then buckled suddenly and collapsed on one side. They heard that awful, muffled sound of splintering bone and then the scream of the tortured horse.

But they gave no heed to that. Hal Sinclair in the fall had been pinned beneath his mount. The huge strength of Quade sufficed to budge the writhing mustang. Lowrie and Sandersen drew Sinclair's pinioned right leg clear and stretched him on the sand.

It was Lowrie who shot the horse.

"You've done a brown turn," said Sandersen fiercely to

the prostrate figure of Sinclair. "Four men and three hosses. A fine partner you are, Sinclair!"

"Shut up," said Hal. "Do something for that foot of mine."

Lowrie cut the boot away dexterously and turned out the foot. It was painfully twisted to one side and lay limp on the sand.

"Do something!" said Sinclair, groaning.

The three looked at him, at the dead horse, at the white-hot desert, at the distant, blue mountains.

"What the devil can we do? You've spoiled all our chances, Sinclair."

"Ride on then and forget me! But tie up that foot before you go. I can't stand it!"

Silently, with ugly looks, they obeyed. Secretly every one of the three was saying to himself that this folly of Sinclair's had ruined all their chances of getting free from the sands alive. They looked across at the skull of the steer. It was still there, very close. It seemed to have grown larger, with a horrible significance. And each instinctively put a man's skull beside it, bleached and white, with shadow eyes. Quade did the actual bandaging of Sinclair's foot, drawing tight above the ankle, so that some of the circulation was shut off; but it eased the pain, and now Sinclair sat up.

"I'm sorry," he said, "mighty sorry, boys!"

There was no answer. He saw by their lowered eyes that they were hating him. He felt it in the savage grip of their hands, as they lifted him and put him into Quade's saddle. Quade was the largest, and it was mutely accepted that he should be the first to walk, while Sinclair rode. It was accepted by all except Quade, that is to say. That big man strode beside his horse, lifting his eyes now and then to glare remorselessly at Sinclair.

It was bitter work walking through that sand. The heel crunched into it, throwing a strain heavily on the back of the thigh, and then the ball of the foot slipped back in the midst of a stride. Also the labor raised the temperature of the body incredibly. With no wind stirring it was suffocating.

And the day was barely beginning!

Barely two hours before the sun had been merely a red ball on the edge of the desert. Now it was low in the sky, but bitterly hot. And their mournful glances presaged the horror that was coming in the middle of the day.

Deadly silence fell on that group. They took their turns by the watch, half an hour at a time, walking and then changing horses, and, as each man took his turn on foot, he cast one long glance of hatred at Sinclair.

He was beginning to know them for the first time. They were chance acquaintances. The whole trip had been undertaken by him on the spur of a moment; and, as far as lay in his cheery, thoughtless nature, he had come to regret it. The work of the trail had taught him that he was mismated in this company, and the first stern test was stripping the masks from them. He saw three ugly natures, three small, cruel souls.

It came Sandersen's turn to walk.

"Maybe I could take a turn walking," suggested Sinclair.

It was the first time in his life that he had had to shift any burden onto the shoulders of another except his brother, and that was different. Ah, how different! He sent up one brief prayer for Riley Sinclair. There was a man who would have walked all day that his brother might ride, and at the end of the day that man of iron would be as fresh as those who had ridden. Moreover, there would have been no questions, no spite, but a free giving. Mutely he swore that he would hereafter judge all men by the stern and honorable spirit of Riley.

And then that sad offer: "Maybe I could take a turn walking, Sandersen. I could hold on to a stirrup and hop along some way!"

Lowrie and Quade sneered, and Sandersen retorted fiercely: "Shut up! You know it ain't possible, but I ought to call your bluff."

He had no answer, for it was not possible. The twisted foot was a steady torture.

In another half hour he asked for water, as they paused for Sandersen to mount, and Lowrie to take his turn on foot. Sandersen snatched the canteen which Quade reluctantly passed to the injured man.

"Look here!" said Sandersen. "We got to split up on this. You sit there and ride and take it easy. Me and the rest has to go through hell. You take some of the hell yourself. You ride, but we'll have the water, and they ain't much of it left at that!"

Sinclair glanced helplessly at the others. Their faces were set in stern agreement.

Slowly the sun crawled up to the center of the sky and stuck there for endless hours, it seemed, pouring down a fiercer heat. And the foothills still wavered in blue outlines that meant distance—terrible distance.

Out of the east came a cloud of dust. The restless eye of Sandersen saw it first, and a harsh shout of joy came from the others. Quade was walking. He lifted his arms to the cloud of dust as if it were a vision of mercy. To Hal Sinclair it seemed that cold water was already running over his tongue and over the hot torment of his foot. But, after that first cry of hoarse joy, a silence was on the others, and gradually he saw a shadow gather.

"It ain't wagons," said Lowrie bitterly at length. "And it ain't riders; it comes too fast for that. And it ain't the wind; it comes too slow. But it ain't men. You can lay to that!"

Still they hoped against hope until the growing cloud parted and lifted enough for them to see a band of wild horses sweeping along at a steady lope. They sighted the men and veered swiftly to the left. A moment later there was only a thin trail of flying dust before the four. Three pairs of eyes turned on Sinclair and silently cursed him as if this were his fault.

"Those horses are aiming at water," he said. "Can't we follow 'em?"

"They're aiming for a hole fifty miles away. No, we can't follow 'em!"

They started on again, and now, after that cruel moment of hope, it was redoubled labor. Quade was cursing thickly with every other step. When it came his turn to ride he drew Lowrie to one side, and they conversed long together, with side glances at Sinclair.

Vaguely he guessed the trend of their conversation, and vaguely he suspected their treacherous meanness. Yet he dared not speak, even had his pride permitted.

It was the same story over again when Lowrie walked. Quade rode aside with Sandersen, and again, with the wolfish side glances, they eyed the injured man, while they talked. At the next halt they faced him. Sandersen was the spokesman.

"We've about made up our minds, Hal," he said deliberately, "that you got to be dropped behind for a time. We're going on to find water. When we find it we'll come back and get you. Understand?"

Sinclair moistened his lips, but said nothing.

Then Sandersen's voice grew screechy with sudden passion. "Say, do you want three men to die for one? Besides, what good could we do?"

"You don't mean it," declared Sinclair. "Sandersen, you don't mean it! Not alone out here! You boys can't leave me out here stranded. Might as well shoot me!"

All were silent. Sandersen looked to Lowrie, and the latter stared at the sand. It was Quade who acted.

Stepping to the side of Sinclair he lifted him easily in his powerful arms and lowered him to the sands. "Now, keep your nerve," he advised. "We're coming back."

He stumbled a little over the words. "It's all of us or none of us," he said. "Come on, boys. *My* conscience is clear!"

They turned their horses hastily to the hills, and, when the voice of Sinclair rang after them, not one dared turn his head.

"Partners, for the sake of all the work we've done together—don't do this!"

In a shuddering unison they spurred their horses and raised the weary brutes into a gallop; the voice faded into a wail behind them. And still they did not look back.

For that matter they dared not look at one another, but pressed on, their eyes riveted to the hills. Once Lowrie turned his head to mark the position of the sun. Once Sandersen, in the grip of some passion of remorse or of fear of death, bowed his head with a strange moan. But, aside from that, there was no sound or sign between them until, hardly an hour and a half after leaving Sinclair, they found water.

At first they thought it was a mirage. They turned away from it by mutual assent. But the horses had scented drink, and they became unmanageable. Five minutes later the animals were up to their knees in the muddy water, and the men were floundering breast deep, drinking, drinking, drinking.

After that they sat about the brink staring at one another in a stunned fashion. There seemed no joy in that delivery, for some reason.

"I guess Sinclair will be a pretty happy gent when he sees us coming back," said Sandersen, smiling faintly.

There was no response from the others for a moment. Then they began to justify themselves hotly.

"It was your idea, Quade."

"Why, curse your soul, weren't you glad to take the idea? Are you going to blame it on to me?"

"What's the blame?" asked Lowrie. "Ain't we going to bring him water?"

"Suppose he ever tells we left him? We'd have to leave these parts pronto!"

"He'll never tell. We'll swear him."

"If he does talk, I'll stop him pretty sudden," said Lowrie, tapping his holster significantly.

"Will you? What if he puts that brother of his on your trail?"

Lowrie swallowed hard. "Well—" he began, but said no more.

They mounted in a new silence and took the back trail slowly. Not until the evening began to fall did they hurry, for fear the darkness would make them lose the position of their comrade. When they were quite near the place, the semidarkness had come, and Quade began to shout in his tremendous voice. Then they would listen, and sometimes they heard an echo, or a voice like an echo, always at a great distance.

"Maybe he's started crawling and gone the wrong way. He should have sat still," said Lowrie, "because—"

"Oh, Lord," broke in Sandersen, "I knew it! I been seeing it all the way!"

He pointed to a figure of a man lying on his back in the sand, with his arms thrown out crosswise. They dismounted and found Hal Sinclair dead and cold. Perhaps the insanity of thirst had taken him; perhaps he had figured it out methodically that it was better to end things before the madness came. There was a certain stern repose about his face that favored this supposition. He seemed much older. But, whatever the reason, Hal Sinclair had shot himself cleanly through the head.

"You see that face?" asked Lowrie with curious quiet. "Take a good look. You'll see it ag'in."

A superstitious horror seized on Sandersen. "What d'you mean, Lowrie? What d'you mean?"

"I mean this! The way he looks now he's a ringer for Riley Sinclair. And, you mark me, we're all going to see Riley Sinclair, face to face, before we die!"

"He'll never know," said Quade, the stolid. "Who knows except us? And will one of us ever talk?" He laughed at the idea.

"I dunno," whispered Sandersen. "I dunno, gents. But we done an awful thing, and we're going to pay—we're going to pay!"

2

Their trails divided after that. Sandersen and Quade started back for Sour Creek. At the parting of the ways Lowrie's last word was for Sandersen.

"You started this party, Sandersen. If they's any hell coming out of it, it'll fall chiefly on you. Remember, because I got one of your own hunches!"

After that Lowrie headed straight across the mountains, traveling as much by instinct as by landmarks. He was one of those men who are born to the trail. He stopped in at Four Pines, and there he told the story on which he and Sandersen and Quade had agreed. Four Pines would spread that tale by telegraph, and Riley Sinclair would be advised beforehand. Lowrie had no desire to tell the gunfighter in person of the passing of Hal Sinclair. Certainly he would not be the first man to tell the story.

He reached Colma late in the afternoon, and a group instantly formed around him on the veranda of the old hotel. Four Pines had indeed spread the story, and the crowd wanted verification. He replied as smoothly as he could. Hal Sinclair had broken his leg in a fall from his horse, and they had bound it up as well as they could. They had tied him on his horse, but he could not endure the pain of travel. They stopped, nearly dying from thirst.

Mortification set in. Hal Sinclair died in forty-eight hours after the halt.

Four Pines had accepted the tale. There had been more deadly stories than this connected with the desert. But Pop Hansen, the proprietor, drew Lowrie to one side.

"Keep out of Riley's way for a while. He's all het up. He was fond of Hal, you know, and he takes this bad. Got an ugly way of asking questions, and—"

"The truth is the truth," protested Lowrie. "Besides—"

"I know—I know. But jest make yourself scarce for a couple of days."

"I'll keep on going, Pop. Thanks!"

"Never mind, ain't no hurry. Riley's out of town and won't be back for a day or so. But, speaking personal, I'd rather step into a nest of rattlers than talk to Riley, the way he's feeling now."

Lowrie climbed slowly up the stairs to his room, thinking very hard. He knew the repute of Riley Sinclair, and he knew the man to be even worse than reputation, one of those stern souls who exact an eye for an eye—and even a little more.

Once in his room he threw himself on his bed. After all there was no need for a panic. No one would ever learn the truth. To make surety doubly sure he would start early in the dawn and strike out for far trails. The thought had hardly come to him when he dismissed it. A flight would call down suspicion on him, and Riley Sinclair would be the first to suspect. In that case distance would not save him, not from that hard and tireless rider.

To help compose his thoughts he went to the washstand and bathed his hot face. He was drying himself when there was a tap on the door.

"Can I come in?" asked a shrill voice.

He answered in the affirmative, and a youngster stepped into the room.

"You're Lowrie?"

"Yep."

"They's a gent downstairs wants you to come down and see him."

"Who is it?"

"I dunno. We just moved in from Conway. I can point him out to you on the street."

Lowrie followed the boy to the window, and there, surrounded by half a dozen serious-faced men, stood Riley Sinclair, tall, easy, formidable. The sight of Sinclair filled Lowrie with dismay. Pushing a silver coin into the hand of the boy, he said: "Tell him—tell him—I'm coming right down."

As soon as the boy disappeared, Lowrie ran to the window which opened on the side of the house. When he looked down his hope fled. At one time there had been a lean-to shed running along that side of the building. By the roof of it he could have got to the ground unseen. Now he remembered that it had been torn down the year before; there was a straight and perilous drop beneath the window. As for the stairs, they led almost to the front door of the building. Sinclair would be sure to see him if he went down there.

Of the purpose of the big man he had no doubt. His black guilt was so apparent to his own mind that it seemed impossible that the keen eyes of Sinclair had not looked into the story of Hal's broken leg and seen a lie. Besides, the invitation through a messenger seemed a hollow lure. Sinclair wished to fight him and kill him before witnesses who would attest that Lowrie had been the first to go for his gun.

Fight? Lowrie looked down at his hand and found that the very wrist was quivering. Even at his best he felt that he would have no chance. Once he had seen Sinclair in action in Lew Murphy's old saloon, had seen Red Jordan get the drop, and had watched Sinclair shoot his man deliberately through the shoulder. Red Jordan was a cripple for life.

Suppose he walked boldly down, told his story, and

trusted to the skill of his lie? No, he knew his color would pale if he faced Sinclair. Suppose he refused to fight? Better to die than be shamed in the mountain country.

He hurried to the window for another look into the street, and he found that Sinclair had disappeared. Lowrie's knees buckled under his weight. He went over to the bed, with short steps, like a drunken man, and lowered himself down on it.

Sinclair had gone into the hotel, and doubtless that meant that he had grown impatient. The fever to kill was burning in the big man. Then Lowrie heard a steady step come regularly up the stairs. They creaked under a heavy weight.

Lowrie drew his gun. It caught twice; finally he jerked it out in a frenzy. He would shoot when the door opened, without waiting, and then trust to luck to fight his way through the men below.

In the meantime the muzzle of the revolver wabbled crazily from side to side, up and down. He clutched the barrel with the other hand. And still the weapon shook.

Curling up his knee before his breast he ground down with both hands. That gave him more steadiness; but would not this contorted position destroy all chance of shooting accurately?

His own prophecy, made over the dead body of Hal Sinclair, that all three of them would see that face again, came back to him with a sense of fatality. Some forward-looking instinct, he assured himself, had given him that knowledge.

The step upon the stairs came up steadily. But the mind of Lowrie, between the steps, leaped hither and yon, a thousand miles and back. What if his nerve failed him at the last moment? What if he buckled and showed yellow and the shame of it followed him? Better a hundred times to die by his own hand.

Excitement, foreboding, the weariness of the long trail—all were working upon Lowrie.

Nearer drew the step. It seemed an hour since he had first heard it begin to climb the stairs. It sounded heavily on the floor outside his door. There was a heavy tapping on the door itself. For an instant the clutch of Lowrie froze around his gun; then he twitched the muzzle back against his own breast and fired.

There was no pain—only a sense of numbness and a vague feeling of torn muscles, as if they were extraneous matter. He dropped the revolver on the bed and pressed both hands against his wound. Then the door opened, and there appeared, not Riley Sinclair, but Pop Hansen.

"What in thunder—" he began.

"Get Riley Sinclair. There's been an accident," said Lowrie faintly and huskily. "Get Riley Sinclair; quick. I got something to say to him.

3

Riley Sinclair rode over the mountain. An hour of stern climbing lay behind him, but it was not sympathy for his tired horse that made him draw rein. Sympathy was not readily on tap in Riley's nature. "Hossflesh" to Riley was purely and simply a means to an end. Neither had he paused to enjoy that mystery of change which comes over mountains between late afternoon and early evening. His keen eyes answered all his purposes, and that they had never learned to see blue in shadows meant nothing to Riley Sinclair.

If he looked kindly upon the foothills, which stepped down from the peaks to the valley lands, it was because they meant an easy descent. Riley took thorough stock of his surroundings, for it was a new country. Yonder, where the slant sun glanced and blinked on windows, must be

Sour Creek; and there was the road to town jagging across the hills. Riley sighed.

In his heart he despised that valley. There were black patches of plowed land. A scattering of houses began in the foothills and thickened toward Sour Creek. How could men remain there, where there was so little elbowroom? He scowled down into the shadow of the valley. Small country, small men.

Pictures failed to hold Riley, but, as he sat the saddle, hand on thigh, and looked scornfully toward Sour Creek, he was himself a picture to make one's head lift. As a rule the horse comes in for as much attention as the rider, but when Riley Sinclair came near, people saw the man and nothing else. Not because he was good-looking, but because one became suddenly aware of some hundred and eighty pounds of lithe, tough muscle and a domineering face.

Somewhere behind his eyes there was a faint glint of humor. That was the only soft touch about him. He was in that hard age between thirty and thirty-five when people are still young, but have lost the illusions of youth. And, indeed, that was exactly the word which people in haste used to describe Riley Sinclair—"hard."

Having once resigned himself to the descent into that cramped country beneath he at once banished all regret. First he picked out his objective, a house some distance away, near the road, and then he brought his mustang up on the bit with a touch of the spurs. Then, having established the taut rein which he preferred, he sent the cow pony down the slope. It was plain that the mustang hated its rider; it was equally plain that Sinclair was in perfect touch with his horse, what with the stern wrist pulling against the bit, and the spurs keeping the pony up on it. In spite of his bulk he was not heavy in the saddle, for he kept in tune with the gait of the horse, with that sway of the body which lightens burdens. A capable rider, he was so judicious that he seemed reckless.

Leaving the mountainside, he struck at a trot across a tableland. Some mysterious instinct enabled him to guide the pony without glancing once at the ground; for Sinclair, with his head high, was now carefully examining the house before him. Twice a cluster of trees obscured it, and each time, as it came again more closely in view, the eye of Riley Sinclair brightened with certainty. At length, nodding slightly to express his conviction, he sent the pony into the shelter of a little grove overlooking the house. From this shelter, still giving half his attention to his objective, he ran swiftly over his weapons. The pair of long pistols came smoothly into his hands, to be weighed nicely, and have their cylinders spun. Then the rifle came out of its case, and its magazine was looked to thoroughly before it was returned.

This done, the rider seemed in no peculiar haste to go on. He merely pushed the horse into a position from which he commanded all the environs of the house; then he sat still as a hawk hovering in a windless sky.

Presently the door of the little shack opened, and two men came out and walked down the path toward the road, talking earnestly. One was as tall as Riley Sinclair, but heavier; the other was a little, slight man. He went to a sleepy pony at the end of the path and slowly gathered the reins. Plainly he was troubled, and apparently it was the big man who had troubled him. For now he turned and cast out his hand toward the other, speaking rapidly, in the manner of one making a last appeal. Only the murmur of that voice drifted up to Riley Sinclair, but the loud laughter of the big man drove clearly to him. The smaller of the two mounted and rode away with dejected head, while the other remained with arms folded, looking after him.

He seemed to be chuckling at the little man, and indeed there was cause, for Riley had never seen a rider so completely out of place in a saddle. When the pony presently broke into a soft lope it caused the elbows of the little man to flop like wings. Like a great clumsy bird he winged his way out of view beyond the edge of the hilltop.

The big man continued to stand with his arms folded, looking in the direction in which the other had disappeared; he was still shaking with mirth. When he eventually turned, Riley Sinclair was riding down on him at a sharp gallop. Strangers do not pass ungreeted in the mountain desert. There was a wave of the arm to Riley, and he responded by bringing his horse to a trot, then reining in close to the big man. At close hand he seemed even larger than from a distance, a burly figure with ludicrously inadequate support from the narrow-heeled riding boots. He looked sharply at Riley Sinclair, but his first speech was for the hard-ridden pony.

"You been putting your hoss through a grind, I see, stranger."

The mustang had slumped into a position of rest, his sides heaving.

"Most generally," said Riley Sinclair, "when I climb into a saddle it ain't for pleasure—it's to get somewhere."

His voice was surprisingly pleasant. He spoke very deliberately, so that one felt occasionally that he was pausing to find the right words. And, in addition to the quality of that deep voice, he had an impersonal way of looking his interlocutor squarely in the eye, a habit that pleased the men of the mountain desert. On this occasion his companion responded at once with a grin. He was a younger man than Riley Sinclair, but he gave an impression of as much hardness as Riley himself.

"Maybe you'll be sliding out of the saddle for a minute?" he asked. "Got some pretty fair hooch in the house."

"Thanks, partner, but I'm due over to Sour Creek by night. I guess that's Sour Creek over the hill?"

"Yep. New to these parts?"

"Sort of new."

Riley's noncommittal attitude was by no means displeasing to the larger man. His rather brutally handsome face continued to light, as if he were recognizing in Riley Sinclair a man of his own caliber.

"You're from yonder?"

"Across the mountains."

"You travel light."

His eyes were running over Riley's meager equipment. Sinclair had been known to strike across the desert loaded with nothing more than a rifle, ammunition, and water. Other things were nonessentials to him, and it was hardly likely that he would put much extra weight on a horse. The only concession to animal comfort, in fact, was the slicker rolled snugly behind the saddle. He was one of those rare Westerners to whom coffee on the trail is not the staff of life. As long as he had a gun he could get meat, and as long as he could get meat, he cared little about other niceties of diet. On a long trip his "extras" were usually confined to a couple of bags of strength-giving grain for his horse.

"Maybe you'd know the gent I'm down here looking for?" asked Riley. "Happen to know Ollie Quade—Oliver Quade?"

"Sort of know him, yep."

Riley went on explaining blandly. "You see, I'm carrying him a sort of a death message."

"H'm," said the big man, and he watched Riley, his eyes grown suddenly alert, his glance shifting from hand to face with catlike uncertainty.

"Yep," resumed Sinclair in a rambling vein. "I come from a gent that used to be a pal of his. Name is Sam Lowrie."

"Sam Lowrie!" exclaimed the other. "You a friend of Sam's?"

"I was the only gent with him when he died," said Sinclair simply.

"Dead!" said the other heavily. "Sam dead!"

"You must of been pretty thick with him," declared Riley.

"Man, I'm Quade. Lowrie was my bunkie!"

He came close to Sinclair, raising an eager face. "How'd Lowrie go out?"

"Pretty peaceful—boots off—everything comfortable."

"He give you a message for me?"

"Yep, about a gent called Sinclair—Hal Sinclair, I think it was." Immediately he turned his eyes away, as if he were striving to recollect accurately. Covertly he sent a side glance at Quade and found him scowling suspiciously. When he turned his head again, his eye was as clear as the eye of a child.

"Yep," he said, "that was the name—Hal Sinclair."

"What about Hal Sinclair?" asked Quade gruffly.

"Seems like Sinclair was on Lowrie's conscience," said Riley in the same unperturbed voice.

"You don't say so!"

"I'll tell you what he told me. Maybe he was just raving, for he had a sort of fever before he went out. He said that you and him and Hal Sinclair and Bill Sandersen all went out prospecting. You got stuck clean out in the desert, Lowrie said, and you hit for water. Then Sinclair's hoss busted his leg in a hole. The fall smashed up Sinclair's foot. The four of you went on, Sinclair riding one hoss, and the rest of you taking turns with the third one. Without water the hosses got weak, and you gents got pretty badly scared, Lowrie said. Finally you and Sandersen figured that Sinclair had got to get off, but Sinclair couldn't walk. So the three of you made up your minds to leave him and make a dash for water. You got to water, all right, and in three hours you went back for Sinclair. But he'd given up hope and shot himself, sooner'n die of thirst, Lowrie said."

The horrible story came slowly from the lips of Riley Sinclair. There was not the slightest emotion in his face until Quade rubbed his knuckles across his wet forehead. Then there was the faintest jutting out of Riley's jaw.

"Lowrie was sure raving," said Quade.

Sinclair looked carelessly down at the gray face of Quade. "I guess maybe he was, but what he asked me to say was: 'Hell is sure coming to what you boys done.'"

"He thought about that mighty late," replied Quade. "Waited till he could shift the blame on me and Sandersen, eh? To hell with Lowrie!"

"Maybe he's there, all right," said Sinclair, shrugging. "But I've got rid of the yarn, anyway."

"Are you going to spread that story around in Sour Creek?" asked Quade softly.

"Me? Why, that story was told me confidential by a gent that was about to go out!"

Riley's frank manner disarmed Quade in a measure.

"Kind of queer, me running on to you like this, ain't it?" he went on. "Well, you're fixed up sort of comfortable up here. Nice little shack, partner. And I suppose you got a wife and kids and everything? Pretty lucky, I'd call you!"

Quade was glad of an opportunity to change the subject. "No wife yet!" he said.

"Living up here all alone?"

"Sure! Why?"

"Nothing! Thought maybe you'd find it sort of lonesome."

Back to the dismissed subject Quade returned, with the persistence of a guilty conscience. "Say," he said, "while we're talking about it, you don't happen to believe what Lowrie said?"

"Lowrie was pretty sick; maybe he was raving. So you're all alone up here? Nobody near?"

His restless, impatient eye ran over the surroundings. There was not a soul in sight. The mountains were growing stark and black against the flush of the western sky. His glance fell back upon Quade.

"But how did Lowrie happen to die?"

"He got shot."
"Did a gang drop him?"
"Nope, just one gent."
"You don't say! But Lowrie was a pretty slick hand with a gun—next to Bill Sandersen, the best I ever seen, almost! Somebody got the drop on him, eh?"
"Nope, he killed himself!"
Quade gasped. "Suicide?"
"Sure."
"How come?"
"I'll tell you how it was. He seen a gent coming. In fact he looked out of the window of his hotel and seen Riley Sinclair, and he figured that Riley had come to get him for what happened to his brother, Hal. Lowrie got sort of excited, lost his nerve, and when the hotel keeper come upstairs, Lowrie thought that it was Sinclair, and he didn't wait. He shot himself."
"You seem to know a pile," said Quade thoughtfully.
"Well, you see, I'm Riley Sinclair." Still he smiled, but Quade was as one who had seen a ghost.
"I had to make sure that you was alone. I had to make sure that you was guilty. And you are, Quade. Don't do that!"
The hand of Quade slipped around the butt of his gun and clung there.
"You ain't fit for a gun fight right now," went on Riley Sinclair slowly. "You're all shaking, Quade, and you couldn't hit the side of the mountain, let alone me. Wait a minute. Take your time. Get all settled down and wait till your hand stops shaking."
Quade moistened his white lips and waited.
"You give Hal plenty of time," resumed Riley Sinclair. "Since Lowrie told me that yarn I been wondering how Hal felt when you and the other two left him alone. You know, a gent can do some pretty stiff thinking before he makes up his mind to blow his head off."
His tone was quite conversational.

"Queer thing how I come to blunder into all this information, partner. I come into a room where Lowrie was. The minute he heard my name he figured I was after him on account of Hal. Up he comes with his gun like a flash. Afterward he told me all about it, and I give him a pretty fine funeral. I'll do the same by you, Quade. How you feeling now?"

"Curse you!" exclaimed Quade.

"Maybe I'm cursed, right enough, but, Quade, I'd let 'em burn me, inch by inch in a fire, before I'd quit a partner, a bunkie in the desert! You hear? It's a queer thing that a gent could have much pleasure out of plugging another gent full of lead. I've had that pleasure once; and I'm going to have it again. I'm going to kill you, Quade, but I wish there was a slower way! Pull your gun!"

That last came out with a snap, and the revolver of Quade flicked out of its holster with a convulsive jerk of the big man's wrist. Yet the spit of fire came from Riley Sinclair's weapon, slipping smoothly into his hand. Quade did not fall. He stood with a bewildered expression, as a man trying to remember something hidden far in the past; and Sinclair fingered the butt of his gun lightly and waited. It was rather a crumbling than a fall. The big body literally slumped down into a heap.

Sinclair reached down without dismounting and pulled the body over on its back.

"Because," he explained to what had been a strong man the moment before, "when the devil comes to you, I want the old boy to see your face, Quade! Git on, old hoss!"

As he rode down the trail toward Sour Creek he carefully and deftly cleaned his revolver and reloaded the empty chamber.

4

Perhaps, in the final analysis, Riley Sinclair would not be condemned for the death of Lowrie or the killing of Quade, but for singing on the trail to Sour Creek. And sing he did, his voice ringing from hill to hill, and the echoes barking back to him, now and again.

He was not silent until he came to Sour Creek. At the head of the long, winding, single street he drew the mustang to a tired walk. It was a very peaceful moment in the little town. Yonder a dog barked, and a coyote howled a thin answer far away, but, aside from these, all other sounds were the happy noises of families at the end of a day. From every house they floated out to him, the clamor of children, the deep laughter of a man, the loud rattle of pans in the kitchen.

"This ain't so bad," Riley Sinclair said aloud and roused the mustang cruelly to a gallop, the hoofs of his mount splashing through inches of pungent dust.

The heaviness of the gallop told him that his horse was plainly spent and would not be capable of a long run before the morning. Riley Sinclair accepted the inevitable with a sigh. All his strong instincts cried out to find Sandersen and, having found him, to shoot him and flee. Yet he had a sense of fatality connected with Sandersen. Lowrie's own conscience had betrayed him, and his craven fear had been his executioner. Quade had been shot in a fair fight with not a soul near by. But, at the third time, Sinclair felt reasonably sure that his luck would fail him. The third time the world would be very apt to brand him with murder.

It was a bad affair, and he wanted to get it done. This stay in Sour Creek was entirely against his will. Accordingly he put the mustang in the stable behind the hotel, looked to his feed, and then went slowly back to get a room. He registered and went in silence up to his room. If there had been the need, he could have kept on riding for a twenty-hour stretch, but the moment he found his journey interrupted, he flung himself on the bed, his arms thrown out crosswise, crucified with weariness.

In the meantime the proprietor returned to his desk to find a long, gaunt man leaning above the register, one brown finger tracing a name.

"Looking for somebody, Sandersen?" he asked. "Know this gent Sinclair?"

"Face looked kind of familiar to me," said the other, who had jerked his head up from the study of the register. "Somehow I don't tie that name up with the face."

"Maybe not," said the proprietor. "Maybe he ain't Riley Sinclair of Colma; maybe he's somebody else."

"Traveling strange, you mean?" asked Sandersen.

"I dunno, Bill, but he looks like a hard one. He's got one of them nervous right hands."

"Gunfighter?"

"I dunno. I'm not saying anything about what he is or what he ain't. But, if a gent was to come in here and tell me a pretty strong yarn about Riley Sinclair, or whatever his name might be, I wouldn't incline to doubt of it, would you, Bill?"

"Maybe I would, and maybe I wouldn't," answered Bill Sandersen gloomily.

He went out onto the veranda and squinted thoughtfully into the darkness. Bill Sandersen was worried—very worried. The moment he saw Sinclair enter the hotel, there had been a ghostly familiarity about the man. And he understood the reason for it as soon a he saw the name on the register. Sinclair! The name carried him back to the picture of the man who lay on his back, with the soft sands already half burying his body, and the round, purple blur in the center of his forehead. In a way it was as if Hal Sinclair had come back to life in a new and more terrible form, come back as an avenger.

Bill Sandersen was not an evil man, and his sin against Hal Sinclair had its qualifying circumstances. At least he had been only one of three, all of whom had concurred in the thing. He devoutly wished that the thing were to be done over again. He swore to himself that in such a case he would stick with his companion, no matter who deserted. But what had brought this Riley Sinclair all the way from Colma to Sour Creek, if it were not an errand of vengeance?

A sense of guilt troubled the mind of Bill Sandersen, but the obvious thing was to find out the reason for Sinclair's presence in Sour Creek. Sandersen crossed the street to the newly installed telegraph office. He had one intimate friend in the far-off town of Colma, and to that friend he now addressed a telegram.

> Rush back all news you have about man calling self Riley Sinclair of Colma—over six feet tall, weight hundred and eighty, complexion dark, hard look.

There was enough meat in that telegram to make the operator raise his head and glance with sharpened eyes at the patron. Bill Sandersen returned that glance with so much interest that the operator lowered his head again and made a mental oath that he would let the Westerners run the West.

With that telegram working for him in far-off Colma, Bill Sandersen started out to gather what information he could in Sour Creek. He drifted from the blacksmith shop to the kitchen of Mrs. Mary Caluson, but both these brimming reservoirs of news had this day run dry. Mrs. Caluson vaguely remembered a Riley Sinclair, a man who fought for the sheer love of fighting. A grim fellow!

Pete Handley, the blacksmith, had even less to say. He also, he averred, had heard of a Riley Sinclair, a man of action, but he could not remember in what sense. Vaguely he seemed to recall that there had been something about guns connected with that name of Riley Sinclair.

Meager information on which to build, but, having seen this man, Bill Sandersen said the less and thought the more. In a couple of hours he went back through the night to the telegraph office and found that his Colma friend had been unbelievably prompt. The telegram had been sent "collect," and Bill Sandersen groaned as he paid the bill. But when he opened the telegram he did not begrudge the money.

Riley Sinclair is harder than he looks, but absolutely honest and will play fairer than anybody. Avoid all trouble. Trust his word, but not his temper. Gunfighter, but not a bully. By the way, your pal Lowrie shot himself last week.

The long fingers of Bill Sandersen slowly gathered the telegram into a ball and crushed it against the palm of his hand. That ball he presently unraveled to reread the telegram; he studied it word by word.

"Absolutely honest!"

It made Sandersen wish to go straight to the gunfighter, put his cards on the table, confess what he had done to Sinclair's brother, and then express his sorrow. Then he remembered the cruel, lean face of Sinclair and the impatient eyes. He would probably be shot before he had half finished his story of the gruesome trip through the desert. Already Lowrie was dead. Even a child could have put two and two together and seen that Sinclair had come to Sour Creek on a mission of vengeance. Sandersen was himself a fighter, and, being a fighter, he knew that in Riley Sinclair he would meet the better man.

But two good men were better than one, even if the one were an expert. Sandersen went straight to the barn behind his shack, saddled his horse, and spurred out along the north road to Quade's house. Once warned, they would be doubly armed, and, standing back to back, they could safely defy the marauder from the north.

There was no light in Quade's house, but there was just a chance that the owner had gone to bed early. Bill Sandersen dismounted to find out, and dismounting, he stumbled across a soft, inert mass in the path. A moment later he was on his knees, and the flame of the sulphur match sputtered a blue light into the dead face of Quade, staring upward to the stars. Bill Sandersen remained there until the match singed his finger tips.

All doubt was gone now. Lowrie and Quade were both gone; and he, Sandersen, alone remained, the third and last of the guilty. His first strong impulse, after his agitation had diminished to such a point that he was able to think clearly again, was to flee headlong into the night and keep on, changing horses at every town he reached until he was over the mountains and buried in the shifting masses of life in some great city.

And then he recalled Riley Sinclair, lean and long as a hound. Such a man would be terrible on the trail—tireless, certainly. Besides there was the horror of flight, almost more awful than the immediate fear of death. Once he turned his back to flee from Riley Sinclair, the gunfighter would become a nightmare that would haunt him the rest of his life. No matter where he fled, every footstep behind him would be the footfall of Riley Sinclair, and behind every closed door would stand the same ominous figure. On the other hand if he went back and faced Sinclair he might reduce the nightmare to a mere creature of flesh and blood.

Sandersen resolved to take the second step.

In one way his hands were tied. He could not accuse Sinclair of this killing without in the first place exposing the tale of how Riley's brother was abandoned in the desert by three strong men who had been his bunkies. And that story, Sandersen knew, would condemn him to worse than death in the mountain desert. He would be loathed and scorned from one end of the cattle country to the other.

All of these things went through his head, as he jogged his mustang back down the hill. He turned in at Mason's place. All at once he recalled that he was not acting normally. He had just come from seeing the dead body of his best friend. And yet so mortal was his concern for his own safety that he felt not the slightest touch of grief or horror for dead Quade.

He had literally to grip his hands and rouse himself to a pitch of semihysteria. Then he spurred his horse down the path, flung himself with a shout out of the saddle, cast open the door of the house without a preliminary knock, and rushed into the room.

"Murder!" shouted Bill Sandersen. "Quade is killed!"

5

Who killed Quade? That was the question asked with a quiet deadliness by six men in Sour Creek. It had been Buck Mason's idea to keep the whole affair still. It was very possible that the slayer was still in the environs of Sour Creek, and in that case much noise would simply serve to frighten him away. It was also Buck's idea that they should gather a few known men to weigh the situation.

Every one of the six men who answered the summons was an adept with fist or guns, as the need might be; every one of them had proved that he had a level head; every one of them was a respected citizen. Sandersen was one; stocky Buck Mason, carrying two hundred pounds close to the ground, massive of hand and jaw, was a second. After that their choice had fallen on "Judge" Lodge. The judge wore spectacles and a judicial air. He had a keen eye for cows and was rather a sharper in horse trades. He gave his costume a semiofficial air by wearing a necktie instead of a bandanna, even at a roundup. The glasses, the necktie, and his little solemn pauses before he delivered an opinion, had given him his nickname.

Then came Denver Jim, a very little man, with nervous hands and remarkable steady eyes. He had punched cows over those ranges for ten years, and his experience had made him a wildcat in a fight. Oscar Larsen was a huge Swede, with a perpetual and foolish grin. Sour Creek had laughed at Oscar for five years, considered him dubiously for five years more, and then suddenly admitted him as a man among men. He was stronger than Buck Mason, quicker than Denver Jim, and shrewder than the judge. Last of all came Montana. He had a long, sad face, prodigious ability to stow away redeye, and a nature as simple and kind and honest as a child's.

These were the six men who gathered about and stared at the center of the floor. Something, they agreed, had to be done.

"First it was old man Collins. That was two years back," said Judge Lodge. "You boys remember how Collins went. Then there was the drifter that was plugged eight months ago. And now it's Ollie Quade. Gents, three murders in two years is too much. Sour Creek'll get a name. The bad ones will begin to drop in on us and use us for headquarters. We got to make an example. We never got the ones that shot Collins or the drifter. Since Quade has been plugged we got to hang somebody. Ain't that straight?"

"We got to hang somebody," said Denver Jim. "The point is—who?"

His keen eyes went slowly, hungrily, from face to face, as if he would not have greatly objected to picking one of his companions in that very room.

"Is they any strangers in town?" asked Larson with his peculiar, foolish grin.

Sandersen stirred in his chair; his heart leaped.

"There's a gent named Riley Sinclair nobody ain't never seen before."

"When did he come in?"

"Along about dark."

"That's the right time for us. You found Quade a long time dead, Bill."

Sandersen swallowed. In his joy he could have embraced Larsen.

"What'll we do?"

"Go talk to Sinclair," said Larsen and rose. "I got a rope."

"He's a dangerous-lookin' gent," declared Sandersen.

Larsen replied mildly: "Mostly they's a pile more interesting when they's dangerous. Come on, boys!"

It had been well after midnight when Mason and Sandersen got back to Sour Creek. The gathering of the posse had required much time. Now, as they filed out to the hotel, to the east the mountains were beginning to roll up out of the night, and one cloud, far away and high in the sky, was turning pink. They found the hotel wakening even at this early hour. At least, the Chinese cook was rattling in the kitchen as he built the fire. When the six reached the door of Sinclair's room, stepping lightly, they heard the occupant singing softly to himself.

"Early riser," whispered Denver Jim.

"Too early to be honest," replied Judge Lodge.

Larsen raised one of his great hands and imposed an absolute silence. Then, stepping with astonishing softness, considering his bulk, he approached the door of Sinclair's room. Into his left hand slid his .45 and instantly five guns glinted in the hands of the others. With equal caution they ranged themselves behind the big Swede. The latter glanced over his shoulder, made sure that everything was in readiness, and then kicked the door violently open.

Riley Sinclair was sitting on the side of his bed, tugging on a pair of riding boots and singing a hushed song. He interrupted himself long enough to look up into the muzzle of Larsen's gun. Then deliberately he finished drawing on the boot, singing while he did so; and, still deliberately, rose and stamped his feet home in the leather. Next he dropped his hands on his hips and considered the posse gravely.

"Always heard tell how Sour Creek was a fine town but I didn't know they turned out reception committees before sunup. How are you, boys? Want my roll?"

Larsen, as one who scorned to take a flying start on any man, dropped his weapon back in its holster. Sinclair's own gun and cartridge belt hung on the wall at the foot of the bed.

"That sounds too cool to be straight," said the judge soberly. "Sinclair, I figure you know why we want you?"

"I dunno, gents," said Sinclair, who grew more and more cheerful in the face of these six pairs of grim eyes. "But I'm sure obliged to the gent that give me the send-off. What d'you want?"

Drawing into the background Larsen said: "Open up on him, judge. Start the questions."

But Sandersen was of no mind to let the slow-moving mind of the judge handle this affair which was so vital to him. If Riley Sinclair did not hang, Sandersen himself was instantly placed in peril of his life. He stepped in front of Sinclair and thrust out his long arm.

"You killed Quade!"

Riley Sinclair rubbed his chin thoughtfully, looking past his accuser.

"I don't think so," he said at length.

"You don't think so? Don't you know?"

"They was two Mexicans jumped me once. One of 'em was called Pedro. Maybe the other was Quade. That who you're talking about?"

"You can't talk yourself out of it, Sinclair," said Denver

Jim. "We mean business, real business, you'll find out!"

"This here is a necktie party, maybe?" asked Riley Sinclair.

"It is, partner," said big Larsen, with his continual smile.

"Sinclair, you come over the mountains," went on Sandersen. "You come to find Quade. You ride down off'n the hills, and you come up to Quade's house. You call him out to talk to you. You're sitting on your horse. All at once you snatch out a gun and shoot Quade down. We know! That bullet ranged down. It was shot from above him, plain murder! He didn't have a chance!"

Throwing out his facts as he saw them, one by one, there was a ring of conviction in his voice. The barren sentences painted a vivid picture of the death. The six accusing faces grew hard and set. Then, to their astonishment, they saw that Sinclair was smiling!

"He don't noways take us serious, gents," declared the judge. "Let's take him out and see if a rope means anything to him. Sinclair, d'you figure this is a game with us?"

Riley Sinclair chuckled. "Gents," he said easily, "you come here all het up. You want a pile of action, but you ain't going to get it off'n me—not a bit! I'll tell you why. You gents are straight, and you know straight talk when you hear it. This dead man—what's his name, Quade?—was killed by a gent that had a reason for killing him. Wanted to get Quade's money, or they was an old grudge. But what could my reason be for wanting to bump off Quade? Can any of you figure that out? There's my things. Look through 'em and see if I got Quade's money. Maybe you think it's a grudge? Gents, I give you my word that I never been into this country before this trip. How could there be any grudge between me and Quade? Is that sense? Then talk sense back to me!"

His mirth had disappeared halfway through this speech, and in the latter part of it his voice rang sternly. Moreover he looked them in the eye, one by one. All of this was noted by Sandersen. He saw suddenly and clearly that he had lost. They would not hang this man by hearsay evidence, or by chance presumption.

Sinclair would go free. And if Sinclair went free, there would be short shrift for Bill Sandersen. For a moment he felt his destiny wavering back and forth on a needle point. Then he flung himself into a new course diametrically opposed to the other.

"Boys, it was me that started this, and I want to be the first to admit it's a cold trail. Men has been hung with less agin' them than we got agin' Sinclair. We know when Quade must have been killed. We know it tallies pretty close with the time when Sinclair come down that same trail, because that was the way he rode into Sour Creek. But no matter how facts look, nobody *seen* that shooting. And I say this gent Sinclair ain't any murderer. Look him over, boys. He's clean, and I register a vote for him. What d'you say? No matter what the rest of you figure, I'm going to shake hands with him. I like his style!"

He had turned his back on Riley while he spoke, but now he whirled and thrust out his hand. The fingers of Sinclair closed slowly over the proffered hand.

"When it comes to the names, partner, seems like you got an edge over me."

"Have I? I'm Sandersen. Glad to know you, Sinclair."

"Sandersen!" repeated the stranger slowly. "Sandersen!"

Letting his fingers fall away nervelessly from the hand of the other, he sighed deeply.

Sandersen with a side-glance followed every changing shade of expression in that hard face. How could Sinclair attack a man who had just defended him from a terrible charge? It could not be. For the moment, at least, Sandersen felt he was safe. In the future, many things might happen. At the very least, he had gained a priceless postponement of the catastrophe.

"Them that do me a good turn is writ down in red," Sinclair was saying; "and them that step on my toes is writ down the same way. Sandersen, I got an idea that for one reason or another I ain't going to forget you in a hurry."

There was a grim double meaning in that speech which Sandersen alone could understand. The others of the self-appointed posse had apparently made up their minds that Sandersen was right, and that this was a cold trail.

"It's like Sinclair says," admitted the judge. "We got to find a gent that had a reason for wishing to have Quade die. Where's the man?"

"Hunt for the reason first and find the man afterward," said big Larsen, still smiling.

"All right! Did anybody owe Quade money, anybody Quade was pressing for it?"

It was the judge who advanced the argument in this solemn and dry form. Denver Jim declared that to his personal knowledge Quade had neither borrowed nor loaned.

"Well, then, had Quade ever made many enemies? We know Quade was a fighter. Recollect any gents that might hold grudges?"

"Young Penny hated the ground he walked on. Quade beat Penny to a pulp down by the Perkin water hole."

"Penny wouldn't do a murder."

"Maybe it was a fair fight," broke in Larsen.

"Fair nothin'," said Buck Mason. "Don't we all know that Quade was fast with a gun? He barely had it out in his hand when the other gent drilled him. And he was shot from above. No, sir, the way it happened was something like this. The murderin' skunk sat on his hoss saying good-by to Quade, and, while they was shaking hands or something like that, he goes for his gun and plugs Quade. Maybe it was a gent that knew he didn't have a chance agin' Quade. Maybe—"

He broke off short in his deductions and smote his hands together with a tremendous oath. "Boys, I got it! It's Cold Feet that done the job. It's Gaspar that done it!"

They stared at Buck vaguely.

"Mason, Cold Feet ain't got the nerve to shoot a rabbit."

"Not in a fight. This was a murder!"

"What's the schoolteacher's reason?"

"Don't he love Sally Bent? Didn't Quade love her?" He raised his voice. "I'm a big fool for forgetting! Didn't I see him ride over the hill to Quade's place and come back in the evening? Didn't I see it? Why else would he have called on Quade?"

There was a round chorus of oaths and exclamations. "The poisonous little skunk! It's him! We'll string him up!"

With a rush they started for the door.

"Wait!" called Riley Sinclair.

Bill Sandersen watched him with a keen eye. He had studied the face of the big man from up north all during the scene, and he found the stern features unreadable. For one instant now he guessed that Sinclair was about to confess.

"If you don't mind seven in one party," said Riley Sinclair, "I think I'll go along to see justice done. You see, I got a sort of secondhand interest in this necktie party."

Mason clapped him on the shoulder. "You're just the sort of a gent we need," he declared.

6

Down in the kitchen they demanded a loaf of bread and some coffee from the Chinese cook, and then the seven dealers of justice took horse and turned into the silence of the long mountain trail.

The sunrise had picked those mountains out of the night, directly above Sour Creek. Riley Sinclair regarded them with a longing eye. That was his country. A man could see up there, and he could see the truth. Down here in the valley everything was askew. Men lived blindly and did blind things, like this "justice" which the six riders were bringing on an innocent man.

Not by any means had Riley decided what he would do. If he confessed the truth he would not only have a man-sized job trying to escape from the posse, but he would have to flee before he had a chance to deal finally with Sandersen. Chiefly he wanted time. He wanted a chance to study Sandersen. The fellow had spoken for him like a man, but Sinclair was suspicious.

In his quandary he turned to sad-faced Montana and asked: "Who's this gent you call Cold Feet?"

"He's a tenderfoot," declared Montana, "and he's queer. He's yaller, they say, and that's why they call him Cold Feet. Besides, he teaches the school. Where's they a real man that would do a schoolma'am's work? Living or dying, he ain't much good. You can lay to that!"

Sinclair was comforted by this speech. Perhaps the schoolteacher was, as Montana stated, not much good, dead or alive. Sinclair had known many men whose lives were not worth an ounce of powder. In this case he would let Cold Feet be hanged. It was a conclusion sufficiently grim, but Riley Sinclair was admittedly a grim man. He had lived for himself, he had worked for himself. On his younger brother, Hal, he had wasted all the better and tenderer side of his nature. For Hal's education and advantage he had sweated and saved for a long time. With the death of Hal, the better side of Riley Sinclair died.

The horses sweated up a rise of ground.

"For a schoolteacher he lives sort of far out of town, I figure," said Riley Sinclair.

"That's on account of Sally Bent," answered Denver Jim. "Sally and her brother got a shack out this way, and Cold Feet boards with 'em."

"Sally Bent! That's an old-maidish-sounding name."

Denver Jim grinned broadly. "Tolerable," he said, "just tolerable old-maidish sounding."

When they reached the top of the knoll, the horses paused, as if by common assent. Now they stood with their heads bowed, sullen, tired already, steam going up from them into the cool of the morning.

"There it is!"

It was as comfortably placed a house as Riley Sinclair had ever seen. The mountain came down out of the sky in ragged, uneven steps. Here it dipped away into a lap of quite level ground. A stream of spring water flashed across that little tableland, dark in the shadow of the big trees, silver in the sunlight. At the back of the natural clearing was the cabin, built solidly of logs. Wood, water, and a commanding position for defense! Riley Sinclair ran his eye appreciatively over these advantages.

"My guns, I'd forgot Sally!" exclaimed the massive Buck Mason.

"Is that her?" asked Riley Sinclair.

A woman had come out of the shadow of a tree and stood over the edge of the stream, a bucket in her hand. At that distance it was quite impossible to make out her features, although Riley Sinclair found himself squinting and peering to make them out. She had on something white over her head and neck, and her dress was the faded blue of old gingham. Then the wind struck her dress, and it seemed to lift the girl in its current.

"I'd forgot Sally Bent!"

"What difference does she make?" asked Riley.

"You don't know her, stranger."

"And she won't know us. Got anything for masks?"

"I'm sure a Roman-nosed fool!" declared Mason. "Of course we got to wear masks."

The girl's pail flashed, as she raised it up from the stream and dissolved into the shadow of a big tree.

"She don't seem noways interested in this here party," remarked Riley.

"That's her way," said Denver Jim, arranging his bandanna to mask the lower part of his face from the bridge of his nose down. "She'll show plenty of interest when it comes to a pinch."

Riley adjusted his own mask, and he did it thoroughly. Out of his vest he ripped a section of black lining, and, having cut eyeholes, he fastened the upper edge of the cloth under the brim of his hat and tied the loose ends behind his head. Red, white, blue, black, and polka dot was that quaint array of masks.

Having completed his arrangements, Larsen started on at a lope, and the rest of the party followed in a lurching, loose-formed wedge. At the edge of the little tableland, Larsen drew down his mount to a walk and turned in the saddle.

"Quick work, no talk, and a getaway," he said as he swung down to the ground.

In the crisis of action the big Swede seemed to be accorded the place of leader by natural right. The others imitated his example silently. Before they reached the door Larsen turned again.

"Watch Jerry Bent," he said softly. "You watch him, Denver, and you, Sandersen. Me and Buck will take care of Cold Feet. He may fight like a rat. That's the way with a coward when he gets cornered." Then he strode toward the door.

"How thick is Sally Bent with this schoolteaching gent?" asked Riley Sinclair of Mason.

"I dunno. Nobody knows. Sally keeps her thinking to herself."

Larsen kicked open the door and at the same moment drew his six-shooter. That example was also imitated by the rest, with the exception of Riley Sinclair. He hung in the background, watching.

"Gaspar!" called Larsen.

There was a voice of answer, a man's thin voice, then the sharp cry of a girl from the interior of the house. Sinclair heard a flurry of skirts.

"Hysterics now," he said into his mask.

She sprang into the doorway, her hands holding the jamb on either side. In her haste the big white handkerchief around her throat had been twisted awry. Sinclair looked over the heads of Mason and Denver Jim into the suntanned face that had now paled into a delicate olive color. Her very lips were pale, and her great black eyes were flashing at them. She seemed more a picture of rage than hysterical fear.

"Why for?" she asked. "What are you-all here for in masks, boys? What you mean calling for Gaspar? What's he done?"

In a moment of waiting Larsen cleared his throat solemnly. "It'd be best we tell Gaspar direct what we're here for."

This seemed to tell her everything. "Oh," she gasped, "you're not really *after* him?"

"Lady, we sure be."

"But Jig—he wouldn't hurt a mouse—he couldn't!"

"Sally, he's done a murder!"

"No, no, no!"

"Sally, will you stand out of the door?"

"It ain't—it ain't a lynching party, boys? Oh, you fools, you'll hang for it, every one of you!"

Sinclair confided to Buck Mason beside him: "Larsen is letting her talk down to him. She'll spoil this here party."

"We're the voice of justice," said Judge Lodge pompously. "We ain't got any other names. They wouldn't be nothing to hang."

"Don't you suppose I know you?" asked the girl, stiffening to her full height. "D'you think those fool masks mean anything? I can tell you by your little eyes, Denver Jim!"

Denver cringed suddenly behind the man before him.

"I know you by that roan hoss of yours, Oscar Larsen. Judge Lodge, they ain't nobody but you that talks about 'justice' and 'voices.' Buck Mason, I could tell you by your build, a mile off. Montana, you'd ought to have masked your neck and your Adam's apple sooner'n your face. And you're Bill Sandersen. They ain't any other man in these parts that stands on one heel and points his off toe like a hoss with a sore leg. I know you all, and, if you touch a hair on Jig's head, I'll have you into court for murder! You hear—murder! I'll have you hung, every man jack!"

She had lowered her voice for the last part of this speech. Now she made a sweeping gesture, closing her hand as if she had clutched their destinies in the palm of her hand and could throw it into their faces.

"You-all climb right back on your hosses and feed 'em the spur."

They stood amazed, shifting from foot to foot, exchanging miserable glances. She began to laugh; mysterious lights danced and twinkled in her eyes. The laughter chimed away into words grown suddenly gentle, suddenly friendly. Such a voice Riley Sinclair had never heard. It walked into a man's heart, breaking the lock.

"Why, Buck Mason, you of all men to be mixed up in a deal like this. And you, Oscar Larsen, after you and me had talked like partners so many a time! Denver Jim, we'll have a good laugh about this necktie party later on. Why, boys, you-all know that Jig ain't guilty of no harm!"

"Sally," said the wretched Denver Jim, "things seemed to be sort of pointing to a—"

There was a growl from the rear of the party, and Riley Sinclair strode to the front and faced the girl. "They's a gent charged with murder inside," he said. "Stand off, girl. You're in the way!"

Before she answered him, her teeth glinted. If she had been a man, she would have struck him in the face. He saw that, and it pleased him.

"Stranger," she said deliberately, making sure that every one in the party should hear her words, "what you need is a stay around Sour Creek long enough for the boys to teach you how to talk to a lady."

"Honey," replied Riley Sinclair with provoking calm, "you sure put up a tidy bluff. Maybe you'd tell a judge that you knowed all these gents behind their masks, but they wouldn't be no way you could *prove* it!"

A stir behind him was ample assurance that this simple point had escaped the cowpunchers. All the soul of the girl stood up in her eyes and hated Riley Sinclair, and again he was pleased. It was not that he wished to bring the schoolteacher to trouble, but it had angered him to see one girl balk seven grown men.

"Stand aside," said Riley Sinclair.

"Not an inch!"

"Lady, I'll move you."

"Stranger, if you touch me, you'll be taught better. The gents in Sour Creek don't stand for suchlike ways!"

Before the appeal to the chivalry of Sour Creek was out of her lips, smoothly and swiftly the hands of Sinclair settled around her elbows. She was lifted lightly into the air and deposited to one side of the doorway.

Her cry rang in the ear of Riley Sinclair. Then her hand flashed up, and the mask was torn from his face.

"I'll remember! Oh, if I have to wait twenty years, I'll remember!"

"Look me over careful, lady. Today's most likely the last time you'll see me," declared Riley, gazing straight into her eyes.

A hand touched his arm. "Stranger, no rough play!"

Riley Sinclair whirled with whiplash suddenness and, chopping the edge of his hand downward, struck away the arm of Larsen, paralyzing the nerves with the same blow.

"Hands off!" said Sinclair.

The girl's clear voice rang again in his ear: "Thank you, Oscar Larsen. I sure know my friends—and the gentlemen!"

She was pouring oil on the fire. She would have a feud blazing in a moment. With all his heart Riley Sinclair admired her dexterity. He drew the posse back to the work in hand by stepping into the doorway and calling: "Hey, Gaspar!"

7

"He's right, Larsen, and you're wrong," Buck Mason said. "She had us buffaloed, and he pulled us clear. Steady, boys. They ain't no harm done to Sally!"

"Oh, Buck, is that the sort of a friend of mine you are?"

"I'm sorry, Sally."

Sinclair gave this argument only a small part of his attention. He found himself looking over a large room which was, he thought, one of the most comfortable he had ever seen—outside of pictures. At the farther end a great fireplace filled the width of the room. The inside of the log walls had been carefully and smoothly finished by some master axman. There were plenty of chairs, homemade and very comfortable with cushions. A little organ stood against the wall to one side. No wonder the schoolteacher had chosen this for his boarding place!

Riley made his voice larger. "Gaspar!"

Then a door opened slowly, while Sinclair dropped his hand on the butt of his gun and waited. The door moved again. A head appeared and observed him.

"Pronto!" declared Riley Sinclair, and a little man slipped into full view.

He was a full span shorter, Riley felt, than a man had any right to be. Moreover, he was too delicately made. He had a head of bright blond hair, thick and rather on end. The face was thin and handsome, and the eyes impressed

Riley as being at once both bright and weary. He was wearing a dressing gown, the first that Riley had ever seen.

"Get your hands out of those pockets!" He emphasized the command with a jerk of his gun hand, and the arms of the schoolteacher flew up over his head. Lean, fragile hands, Riley saw them to be. Altogether it was the most disgustingly inefficient piece of manhood that he had ever seen.

"Slide out here, Gaspar. They's some gents here that wants to look you over."

The voice that answered him was pitched so low as to be almost unintelligible. "What do they want?"

"Step lively, friend! They want to see a gent that lets a woman do his fighting for him."

He had dropped his gun contemptuously back into its holster. Now he waved the schoolteacher to the door with his bare hands.

Gaspar sidled past as if a loaded gun were about to explode in his direction. He reached the door, his arms still held stiffly above his head, but, at the sight of the masked faces, one arm dropped to his side, and the other fell across his face. He slumped against the side of the door with a moan.

It was Judge Lodge who broke the silence. "Guilty, boys. Ain't one look at the skunk enough to prove it?"

"Make it all fair and legal, gents," broke in Larsen.

Buck Mason strode straight up to the prisoner.

"Was you over to Quade's house yesterday evening?"

The other shrank away from the extended, pointing arm. "Yes," he stammered. "I—I—what does all this mean?"

Mason whirled on his companions, still pointing to the schoolmaster. "Take a slant at him, boys. Can't you read it in his face?"

There was a deep and humming murmur of approval. Then, without a word, Mason took one of Gaspar's arms and Montana took the other. Sally Bent ran forward at them with a cry, but the long arm of Riley Sinclair barred her way.

"Man's work," he said coldly. "You go inside and cover your head."

She turned to them with extended hands.

"Buck, Montana, Larsen—boys, you-all ain't going to let it happen? He *couldn't* have done it!"

They lowered their heads and returned no answer. At that she whirled with a sob and ran back into the house. The procession moved on, Buck and Montana in the lead, with the prisoner between them. The others followed, Judge Lodge uncoiling a horribly significant rope. Last of all came Bill Sandersen, never taking his eyes from the face of Riley Sinclair.

The latter was thoughtful, very thoughtful. He seemed to feel the eyes of Sandersen upon him, for presently he turned to the other. "What good's a coward to the world, Sandersen?"

"None that I could see."

"Well, look at that. Ever see anything more yaller?"

Gaspar walked between his two guards. Rather he was dragged between them, his feet trailing weakly and aimlessly behind him, his whole body sinking with flabby terror. The stern lip of Riley Sinclair curled.

"He's going to let it go through," said Sandersen to himself. "After all nobody can blame him. He couldn't put his own neck in the noose."

Over the lowest limb of a great cottonwood Judge Lodge accurately flung the rope, so that the noose dangled a significant distance from the ground. There was a businesslike stir among the others. Denver, Larsen, the judge, and Sandersen held the free end of the rope. Buck Mason tied the hands of the prisoner behind him. Montana spoke calmly through his mask.

"Jig, you sure done a rotten bad thing. You hadn't ought to of killed him, Jig. These here killings has got to stop. We ain't hanging you for spite, but to make an example."

Then with a dexterous hand he fitted the noose around the neck of the schoolteacher. As the rough rope grated against Gaspar's throat, he shrieked and jerked against the rope end that bound his hands. Then, as if he realized that struggling would not help him, and that only speech could give him a chance for life, he checked the cry of horror and looked around him. His glances fell on the grim masks, and it was only natural that he should address himself to the only uncovered face he saw.

"Sir," he said to Riley in a rapid, trembling voice, "you look to me like an honest man. Give me—give me time to speak."

"Make it pronto," said Riley Sinclair coldly.

The four waited, with their hands settled high up on the rope, ready for the tug which would swing Gaspar halfway to his Maker.

"We're kind of pushed for time, ourselves," said Riley. "So hurry it on, Gaspar."

Bill Sandersen was a cold man, but such unbelievable heartlessness chilled him. Into his mind rushed a temptation suddenly to denounce the real slayer before them all. He checked that temptation. In the first place it would be impossible to convince five men who had already made up their minds, who had already acquitted Sinclair of the guilt. In the second place, if he succeeded in convincing them, there would be an instant gunplay, and the first man to come under Sinclair's fire, he knew well enough, would be himself. He drew a long breath and waited.

"Good friends, gentlemen," Gaspar was saying, "I don't even know what you accuse me of. Kill a man? Why should I wish to kill a man? You know I'm not a fighter. Gentlemen—"

"Jig," cut in Buck Mason, "you was as good as seen to murder Quade. You're going to hang. If you got anything to say make a confession."

Gaspar attempted to throw himself on his knees, but his weight struck against the rope. He staggered back to his feet, struggling for breath.

"For mercy's sake—" began Gaspar.

"Cut it short, boys!" cried Buck Mason. "Up with him!"

The four men at the rope reached a little higher and settled their grips. In another moment Gaspar would dangle in the air. Now Riley Sinclair made his decision.

The agonized eyes of the condemned man, wide with animal terror, were fixed on his face. Sinclair raised his hand.

"Wait!"

The arms, growing tense for the jerk, relaxed.

"How long is this going to be dragged out?" asked the judge in disgust. "The worst lynching I ever see, that's what I call it! They ain't no justice in it—it's just plain torture."

"Partner," declared Riley Sinclair, "I'm sure glad to see that you got a good appetite for a killing. But it's just come home to me that in spite of everything, this here gent might be innocent. And if he is, heaven help our souls. We're done for!"

"Bless you for that!" exclaimed Gaspar.

"Shut up!" said Sinclair. "No matter what you done, you deserve hangin' for being yaller. But concerning this here Quade matter, gents, it looks to me like it'd be a pretty good idea to have a fair and square trial for Gaspar."

"Trial?" asked Buck Mason. "Don't we all know what trials end up with? Law ain't no good, except to give lawyers a living."

"Never was a truer thing said," declared Sinclair. "All I mean is, that you and me and the rest of us run a trial for ourselves. Let's get in the evidence and hear the witness and make out the case. If we decide they ain't enough agin' Gaspar to hang him, then let him go. If we decide to stretch him up, we'll feel a pile better about it and nearer to the truth."

He went on steadily in spite of the groans of disapproval on every side. "Why, this is all laid out nacheral for a court-room. That there stump is for the judge, and the black rock yonder is where the prisoner sits. That there nacheral bench of grass is where the jury sits. Gents, could anything be handier for a trial than this layout?"

To the theory of the thing they had been entirely unresponsive, but to the chance to play a game, and a new game, they responded instantly.

"Besides," said Judge Lodge, "I'll act as the judge. I know something about the law."

"No, you won't," declared Riley. "I thought up this little party, and I'm going to run it." Then he stepped to the stump and sat down on it.

8

Denver Jim was already heartily in the spirit of the thing.

"Sit down on that black rock, Jig," he said, taking Gaspar to the designated stone as he spoke, and removing the noose from the latter's neck. "Black is a sign you're going to swing in the end. Jest a triflin' postponement, that's all."

Riley placated the judge with his first appointment. "Judge Lodge," he said, "you know a pile about these here things. I appoint you clerk. It's your duty to take out that little notebook you got in your vest pocket and write down a note for the important things that's said. Savvy?"

"Right," replied Lodge, entirely won over, and he settled himself on the grass, with the notebook on his knee and a stub of a pencil poised over it.

"Larsen, you're sergeant-at-arms."

"How d'you mean that, Sinclair?"

"That's what they call them that keeps order; I disremember where I heard it. Larsen, if anybody starts raising a rumpus, it's up to you to shut 'em up."

"I'll sure do it," declared Larsen. "You can sure leave that to me, judge." He hoisted his gun belt around so that the gun butt hung more forward and readier to his hand.

"Denver, you're the jailer. You see the prisoner don't get away. Keep an eye on him, you see?"

"Easy, judge," replied Denver. "I can do it with one hand."

"Montana, you keep the door."

"What d'you mean—door, judge?"

"Ain't you got no imagination whatever?" demanded Sinclair. "You keep the door. When I holler for a witness you go and get 'em. And Sandersen, you're the hangman. Take charge of that rope!"

"That ain't such an agreeable job, your honor."

"Neither is mine. Go ahead."

Sandersen, glowering, gathered up the rope and draped it over his arm.

"Buck Mason, you're the jury. Sit down over there on your bench, will you? This here court being kind of short-handed, you got to do twelve men's work. If it's too much for you, the rest of us will help out."

"Your honor," declared Buck, much impressed, "I'll sure do my best."

"The jury's job," explained Sinclair, "is to listen to everything and not say nothing, but think all the time. You'll do your talking in one little bunch when you say guilty or not guilty. Now we're ready to start. Gaspar, stand up!"

Denver Jim officiously dragged the schoolteacher to his feet.

"What's your name?"

"Name?" asked the bewildered Gaspar. "Why, everybody knows my name!"

"Don't make any difference," announced Sinclair. "This is going to be a strictly regular hanging with no frills left out. What's your name?"

"John Irving Gaspar."

"Called Jig for short, and sometimes Cold Feet," put in the clerk.

Sinclair cleared his throat. "John Irving Gaspar, alias Jig, alias Cold Feet, d'you know what we got agin' you? Know what you're charged with?"

"With—with an absurd thing, sir."

"Murder!" said Sinclair solemnly. "Murder, Jig! What d'you say, guilty or not guilty! Most generally you'd say not guilty."

"Not guilty—absolutely not guilty. As a matter of fact, Mr. Sinclair—"

"Denver, shut him up and make him sit down."

One hard, brown hand was clapped over Jig's mouth. The other thrust him back on the black rock.

"Gentlemen of the jury," said his honor, "you've heard the prisoner say he didn't do it. Now we'll get down to the truth of it. What's the witnesses for the prosecution got to say?"

There was a pause of consideration.

"Speak up pronto," said Sinclair. "Anybody know anything agin' the prisoner?"

Larsen stepped forward. "Your honor, it's pretty generally known—"

"I don't give a doggone for what's generally known. What d'you know?"

The Swede's smile did not alter in the slightest, but his voice became blunter, more acrid. From that moment he made up his mind firmly that he wanted to see John Irving Gasper, otherwise Jig, hanged from the cottonwood tree above them.

"I was over to Shorty Lander's store the other day—"

His honor raised his hand in weary protest, as he smiled apologetically at the court. "Darned if I didn't plumb forget one thing," he said. "We got to swear in these witnesses before they can chatter. Is there anybody got a Bible around 'em? Nope? Montana, I wished you'd lope over to that house and see what they got in the line of Bibles."

Montana strode away in the direction of the house, and quiet fell over that unique courtroom. Larsen, so pleasant of face and so unbending of heart, was the first to speak.

"Looks to me, gents, like we're wasting a lot of time on a rat!"

The blond head of Cold Feet turned, and his large, dark eyes rested without expression upon the face of the Swede. He seemed almost literally to fold his hands and await the result of his trial. The illusion was so complete that even Riley Sinclair began to feel that the prisoner might be guilty—of an act which he himself had done! The opportunity was indeed too perfect to be dismissed without consideration. It was in his power definitely to put the blame on another man; then he could remain in this community as long as he wished, to work his will upon Sandersen.

Sandersen himself was a great problem. If Bill had spoken up in good faith to save Sinclair from the posse that morning, then Riley felt that he was disarmed. But a profound suspicion remained with him that Sandersen guessed his mission, and was purposely trying to brush away the wrath of the avenger. It would take time to discover the truth, but to secure that time it was necessary to settle the blame for the Quade killing. Cold Feet was a futile, weak-handed little coward. In the stern scheme of Sinclair's life, the death of such a man was almost less than nothing.

"Wasting a lot of time on a rat!"

The voice of Larsen fell agreeably upon the ear of his honor. Behind that voice came a faraway murmur, the scream of a hawk. He bent his head back and looked up through the limbs of the cottonwood into the pale blue-white haze of the morning sky.

A speck drifted across it, the hawk sailing in search of prey. Under the noble arch of heaven floated that fierce, malignant creature!

Riley Sinclair lowered his head with a sigh. Was not he

himself playing the part of the hawk? He looked straight into the eyes of the prisoner, and Jig met that gaze without flinching. He merely smiled in an apologetic manner, and he made a little gesture with his right hand, as if to admit that he was helpless, and that he cast himself upon the good will of Riley Sinclair. Riley jerked his head to one side and scowled. He hated that appeal. He wanted this hanging to be the work of seven men, not of one.

Montana returned, bringing with him a yellow-covered, red-backed book. "They wasn't a sign of a Bible in the house," he stated, "but I found this here history of the United States, with the Declaration of Independence pasted into the back of it. I figure that ought to do about as well as a Bible."

"You got a good head, Montana," said his honor. "Open up to that there Declaration. Here, Larsen, put your hand on this and swear you're telling the truth, the whole truth, and nothing but the truth. They ain't going to be any bum testimony taken in this court. We ain't going to railroad this lynching through."

He caught a glistening light of gratitude in the eyes of the schoolteacher. Riley's own breast swelled with a sense of virtue. He had never before taken the life of a helpless man; and now that it was necessary, he would do it almost legally.

Larsen willingly took the oath. "I'm going to tell the truth, the whole truth, and nothing but the truth, damn me if I don't! I was over to Shorty Lander's store the other day—"

"What day?"

"Hmm! Last Tuesday, I reckon."

"Go on, Larsen, but gimme nothin' but the facts."

"I seen Jig come into the store. 'I want to look at a revolver,'" he said.

"'The deuce you do! What might you want to do with a revolver, Jig?' says Shorty. 'You mean you want a toy gun?'

"I remember them words particular clear, because I

didn't see how even a spineless gent like Jig could stand for such a pile of insult. But he just sort of smiled with his lips and got steady with his eyes, like he was sort of grieved.

" 'I want a gun that'll kill a man,' he says to Shorty.

"Shorty and me both laughed, but, when Shorty brung out a forty-five, doggone me if Jig didn't buy the gun.

" 'Look here,' says he, 'is this the way it works?'

"And he raises it up in his skinny hand. I had to laugh.

" 'Hold it in both hands,' says I.

" 'Oh,' says he, and darned if he didn't take it in both hands.

" 'It seems much easier to handle in this way,' says he.

"But that's what I seen. I seen him buy a gun to kill a man. Them was his words, and I figure they're a mouthful."

Larsen retired.

"Damagin' evidence, they ain't no question," said Mr. Clerk severely. "But I can lay over it, your honor."

"Blaze away, judge."

Lodge took the oath. "I'm going to show you they was bad feelings between the prisoner and the dead man, your honor. I was over to the dance at the Woodville schoolhouse a couple of weeks ago. Jig was there, not dancing or nothing, but sitting in a corner, with all the girls, mostly, hanging around him. They keep hanging around looking real foolish at him, and Jig looks back at 'em as if they wasn't there. Well, it riles the boys around these parts. Quade comes up to him and takes him aside.

"Look here," he says, "why don't you dance with one girl instead of hogging them all?"

" 'I don't dance,' says Jig.

" 'Why do you stay if you won't dance?' asks Quade.

" 'It is my privilege,' says Jig, smiling in that ornery way of his, like his thoughts was too big for an ordinary gent to understand 'em.

" 'You stay an' dance an' welcome,' says Quade, 'but if you won't dance, get out of here and go home where you belong. You're spoiling the party for us, keeping all the girls over here.'

"'Is that a threat?' says Jig, smiling in that way of his.

"'It sure is. And most particular I want you to keep away from Sally Bent. You hear?'

"'You take advantage of your size,' says Jig.

"'Guns even up sizes,' says Quade.

"'Thank you,' says Jig. 'I'll remember.'

"Right after that he went home because he was afraid that Quade would give him a dressing. But they was bad feelings between him and Quade. They was a devil in them eyes of Jig's when he looked at big Quade. I seen it, and I knowed they'd be trouble!" Lodge then retired.

"Gents," said his honor, "it looks kind of black for the prisoner. We know that Gaspar had a grudge agin' Quade, and that he bought a gun big enough to kill a man. It sure looks black for you, Gaspar."

The prisoner looked steadily at Sinclair. There was something unsettling in that gaze.

"All we got to make sure of," said the judge, "is that that quarrel between Gaspar and Quade was strong enough to make Gaspar want to kill him, and—"

"Your honor," broke in Gaspar, "don't you see that I could never kill a man?" The prisoner stretched out his hands in a gesture of appeal to Sinclair.

Riley gritted his teeth. Suddenly a chill had passed through him at the thought of the hanging noose biting into that frail, soft throat. "You shut up till you're asked to talk," he said, frowning savagely. "I think we got a witness here that'll prove that you *did* have sufficient cause to make you want to get rid of Quade. And, if we have that proof, heaven help you. Montana, go get Sally Bent!"

Gaspar started up with a ring in his voice. "No, no!"

In response to a gesture from Sinclair, Denver Jim jerked the prisoner back onto the black rock. With blazing blue eyes, Gaspar glared at the judge, his delicate lips trembling with unspoken words.

Sinclair knew, with another strange falling of the heart, that the prisoner was perfectly aware that his judge had not the slightest suspicion of his guilt. An entente was established between them, an entente which distressed Sinclair, and which he strove to destroy. But, despite himself, he could not get rid of the knowledge that the great blue eyes were fixed steadily upon him, as if begging him to see that justice was done. Consequently, the judge made himself as impersonal as possible.

9

Sally Bent came willingly, even eagerly. It was the eagerness of an angry woman who wanted to talk.

"What is your name?"

"A name, you'll come to wish you'd never heard," said the girl, "if any harm comes to John Gaspar. Poor Jig, they won't *dare* to touch a hair of your head!"

With a gentle voice she had turned to Gaspar to speak these last words. A faint smile came on the lips of Gaspar, and his gaze was far away, as if he were in the midst of an unimportant dream, with Sally Bent the least significant part of it all. The girl flushed and turned back to Riley.

"I asked you your name," said his honor gravely.

"What right have you to ask me my name, or any other question?"

"Mr. Lodge," said his honor, "will you loosen up and tell this lady where we come in?"

"Sure," said the judge, clearing his throat. "Sally, here's the point. They ain't been much justice around here. We're simply giving the law a helping hand. And we start in today on the skunk that shot Quade. Quade may have had faults, but he was a man. And look at what done the killing! Sally, I ask you to look! That bum excuse for a man! That Gaspar!"

Following the command, Sally looked at Gaspar, the smile of pity and sympathy trembling on her lips again. But Gaspar took no notice.

"How dare you talk like that?" asked Sally. "Gaspar is worth all seven of you put together!"

"Order!" said Riley Sinclair. "Order in this here court. Mr. Sergeant-at-arms, keep the witness in order."

Larsen strode near authoritatively. "You got to stop that fresh talk, Sally. Sinclair won't stand for it."

"Oscar Larsen," she cried, whirling on him, "I always thought you were a man. Now I see that you're only big enough to bully a woman. I—I never want to speak to you again!"

"Silence!" thundered Riley Sinclair, smiting his hard brown hands together. "Take that witness away and we'll hang Gaspar without her testimony. We don't really need it—anyways."

There was a shrill cry from Sally. "Let me talk!" she pleaded. "Let me stay! I won't make no more trouble, Mr. Sinclair."

"All right," he decided without enthusiasm. "Now, what's your name?"

"Sally Bent." She smiled a little as she spoke. That name usually brought an answering smile, particularly from the men of Sour Creek. But Sinclair's saturnine face showed no softening.

"Mr. Clerk, swear the witness."

Judge Lodge rose and held forth the book and prescribed the oath.

During that interval, Riley Sinclair raised his head to escape from the steady, reproachful gaze of John Gaspar. Down in the valley bottom, Sour Creek flashed muddy-yellow and far away. Just beyond, the sun gleamed on a chalk-faced cliff. Still higher, the mountains changed between dawn and full day. There was the country for Riley Sinclair. What he did down here in the valleys did not matter. Purification waited for him among the summit snows. He turned back to hear the last of Sally Bent's voice, whipping his eyes past Gaspar to avoid meeting again that clinging stare.

"Sally Bent," he said, "do you know the prisoner?"

"You know I know him. John Gaspar boards with us."

"Ah, then you know him!"

"That's a silly question. What I want to say is—"

"Wait till you're asked, Sally Bent."

She stamped her foot. Quietly Sinclair compared the girl and the accused man.

"Here's the point," he said slowly. "You knew Quade, and you knew John Gaspar."

"Yes."

"You know Quade's dead?"

"I've just heard it."

"You didn't like him much?"

"I used to like him."

"Until Gaspar blew in?"

"You've got no right to ask those questions."

"I sure have. All right, I gather you were pretty sweet on Quade till Gaspar come along."

"I never said so!"

"Girl," pronounced Riley solemnly, "ain't it a fact that you went around to a lot of parties and suchlike things with Quade?"

She was silent.

"It's the straight thing you're giving her," broke in Larsen. "After Gaspar come, she didn't have no time for none of us!"

"Ah!" said his honor significantly, scowling on Sally Bent. "After you cut out Quade, he got ugly, didn't he?"

"He sure did!" said Sally. "He said things that no gentleman would of said to a lady."

"Such as what?"

"Such as that I was a flirt. And he said, I swear to it, that he'd get Gaspar!" She stopped, panting with excitement. "He wanted to murder John Gaspar!"

Riley Sinclair lifted his heavy brows. "That's a pretty serious thing to say, Sally Bent."

"But, it's the truth! And I've even heard him threaten Gaspar!"

"But you tried to make them friends? You tried to smooth Quade down?"

"I wouldn't waste my time on a bully! I just told John to get a gun and be ready to defend himself."

"And he done it?"

"He done it. But he never fired the gun."

"What was the last time Quade seen you?"

"The day before yesterday. He come up here and told me that he knew me and John Gaspar was going to get married, and that he wouldn't stand still and see the thing go through."

"But what he said was right, wasn't it? Gaspar had asked you to marry him?"

She dropped her head. "No."

"What? You mean to say that Gaspar hadn't told you he loved you?"

"Never! But now that John's in this trouble, I don't care if the whole world knows it! I love John Gaspar!"

What a voice! What a lighted face, as she turned to the prisoner. But, instead of a flush of happiness, John Gaspar rose and shrank away from the outstretched hands of the girl. And he was pale—pale with sorrow, and even with pity, it seemed to Sinclair.

"No, no," said the soft voice of Gaspar. "Not that, Sally. Not that!"

Decidedly it would not do to let this scene progress.

"Take away the witness, Montana."

Montana drew her arm into his, and she went away as one stunned, staring at John Gaspar as if she could not yet understand the extent of the calamity which had befallen her. She had been worse than scorned. She had been rejected with pity!

As she disappeared into the door of her house, Sinclair looked at the bowed head of John Gaspar.

"Denver!" he called suddenly.

"Yes, your honor."

"The prisoner's hands are tied. Wipe the sweat off'n his face, will you?"

"Sure!"

With a large and brilliant bandanna Montana obeyed. Then he paused in the midst of his operation.

"Your honor."

"Well?"

"It ain't sweat. It's tears!"

"Tears!" Riley Sinclair started up, then slumped back on his stump with a groan. "Tears!" he echoed, with a voice that was a groan. "John Gaspar, what kind of a man are you?"

He turned back to the court with a frown.

"Mr. Jury," he said, "look at this prisoner we got. Look him over considerable. I say, did you ever see a man like that? A man that ain't able to love a girl like Sally Bent when she just about throws herself at his head? Is he worth keeping alive? Look at him, and then listen to me. I see the whole of it, Mr. Jury."

Buck Mason leaned forward with interest, glowering upon John Gaspar.

"This skunk of a John Gaspar gets Sally all tied up with his sappy talk. Gets her all excited because he's something brand new and different. Quade gets sore, nacherallike. Then he comes to Gaspar and says: 'Cut out this soft talk to Sally, or I'll bust your head.' Gaspar don't love Sally, but he's afraid of Quade. He goes and gets a gun. He goes to Quade's house and tries to be friends. Quade kicks him out. Gaspar climbs back on his hoss and, while he's sitting there, pulls out a gun and shoots poor Quade dead. Don't that sound nacheral? He wouldn't marry Sally, but he didn't want another man to have her. And he wouldn't give up his soft berth in the house of Sally's brother. He knew Quade would never suspect him of having the nerve to fight. So he takes Quade unready and plugs him, while Quade ain't looking. Is that clear?"

"It sure sounds straight to me," said Buck Mason.

"All right! Stand up."

Mason rose.

"Take off your hat."

The sombrero was withdrawn with a flourish.

"God's up yonder higher'n that hawk, but seeing you clear, Buck. Tell us straight. Is Gaspar guilty or not?"

"Guilty as hell, your honor!"

A sigh from the prisoner. The last of life seemed to go from him, and Sinclair braced himself to meet a hysterical appeal. But there was only that slight drooping of the shoulders and declining of the head.

It was an appalling thing for Sinclair to watch. He was used to power in men and beasts. He understood it. A cunning devil of a fighting outlaw horse was his choice for a ride. "The meaner they are, the longer they last," he used to say. He respected men of evil as long as they were men of action. He was perfectly at home and contented among men, where one's purse and life were at constant hazard, where a turned back might mean destruction.

To him this meek surrender of hope was incomprehensibly despicable. If he had hesitated before, his hard soul was firm now in the decision that John Gaspar must die, and so leave Sinclair's own road free. With all suspicion of a connection between him and Quade's death gone, Riley could play a free hand against Sandersen. He turned a face of iron upon the prisoner.

"Sandersen and Denver Jim, bring the prisoner before me."

They obeyed. But when they reached down their hands

to Gaspar's shoulders to drag him to his feet, he avoided them with a shudder and of his own free will rose and walked between them.

"John Irving Gaspar," said Sinclair sternly, "alias Jig, alias Cold Feet—which is a fitting and proper name for you—have you got anything to say that won't take too long before I pronounce sentence on you?"

He had to set his teeth. The sad eyes of John Gaspar had risen from the ground and fixed steadily, darkly upon the eyes of his judge. There was infinite understanding, infinite patience in that look, the patience of the weak man, schooled in enduring buffets. For the moment Sinclair almost felt that the man was pitying him!

"I have only a little to say," said John Gaspar.

"Speak up then. Who d'you want to give the messages to?"

"To no living man," said John Gaspar.

"All right then, Gaspar. Blaze away with the talk, but make it short."

John Gaspar raised his head until he was looking through the stalwart branches of the cottonwood tree, into the haze of light above.

"Our Father in Heaven," said John Gaspar, "forgive them as I forgive them!"

Riley Sinclair, quivering under those words, looked around him upon the stunned faces of the rest of the court, then back to the calm of Gaspar. Strength seemed to have flooded the coward. At the moment when he lost all hope, he became glorious. His voice was soft, never rising, and the great, dark eyes were steadfast. A sudden consciousness came to Riley Sinclair that God must indeed be above them, higher than the flight of the hawk, robed in the maze of that lofty cloud, seeing all, hearing all. And every word that Gaspar spoke was damning him, dragging him to hell.

But Riley Sinclair was not a religious man. Luck was his divinity. He left God and heaven and hell inside the pages of the Bible, undisturbed. The music of the school-teacher's voice reminded him of the purling of some tiny waterfall in the midst of a mountain wilderness.

"I have no will to fight for life. For that sin, forgive me, and for whatever else I have done wrong. Let no knowledge of the crime they are committing come to these men. Fierce men, fighters, toilers, full of hate, full of despair, full of rage, how can they be other than blind? Forgive them, as I forgive them without malice. And most of all, Lord God, forgive this most unjust judge."

"Louder!" whispered Sandersen, his hand cupped behind his ear.

"Amen," said John Gaspar, as his head bowed again. The fascinated posse seemed frozen, each man in his place, each in his attitude.

"John Gaspar," said his honor, "here's your sentence: You're to be hanged by the neck till you're dead."

John Gaspar closed his eyes and opened them again. Otherwise he made no move of protest.

"But not," continued Sinclair, "from this cottonwood tree."

A faint sigh, indubitably of relief, came from the posse.

Riley Sinclair arose. "Gents," he said, "I been thinking this over. They ain't any doubt that the prisoner is guilty, and they ain't any doubt that John Gaspar is no good, anyway you look at him. But a gent that can put the words together like he can, ought to get a chance to talk in front of a regular jury. I figure we'd better send for the sheriff to come over from Woodville and take the prisoner back there. One of you gents can slide over there today, and the sheriff'll be here tomorrow, mostlike."

"But who'll take charge of Gaspar?"

"Who? Why me, of course! Unless somebody else would like the job more? I'll keep him right here in the Bent cabin."

"Sinclair," protested Buck Mason, "you're a pretty capable sort. They ain't no doubt of that. But what if Jerry Bent comes home, which he's sure to do before night? There'd be a mess, because Jerry'd fight for Gaspar, I know!"

"Partner," said Riley Sinclair dryly, "if it come to that, then I guess I'd have to fight back."

It was foolish to question the power in that grave, sardonic face. The other men gave way, nodding one by one. Secretly each man, now that the excitement was gone, was glad that they had not proceeded to the last extremity. In five minutes they were drifting away, and all this time Sinclair watched the face of John Gaspar, as the sorrow changed to wonder, and the wonder to the vague beginnings of happiness.

Suddenly he felt that he had the clue to the mystery of Cold Feet. As a matter of fact John Gaspar had never grown up. He was still a weak, dreamy boy.

10

The posse had hardly thrown its masks to the wind and galloped down the road when Sally Bent came running from the house.

"I knew they couldn't," she cried to John Gaspar. "I knew they wouldn't dare. The cowards! I'll remember every one of them!"

"Hush!" murmured Gaspar. His faint smile was for Riley Sinclair. "One of them is still here, you see!"

With wrath flushing her face, the girl looked at Riley.

"How do you dare to stay here and face me—after the things you said!"

"Lady," replied Sinclair, "you mean after the things I made you say."

"Just wait till Jerry comes," exclaimed Sally.

At this Sinclair grew more sober.

"Honey," he said dryly, "when your brother drops in, you just calm him down, will you? Because if him and Gaspar together was to start in raising trouble—well, they'd be more action than you ever seen in that cabin before. And, after it was all over, they'd have a dead Gaspar to cart over to Woodville. You can lay to that!"

It took Sally somewhat aback, this confident ferociousness.

"Them that brag ain't always the ones that do things," she declared. "But why are you staying here?"

"To keep Gaspar till the sheriff comes for him."

Sally grew white.

"Don't you see that there's nothing to be afraid of?" asked John Gaspar. "See how close I came to death, and yet I was saved. Why, God doesn't let innocent men be killed, Sally."

For a moment the girl stared at the schoolteacher with tears in her eyes; then she flashed at Riley a glance of utter scorn, as if inviting him to see what an angel upon the earth he was persecuting. But Sinclair remained unmoved.

He informed them of the conditions of his stay. He must be allowed to keep John Gaspar in sight at all times. Only suspicious moves he would resent with violence. Sally Bent heard all of this with openly expressed hatred and contempt. John Gaspar showed no emotion whatever.

"By heaven," declared Sinclair, when the girl had gone about some housework, "I'd actually think you believed that God was on your side. You talk about Him so familiar—like you and Him was partners."

John Gaspar smiled one of his rare smiles. He had a way of looking for a long moment at another before he spoke. All that he was about to say was first registered in his face. It was easy to understand how Sally Bent had been entrapped by the classic regularity of those features and the strange manner of the schoolteacher. She lived in a country where masculine men were a drug on the market. John Gaspar was the pleasant exception.

"You see," explained Gaspar, "I had to cheer Sally by saying something like that. Women like to have such things said. She'll be absolutely confident now, because she thinks I'm not disturbed. Very odd, but very true."

"And it seems to me," said Sinclair, frowning, "that you're not much disturbed, Gaspar. How does that come?"

"What can I do?"

"Maybe you'd be man enough to try to break away."

"From you? Tush! I know it is impossible. I'd as soon try to hide myself in an open field from that hawk. No, no! I'll give you my parole, my word of honor that I'll make no escape."

But Sinclair struck in with: "I don't want your parole. Hang it, man, just do your best, and I'll do mine. You try to give me the slip, and I'll try to keep you from it. That's square all around."

Gaspar observed him with what seemed to be a characteristic air of judicious reserve, very much as if he suspected a trap. A great many words came up into the throat of Riley Sinclair, but he refrained from speech.

In a way he was beginning to detest John Gaspar as he had never detested any human being before or since. To him no sin was so great as the sin of weakness in a man, and certainly Gaspar was superlatively weak. He had something in place of courage, but just what that thing was, Sinclair could not tell.

Curiosity drew him toward the fellow; and these weaknesses repulsed him. No wonder that he stared at him now in a quandary. One certainty was growing upon him. He wished Gaspar to escape. It would bring him shame in Sour Creek, but for the opinion of these men he had not the slightest respect. Let them think as they pleased.

It came home to Riley that this was a man whose like he had never known before, and whom he must not, therefore, judge as if he knew him. He softened his voice.

"Gaspar," he said, "keep your head up. Make up your

mind that you'll fight to the last gasp. Why, it makes me plumb sick to see a grown man give up like you do!"

His scorn rang in his voice, and Gaspar looked at him in wonder.

"You'd ought to be packing yourself full of courage," went on Sinclair. "Here's your pal, Jerry Bent, coming back. Two agin' one, you'll be. Ain't that a chance, I ask you?"

But Gaspar shook his head. He seemed even a little amused.

"Not against a man like you, Sinclair. You love fighting, you see. You're made for fighting. You make me think of that hawk. All beak and talons, made to tear, remorseless, crafty."

"That's overrating me a pile," muttered Riley, greatly pleased by this tribute, as he felt it to be. "If you tried, maybe you could do a lot yourself. You're full of nerves, and a gent that's full of nerves makes a first-class fighting man, once he finds out what he can do. With them fingers of yours you could learn to handle a gun like a flash. Start in and learn to be a man, Gaspar!"

Sinclair stretched a friendly hand toward the shoulder of the smaller man. The hand passed through thin air. Gaspar had slipped away. He stood at a greater distance. On his face there was a strong expression of displeasure.

Sinclair scowled darkly. "Now what d'you mean by that?"

"I mean that I don't envy you," said Gaspar steadily. "I'd rather have the other thing."

"What other thing, Jig?"

Gaspar overlooked the contemptuous nickname, doubly contemptuous on the lips of a stranger.

"You go into the world and take what you want. I'm stronger than that."

"How are you stronger?" asked Riley.

"Because I sit in my room, and I can make the world come to me."

"Jig, I was never smart at riddles. Go ahead and clear yourself up with a few more words."

The other hesitated—not for words, but as if he wondered if it might be worth while for him to explain. Never in Riley Sinclair's life had he been taken so lightly.

"Will you follow me into the house?" asked Gaspar at length.

"I'll follow you, right enough," said Sinclair. "That's my job. Lead on."

He was brought through the living room of the cabin and into a smaller room to the side.

Comfort seemed to fill this smaller room. Bookcases ranged along one wall were packed with books. The couch before the window was heaped with cushions. There was an easy chair with an adjustable back, so that one could either sit or lie in it. There was a lamp with a big greenish-yellow shade.

"This is what I mean," murmured Jig.

Riley Sinclair's bold eye roved swiftly, contemptuously. "Well, you got this place fixed up pretty stuffy," he answered. "Outside of that, hang me if I see what you mean."

Cold Feet slipped into a chair and, interlacing those fingers whose delicacy baffled and disturbed Sinclair, stared over them at his companion.

"I really shouldn't expect you to understand, my friend."

"Friend!" Sinclair exploded. "You're a queer bird, Jig. What do you mean by 'friend'?"

"Why not?" asked this amazing youth, and the quiet of his face brightened into a smile. "I'd be swinging from the end of a rope if it weren't for you, you know."

Sinclair shrugged away this rejoinder. He trod heavily to the bookshelves, took up two or three random volumes, and tossed them heedlessly back into place.

"Well, kid, you're going to be yanked out of this little imitation world of yours pretty pronto."

"Ah, but perhaps not!"

"Eh?"

"Something may happen."

"What can happen?"

"Just something like you, my friend."

The insistence on that word irritated Riley Sinclair.

"Don't call me that," he replied in his most brutal manner. "Jig, d'you know what a friend means?" he asked. "How d'you figure that word out?"

Jig considered. "A friend is somebody you know and like and are glad to have around."

Contempt spread on the face of Sinclair. "That's just about what I knew you'd say."

"Am I wrong?"

"Son, they ain't anything right about you, as far as I can make out. Wrong? You're as wrong as a yearling in a blizzard. Wrong? I should tell a man you're wrong! Lemme tell you what a friend is. He's the bunkie that guards your back in a fight; he's the man that can ask for your hoss or your gun or your life, no matter how bad you want 'em; he's the gent that trusts you when the world calls you a liar; he's the one that don't grin when you're in trouble, who gives a cheer when you're going good. With a friend you let down the bars and turn your mind loose like wild hosses. I take out my soul like a gun and show it to my friend in the palm of my hand. It's sure full of holes and stains, this life of mine, but my friend checks off the good agin' the bad, and when you're through he says: 'Partner, now I like you better because I know you better.'

"Son, I don't know what God means very well, and I ain't any bunkie of the law, but I'm tolerable well acquainted with what the word 'friend' means. When you use it, you want to look sharp."

"I really believe," Jig said, "that you would be a friend like that. I think I understand."

"You don't, though. To a friend you give yourself away,

and you get yourself back bigger and stronger."

"I didn't know," said Jig softly, "that friendship could mean all that. How many friends have you had?"

The big cowpuncher paused. Then he said gently at length, "One friend."

"In all your life?"

"Sure! I was lucky and had one friend."

Cold Feet leaned forward, eagerness in his eyes. "Tell me about him!

"I don't know you well enough, son."

That jarring speech thrust Jig back into his chair, as if with a physical hand. There, as though in covert, he continued to study Sinclair. Presently he began to nod.

"I knew it from the first, in spite of appearances."

"Knew what?"

"Knew that we'd get along."

"And are we getting along, Jig?"

"I think so."

"Glad of that," muttered the cowpuncher dryly.

"Ah," cried John Gaspar, "you're not as hard as you seem. One of these days I'll prove it. Besides, you won't forget me."

"What makes you so sure of that?"

Jig rose from his chair and stood leaning against it, his hands dropped lightly into the pockets of his dressing gown. He looked extraordinarily boyish at that moment, and he seemed to have the fearlessness of a child which knows that the world has no real account against it. Riley Sinclair set his teeth to keep back a flood of pity that rose in him.

"You wait and see," said Jig. He raised a finger at Sinclair. "I'll keep coming back into your mind a long time after you leave me; and you'll keep coming back into my mind. Oh, I know it!"

"How in thunder do you?"

"I don't know. Just because—well, how did I understand

at the trial that you knew I was innocent, and that you would let no harm come to me?"

"Did you know that?" asked Sinclair.

Instead of answering, Jig broke into his soft, pleasant laughter.

11

"Laugh and be hanged," declared Sinclair. "I'm going outside. And don't try no funny breaks while I'm gone," he said. "I'll be watching and waiting when you ain't expecting." With that he was gone.

At the door of the house a gust of hot wind struck him, for the day was verging on noon, and there seemed more heat than light in the sun. Even to that hot gust Sinclair jerked his bandanna knot aside and opened his throat gratefully. He felt as if he had been under a hard nervous strain for some time past. Cold Feet, the craven, the weak of hand and the frail of spirit, had tested him in a new way. He had been confronting a novel and unaccountable thing. He felt very oddly as if someone had been prodding into corners of his nature yet unknown even to himself. He tingled from the rapier touches of that last laughter.

Now his eye roamed with relief across the valley. Heat waves blurred the hollow and pushed Sour Creek away until it seemed a river of mist—yellow mist. He raised his attention out of that sweltering hollow to the cool, blue, mighty mountains—his country!

Presently he had forgotten all this. He settled his hat on the back of his head and began to kick a stone before him, following it aimlessly.

Someone was humming close to him, and he turned

sharply to see Sally Bent go by, carrying a bucket. She smiled generously, and though he knew that she doubtless hated him in her heart and smiled for a purpose, he had to reply with a perfunctory grin. He stalked after her to the little leaping creek and dipped out a full bucket.

"Thanks," said Sally, wantonly meeting his eye.

As well try to soften a sphinx. Sinclair carried the dripping bucket on the side nearest the girl and thereby gained valuable distance.

"I'm mighty glad it's you and not one of the rest," confided Sally, still smiling firmly up to him.

He avoided that appeal with a grunt.

"Like Sandersen, say," went on the girl.

"Why not him?"

"He's a bad hombre," said the girl. "Hate to have Jig in his hands. With you it's different."

Sinclair waited until he had put down the bucket in the kitchen. Then he faced Sally thoughtfully.

"Why?" he asked.

"Because you're reasonable."

"Did Jig tell you that?"

"And a pile more. Jig says you're a pretty fine sort. That's his words."

The cowpuncher caressed the butt of his gun with his fingertips, his habitual gesture when in doubt.

"Lady," he said at length, "suppose I cut this short? You think I ain't going to keep Cold Feet here till the sheriff comes for him?"

"You see what it would mean?" she asked eagerly. "It wouldn't be a fair trial. You couldn't get a fair jury for Jig around Sour Creek and Woodville. They hate him—all the young men do. D'you know why? Simply because he's different! Simply because—"

"Because all the girls are pretty fond of him, eh?"

"You can put it that way if you want," she answered steadily enough, though she flushed under his stare.

Then: "You'll keep that in mind, and you're man enough to do what you think is right, ain't you, Mr. Sinclair?"

He shifted away from the hand which was moving toward him.

"I'll tell you what," he answered. "I'm man enough to be afraid of a girl like you, Sally Bent."

Then he saw her head fall in despair, as he turned away. When he reached the shimmering heat of the outdoors again, he was feeling like a murderer. His reason told him that Cold Feet was "yaller," not worth saving. His reason told him that he could save Jig only by a confession that would drive him, Sinclair, away from Sour Creek and his destined victim, Sandersen. Or he could save Jig by violating the law, and that also would drive him from Sour Creek and Sandersen.

Suddenly he halted in the midst of his pacing to and fro. Why was he turning these alternatives back and forth in his mind? Because, he understood all at once, he had subconsciously determined that Cold Feet must not die!

The face of his brother rose up and looked into his eyes. That was the friend of whom he would not speak to Jig, brother and friend at once. And as surely as ever ghost called to living man, that face demanded the death of Sandersen. He blinked the vision away.

"I *am* going nutty," muttered Sinclair. "Whether Sandersen lives or dies, Jig ain't going to dance at a rope's end!"

Presently Sally called him in to lunch, and Riley ate half-heartedly. All during the meal neither Sally nor John Gaspar had more than a word for him, while they talked steadily together. They seemed to understand each other so well that he felt a hidden insult in it.

Once or twice he made a heavy attempt to enter the conversation, always addressing his remarks to Sally Bent. He was received graciously, but his remarks always fell dead, and a moment later Cold Feet had picked up the frayed ends of his own talk and won the entire attention of Sally. Riley was beginning to understand why the youth of that district detested Cold Feet.

"Always takes some soft-handed dude to make a winning with a fool girl," he comforted himself.

He expected the arrival of Jerry Bent before nightfall, and with that arrival, perhaps, there would be a new sort of attack on him. Sally and Cold Feet were trying persuasion, but they might encourage Jerry Bent to attempt physical force. With all his heart Riley Sinclair hoped so. He had a peculiar desire to do something significant for the eyes of both Sally and Jig.

But nightfall came, and then supper, and still no Jerry appeared. Afterward, Sinclair made ready to sleep in Jig's room. Cold Feet offered him the couch.

"Beds and me don't hitch" declared Riley, throwing two or three of the rugs together. "I ain't particular partial to a floor, neither, but these here rugs will give it a sort of a ground softness."

He sat cross-legged on the low pile of rugs, while he pulled off his boots and smoked his good-night cigarette. Jig coiled up in a big chair, while he studied his jailer.

"But how can you go to bed so early?" he asked.

"Early? It ain't early. Sun's down, ain't it? Why do they bring on night, except for folks to go to sleep?"

"For my part the best part of the day generally begins when the sun goes down."

With patient contempt Riley considered John Gaspar. "You look kind of that way," he decided aloud. "Pale and not much good with your shoulders. Now, what d'you most generally do with your time in the evening?"

"Why—talk."

"Talk? Huh! A fine way of wasting time for a growed-up man."

"And I read, you know."

"I can see by the looks of them shelves that you do. How many of them books might you have read, Jig?"

"All of them."

"I ask you, man to man, ain't they mostly somebody's idea of what life is?"

"I suppose that's a short way of putting it."

"And I ask you ag'in, what's better to take a secondhand hunch out of what somebody else thinks life might be, or to go out and do some living on your own hook?"

Cold Feet had been smiling faintly up to this point, as though he had many things in reserve which might be said at need. Now his smile disappeared.

"Perhaps you're right."

"And maybe I ain't." Sinclair brushed the entire argument away into a thin mist of smoke. "Now, look here, Cold Feet, I'm about to go to sleep, and when I sleep, I sure sleep sound, taking it by and large. They's times when I don't more'n close one eye all night, and they's times when you'd have to pull my eyes open, one by one, to wake me up. Understand? I'm going to sleep the second way tonight. About eight hours of the soundest sleep you ever heard tell of."

Jig considered him gravely.

"I'm afraid," he answered, "that I won't sleep nearly as well."

Riley Sinclair smiled. "Wouldn't be no ways nacheral for you to do much sleeping," he agreed. "Take a gent that's in danger of having his neck stretched, like you, and most generally he don't do much sleeping. He lies around awake, cussing his luck, I s'pose. Take you, now, Cold Feet, and I s'pose you'll be figuring on how far a hoss could carry you in the eight hours that I'll be sleeping. Eh?"

There was a suggestive lift of the eyebrows, as he spoke, but before Jig had a chance to study his face, he had turned and wrapped himself in one of the rugs. He lay perfectly still, stretched on one side, with his back turned to Jig. He stirred neither hand nor foot.

Outside, a door slammed heavily; Cold Feet heard the heavy voice of Jerry Bent and the beat of his heels across the floor. In spite of those noises Riley Sinclair was presently sound asleep, as he had promised. Gaspar knew it by the rise and fall of the arm which lay along Sinclair's side, also by the sound of his breathing.

Cold Feet went to the window and looked out on the mountains, black and huge, with a faint shimmer of snow on the farthest summits. At the very thought of trying to escape into that wilderness and wandering alone among the peaks, he shuddered. He came back and studied the sleeper. Something about the nonchalance with which Sinclair had gone to sleep under the very eye of his prisoner affected John Gaspar strangely. Doubtless it was sheer contempt for the man he was guarding. And, indeed, something assured Jig that, no matter how well he employed the next eight hours in putting a great distance between himself and Sour Creek, the tireless riding of Sinclair would more than make up the distance.

Gaspar went to the door, then turned sharply and glanced over his shoulder at the sleeper; but the eyes of Sinclair were still closed, and his regular breathing continued. Jig turned the knob cautiously and slipped out into the living room.

Jerry and Sally beckoned instantly to him from the far side of the room. The beauty of the family had descended upon Sally alone. Jerry was a swart-skinned, squat, bowlegged, efficient cowpuncher. He now ambled awkwardly to meet John Gaspar.

"Are you all set?" he asked.

"For what?"

"To start on the trail!" exclaimed Jerry. "What else? Ain't Sinclair asleep?"

"How d'you know?"

"I listened at the door and heard his breathing a long time ago. Thought you'd never come out."

Sally Bent was already on the other side of Gaspar, drawing him toward the door.

"You can have my hoss, Jig," she offered. "Meg is sure as

sin in the mountains. You won't have nothing to fear on the worst trail they is."

"Not a thing," asserted Jerry.

They half led and half dragged Cold Feet to the door.

"I'll show you the best way. You see them two peaks yonder, like a pair of mule's ears? You start—"

"I don't know," said Jig. "It seems very difficult, even to think of riding alone through those mountains."

Sally was white with fear. "You ain't going to throw away this chance, Jig? It'll mean hanging sure, if you don't run now. Ask Jerry what they're saying in Sour Creek tonight?"

Jerry volunteered the information. "They're all wondering why you wasn't strung up today, when they got so much evidence agin' you. Also they're thinking that the boys played plumb foolish in turning you over to this stranger, Sinclair, to guard. But they're waiting for Sheriff Kern to come over from Woodville an' nab you in the morning. They's some that says that they won't wait, if it looks like the law is going to take too long to hang you. They'll get up a necktie party and break the jail and do their own hanging. I heard all them things and more, Jig."

John Gaspar looked uncertainly from one to the other of his friends.

"You've *got* to go!" cried Sally.

"I've got to go," admitted Cold Feet in a whisper.

"I've got Meg saddled for you already. She's plumb gentle."

"Just a minute. I've forgotten something."

"You don't mean you're going back into that room where Sinclair is?"

"I won't waken him. He's sleeping like the dead."

Jig turned away from them and hurried back to his room. Having opened and closed the door softly, he went to a chest of drawers near the window and fumbled in the half-light of the low-burning lamp. He slipped a small leather case into the breast pocket of his coat, and then stole back toward the door, as softly as before. With his hand on the knob, he paused and looked back. For all he knew, Sinclair might be really awake now, watching his quarry from beneath those heavy lashes, waiting until his prisoner should have made a definite attempt to escape.

And then the big man would rise to his feet as soon as the door was closed. The picture became startlingly real to John Gaspar. Sinclair would slip out that window, no doubt, and circle around toward the horse shed. There he would wait until his prisoner came out on Meg, and then without warning would come a shot, and there would be an end of Sinclair's trouble with his prisoner. Gaspar could easily attribute such cunning cruelty to Sinclair. And yet there was something untested, unprobed, different about the rangy fellow.

Whatever it was, it kept Gaspar staring down into the lean face of Sinclair for a long moment. Then he went resolutely back into the living room and faced Sally Bent; Jerry was already waiting outdoors.

"I'm not going," said Gaspar slowly. "I'll stay."

Sally cried out. "Oh, Jig, have you lost your nerve ag'in? Ain't you got *no* courage?"

The schoolteacher sighed. "I'm afraid not, Sally. I guess my only courage comes in waiting and seeing how things turn out."

He turned and went gloomily back to his room.

12

With the first brightness of dawn, Sinclair wakened even more suddenly that he had fallen asleep. There was no slow adjusting of himself to the requirements of the day. One prodigious stretching of the long arms, one great yawn, and he was as wide awake as he would be at noon.

He jerked on his boots and rose, and not until he stood up, did he see John Gaspar asleep in the big chair, his head inclining to one side, the book half-fallen from his hand, and the lamp sputtering its last beside him. But instead of viewing the weary face with pity, Sinclair burst into sudden and amazed profanity.

The first jarring note brought Gaspar up and awake with a start, and he stared in astonishment at the uninterrupted flood which rippled from the lips of the cowpuncher. It concluded: "Still here! Of all the shorthorned fatheads that I ever seen, the worst is this Gaspar—this Jig—this Cold Feet. Say, man, ain't you got no spirit at all?"

"What do you mean?" asked Gaspar. "Still here? Of course I'm still here! Did you expect me to escape?"

Sinclair flung himself into a chair, speechless with rage and disgust.

"Did you think I was joking when I told you I was going to sleep eight hours without waking up?"

"It might very well have been a trap, you know."

Sinclair groaned. "Son, they ain't any man in the world that'll tell you that Riley Sinclair sets his traps for birds that ain't got their stiff feathers growed yet. Trap for you? What in thunder should I want you for, eh?"

He strode to the window, still groaning.

"There's where you'd ought to be, over yonder behind them mule ears. They'd never catch you in a thousand years with that start. Eight hours start! As good as have eight years, kid—just as good. And you've throwed that chance away!"

He turned and stared mournfully at the schoolteacher.

"It ain't no use," he said sadly. "I see it all now. You was cut out to end in a rope collar."

Not another word could be pried from his set lips during breakfast, a gloomy meal to which Sally Bent came with red eyes, and Jerry Bent sullenly, with black looks at Sinclair. Jig was the cheeriest one of the party. That cheer at last brought another explosion from Sinclair. They stood in front of the house, watching a horseman wind his way up the road through the hills.

"It's Sheriff Kern," said Jerry Bent. "I can tell by the way he rides, sort of slanting. It's Kern, right enough."

Sally Bent choked, but Jig continued to hum softly.

"Singin'?" asked Riley Sinclair suddenly. "Ain't you no more worried than that?"

The voice of the schoolteacher in reply was as smooth as running water. "I think you'll bring me out of the trouble safely enough, Mr. Sinclair."

"Mr. Sinclair'll see you damned before he lifts a hand for you!" Riley retorted savagely.

He strode to his horse and expended his wrath by viciously jerking at the cinches, until the mustang groaned. Sheriff Kern came suddenly into clear view around the last turn and rode quickly up to them, a very short man, muscular, sweaty. He always gave the impression that he had been working ceaselessly for a week, and certainly he found time to shave only once in ten days. Dense bristle clouded the lower features of his face. He was a taciturn man. His greetings took the form of a single grunt. He took possession of John Gaspar with a single glance that sent the latter nervously toward his saddle horse.

"I see you got this party all ready for me," said the sheriff more amiably to Riley Sinclair, who was watching in disgust the clumsy method of Jig's mounting. "You're Sinclair, I guess?"

"I'm Sinclair, sheriff."

They shook hands.

"Nice bit of work you done for me, Sinclair, keeping the boys from stringing up Jig, yonder. These here lynchings don't set none too well on the reputation of a sheriff. I guess we're ready to start. S'long Sally—Jerry. Are you riding our way, Sinclair?"

"I thought I'd happen along. Ain't never seen Woodville yet."

"Glad to have you. But they ain't much to see unless you look twice at the same thing."

They started down the trail three abreast.

"Ride on ahead," commanded Sinclair to Jig. "We don't want you riding in the same line with men. Git on ahead!"

John Gaspar obeyed that brutal order with bowed head. He rode listlessly, with loose rein, letting the pony pick its own way. Once Sinclair looked back to Sally Bent, weeping in the arms of her brother. Again his face grew black.

"And yet," confided the sheriff softly, "I ain't never heard no trouble about this Gaspar before."

"He's poison," declared Sinclair bitterly, and he raised his voice that it would unmistakably carry to the shrinking figure before them. "He's such a yaller-hearted skunk, sheriff, that it makes me ashamed of bein' a man!"

"They's only one thing I misdoubt," said the sheriff. "How'd that sort of a gent ever get the nerve to murder a man like Quade? Quade wasn't no tenderfoot, and he could shoot a bit, besides."

"Speaking personal, sheriff, I don't think he done it, now I've had a chance to go over the evidence."

"Maybe he didn't, but most like he'll hang for it. The boys is dead set agin' him. First, he's a dude; second, he's a coward. Sour Creek and Woodville wasn't never cut out for that sort. They ain't wanted around."

That speech made Riley Sinclair profoundly thoughtful. He had known well enough before this that there were small chances of Jig escaping from the damning judgment of twelve of these cowpunchers. The statement of the sheriff made the belief a fact. The death sentence of Jig was pronounced the moment the doors of the jail at Woodville clanged upon him.

They struck the trail to Sour Creek and almost immediately swung off on a branch which led south and west, in the opposite direction from the creek. It was a day of high-driving clouds, thin and fleecy, so that they merely filtered the sunlight and turned it into a haze without decreasing the heat perceptibly, and that heat grew until it became difficult to look down at the blazing sand.

Now the trail climbed among broken hills until they reached a summit. From that point on, now and again the road elbowed into view of a wide plain, and in the center of the plain there was a diminutive dump of buildings.

"Woodville," said the sheriff. "Hey, you, Jig, hustle that hoss along!"

Obediently the drooping Gaspar spurred his horse. The animal broke into a gallop that set Gaspar jolting in the seat, with wildly flopping elbows.

"Look at that," said Sinclair. "Would you ever think that men could be born as awkward as that? Would you ever think that men would be born that didn't have no use in the world?"

"He ain't altogether useless," decided the sheriff. "Seems as how he's done noble in the school. Takes on with the little boys and girls most amazing, and he knows how to keep even the eighth graders interested. But what can you expect of a gent that ain't got no more pride than to be a schoolteacher, eh?"

Sinclair shook his head.

The trail drifted downward now less brokenly, and Woodville came into view. It was a wretched town in a wretched landscape, far different from the wild hills and the rich plowed grounds around Sour Creek. All that came to life in the brief spring, the long summer had long since burned away to drab yellows and browns. A horrible place to die in, Sinclair thought.

"Speaking of hosses, that's a wise-looking hoss you got, sheriff."

"Rode him for five years," said the sheriff. "Raised him and busted him and trained him all by myself. Ain't nobody but me ever rode him. He can go so soft-footed he wouldn't bust eggs, sir, and he can turn loose and run like the wind. They ain't no better hoss than this that's come under my eye, Sinclair. Are you much on the points of a hoss?"

"I use hosses—I don't love 'em," said Sinclair gloomily. "But I can read the points tolerable."

The sheriff eyed Sinclair coldly. "So you don't love hosses, eh?" he said, returning distantly to the subject. It was easy to see where his own heart lay by the way his roan picked up its head whenever its master spoke.

"Sheriff," explained Sinclair, "I'm a single-shot gent. I don't aim to have no scatter fire in what I like. They's only one man that I ever called friend, they's only one place that I ever called home—the mountains, yonder—and they's only one hoss that I ever took to much. I raised Molly up by hand, you might say. She was ugly as sin, but they wasn't nothing she couldn't do—nothing!" He paused. "Sheriff, I used to talk to that hoss!"

The sheriff was greatly moved. "What became of her?" he asked softly.

"I took after a gent once. He couldn't hit me, but he put a slug through Molly."

"What became of the gent?" asked the sheriff still more softly.

"He died just a little later. Just how I ain't prepared to state."

"Good!" said the sheriff. He actually smiled in the pleasure of newfound kinship. "You and me would get on proper, Sinclair."

"Most like."

"This hoss of mine, now, has sense enough to take me home without me touching a rein. Knows direction like a wolf."

"Could you guide her with your knees?"

"Sure."

"And she's plumb safe with you?"

"Sure."

"I knowed a gent once that said he'd trust himself tied hand and foot on his hoss."

"That goes for me and my hoss, too, Sinclair."

"Well, then, just shove up them hands, sheriff!"

The sheriff blinked, as the sun flashed on the revolver in the steady hand of Sinclair. There was a significant little jerking up of the revolver. Each time the muzzle stirred, the hands of the sheriff jumped higher and higher until his arms were stiffly stretched. Gaspar had halted his horse and looked back in amazement.

"I hate to do it," declared Sinclair. "Right off I sort of took to you, sheriff. But this has got to be done."

"Sinclair, have you done much thinking before you figured this all out?"

"Enough! If I knowed you one shade better, sheriff, I'd take your word that you'd ride on into Woodville, good and slow, and not start no pursuit. But I don't know you that well. I got to tie you on the back of that steady old hoss of yours and turn you loose. We need that much start."

He dismounted, still keeping careful aim, took the rope coiled beside the sheriff's own saddle horn and began a swift and sure process of tying. He worked deftly, without undue fear or haste, and Gaspar came back to look on with scared eyes.

"You're a fool, Sinclair," murmured the sheriff. "You'll never get shut of me. I'll foller you till I drop dead. I'll never forget you. Change your mind now, and we'll say nothing has happened. But if you keep on, you're done for as sure as my name is Kern. Take you by yourself, and you'd be a handful to catch. But two is easier than one, and, when one of them two is a deadweight like Gaspar, they ain't nothing to it."

He finished his appeal completely trussed.

"I ain't tied you on the hoss," said Sinclair. "Take note of that. Also I'm leaving you your guns, sheriff."

"I hope you'll have a chance to see 'em come out of the holster later on, Sinclair."

The cowpuncher took no notice of this bitterness. Gaspar, who looked on, was astonished by a certain deferential politeness on the part of the big cowpuncher.

"Speaking personal, I hope I don't never have no trouble with you, sheriff. I like you, understand?"

"Have your little joke, Sinclair!"

"I mean it. I know I'm usin' you like a skunk. But I got a special need, and I can't take no chances. Sheriff, I tell you out of my heart that I'm sorry! Will you believe me?"

The sheriff smiled. "The same as you'll believe me when we change parts, Sinclair."

The big man sighed. "I s'pose it's got to be that way," he said. "But if you come for me, Kern, come all primed for action. It'll be a hard trail."

"That's my specialty."

"Well, sheriff, s'long—and good luck!"

The sheriff nodded. "Thanks!"

Pressing his horse with his knees, Kern started down the trail at a slow canter. Sinclair followed the retiring figure, nodding with admiration at the skill with which the sheriff kept his mount under control, merely by power of voice. Presently the latter turned a corner of the trail and was out of sight.

"But—I knew—I knew!" exclaimed John Gaspar. "Only, why did you let him go on into town?"

The cold glance of Sinclair rested on his companion. "What would you have done?"

"Tied him up and left him here."

"I think you would—to die in the sun!" He swung up into his saddle. "Now, Gaspar, we've started on what's like to prove the last trail for both of us, understand? By night we'll both be outlawed. They'll have a price on us, and long before night, Kern will be after us. For the first time in your soft-headed life you've got to work, and you've got to fight."

"I'll do it, Mr. Sinclair!"

"Bah! Save your talk. Talk's dirt cheap."

"I only ask one thing. Why have you done it?"

"Because, you fool, I killed Quade!"

13

From the first there was no thought in the sheriff's mind of riding straight into Woodville, trussed and helpless as he was. Woodville respected him, and the whole district was proud of its sheriff. He knew that five minutes of laughter can blast the finest reputation that was ever built by a lifetime of hard labor. He knew the very faces of the men who would never let the story die, of how the sheriff came into town, not only without his prisoner, but tied hand and foot, helpless in the saddle.

Without his prisoner!

Never before in his twenty years as sheriff had a criminal escaped from his hands. Many a time they had tried, and on those occasions he had brought back a dead body for the hand of the law.

This time he had ample excuse. Any man in the world might admit that he was helpless when such a fellow as Riley Sinclair took him by surprise. He knew Sinclair well by reputation, and he respected all that he had heard.

No matter for that. The fact remained that his unbroken string of successes was interrupted. Perhaps Woodville would explain his failure away. No doubt some of the men knew of Sinclair and would not wonder. They would stand up doughtily for the prowess of their sheriff. Yet the fact held that he had failed. It was a moral defeat more than anything else.

His mind was made up to remain in the mountains until he starved, or until he had removed those shameful ropes—his own rope! At that thought he writhed again. But here an arroyo opening in the ragged wall of a cliff caught his eye. He turned his horse into it and continued on his way until he saw a projecting rock with a ragged edge, left where a great fragment had recently fallen away.

Here he found it strangely awkward and even perilous to dismount without his hands to balance his weight, as he shifted out of the stirrups. In spite of his care, he stumbled over a loose rock as he struck the ground and rolled flat on his back. He got up, grinding his teeth. His hands were tied behind him. He turned his back on the broken rock and sawed the ropes against it. To his dismay he felt the rock edge crumble away. It was some chalky, friable stuff, and it gave at the first friction.

Beads of moisture started out on the sheriff's forehead. Hastily he started on down the arroyo and found another rock, with an edge not nearly so favorable in appearance, but this time it was granite. He leaned his back against it and rubbed with a short shoulder motion until his arms ached, but it was a happy labor. He felt the rock edge taking hold of the ropes, fraying the strands to weakness, and then eating into them. It was very slow work!

The sun drifted up to noon, and still he was leaning against that rock, working patiently, with his head near to bursting, and perspiration, which he could not wipe away, running down to blind him. Finally, when his brain was beginning to reel with the heat, and his shoulders ached to numbness, the last strand parted. The sheriff dropped down to the ground to rest.

Presently he drew out his jackknife and methodically cut the remaining bonds. It came to him suddenly, as he stood up, that someone might have seen this singular performance and carried the tale away for future laughter. The thought drove the sheriff mad. He swung savagely into the saddle and drove his horse at a dead run among the perilous going of that gorge. When he reached the plain he paused, hesitant between a bulldog desire to follow the trail single-handed into the mountains and run down the pair, and a knowledge that he who retreats has an added power that would make such a pursuit rash beyond words.

A phrase which he had coined for the gossips of Woodville, came back into his mind. He was no longer as young as he once was, and even at his prime he shrewdly doubted his ability to cope with Riley Sinclair. With the weight of Gaspar thrown in, the thing became an impossibility. Gaspar might be a weakling, but a man who was capable of a murder was always dangerous.

To have been thwarted once was shame enough, but he dared not risk two failures with one man. He must have help in plenty from Woodville, and, fate willing, he would one day have the pleasure of looking down into the dead face of Sinclair; one day have the unspeakable joy of seeing the slender form of Gaspar dangling from the end of a rope.

His mind was filled with the wicked pleasure of these pictures until he came suddenly upon Woodville. He drew his horse back to a dogtrot to enter the town.

It was a short street that led through Woodville, but, short though it was, the news that something was wrong with the sheriff reached the heart of the town before he did. Men were already pouring out on the veranda of the hotel.

"Where is he, sheriff?" was the greeting.

Never before had that question been asked. He switched to one side in his saddle and made the speech that startled the mind of Woodville for many a day.

"Boys, I've been double-crossed. Have any of you heard tell of Riley Sinclair?"

He waited apparently calm. Inwardly he was breathless with excitement, for according to the size of Riley's reputation as a formidable man would be the size of his disgrace. There was a brief pause. Old Shaw filled the gap, and he filled it to the complete satisfaction of the sheriff.

"Young Hopkins was figured for the hardest man up in Montana way,"he said. "That was till Riley Sinclair beat him. What about Sinclair?"

"It was him that double-crossed me," said the sheriff, vastly relieved. "He come like a friend, stuck me up on the trail when I wasn't lookin' for no trouble, and he got away with Gaspar."

A chorus, astonished, eager. "What did he do it for?"

"No man'll ever know," said the sheriff.

"Why not?"

"Because Sinclair'll be dead before he has a chance to look a jury in the face."

There were more questions. The little crowd had got its breath again, and the words came in volleys. The sheriff cut sharply through the noise.

"Where's Bill Wood?"

"He's in town now."

"Charley, will you find Billy for me and ask him to slide over to my office? Thanks! Where's Arizona and Red Chalmers?"

"They went back to the ranch."

"Be a terrible big favor if you'd go out and try to find 'em for me, boys. Where's Joe Stockton?"

"Up to the Lewis place."

Old Shaw struck in: "You ain't makin' no mistake in picking the best you can get. You'll need 'em for this Riley Sinclair. I've heard tell about him. A pile!"

The very best that Woodville and its vicinity could offer, was indeed what the sheriff was selecting. Another man would have looked for numbers, but the sheriff knew well enough that numbers meant little speed, and speed was one of the main essentials for the task that lay before him. He knew each of the men he had named, and he had known them for years, with the exception of Arizona. But the latter, coming up from the southland, had swiftly proved his ability in many a brawl.

Bill Wood was a peerless trailer; Red Chalmers would, the sheriff felt, be one day a worthy aspirant for the office which he now held, and Red was the only man the sheriff felt who could succeed to that perilous office. As for Joe Stockton, he was distinctly bad medicine, but in a case like this, it might very well be that poison would be the antidote for poison. Of all the men the sheriff knew, Joe was the neatest hand with a gun. The trouble with Joe was that he appreciated his own ability and was fond of exhibiting his prowess.

Having sent out for his assistants on the chase, the sheriff retired to his office and set his affairs in order. There was not a great deal of paper work connected with his position; in twenty minutes he had cleared his desk, and, by the time he had finished this task, the first of his posse had sauntered into the doorway and stood leaning idly there, rolling a cigarette.

"Have a chair, Bill, will you?" said the sheriff. He tilted back in his own and tossed his heels to the top of his desk. "Getting sort of warm today, ain't it?"

Bill Wood had never seen the sheriff so cheerful. He sat down gingerly, knowing well that some task of great danger lay before them.

14

All that Gaspar dreaded in Riley Sinclair had come true. The schoolteacher drew his horse as far away as the trail allowed and rode on in silence. Finally there was a stumble, and it seemed as if the words were jarred out from his lips, hitherto closely compressed: "*You* killed Quade!"

A scowl was his answer.

But he persisted in the inquiry with a sort of trembling curiosity, though he could see the angry emotions rise in Sinclair. The emotion of a murderer, perhaps?

"How?"

"With a gun, fool. How d'you think?"

Even that did not halt John Gaspar.

"Was it a fair fight?"

"Maybe—maybe not. It won't bring him back to life!"

Riley laughed with savage satisfaction. Gaspar watched him as a bird might watch a snake. He had heard tales of men who could find satisfaction in a murder, but he had never believed that a human being could actually gloat over his own savagery. He stared at Riley as if he were looking at a wild beast that must be placated.

Thereafter the talk was short. Now and again Sinclair gave some curt direction, but they put mile after mile behind them without a single phrase interchanged. Gaspar began to slump in the saddle. It brought a fierce rebuke from Sinclair.

"Straighten up. Put some of your weight in them stirrups. D'you think any hoss can buck up when it's carrying a pile of lead? Come alive!"

"It's the heat. It takes my strength," protested Gaspar.

"Curse you and your strength! I wouldn't trade all of you for one ear of the hoss you're riding. Do what I tell you!"

Without protest, without a flush of shame at this brutal abuse, John Gaspar attempted to obey. Then, as they topped a rise and reached the crest of a range of hills, Gaspar cried out in surprise. Sour Creek lay in the hollow beneath them.

"But you're running straight into the face of danger!"

"Don't tell me what I'm doing. I know maybe, all by myself!"

He checked his horse and sat his saddle, eying Gaspar

with such disgust, such concentrated scorn and contempt, that the schoolteacher winced.

"I've brought you in sight of the town so's you can go home."

"And be hanged?"

"You won't be hanged. I'll send a confession along with you. I've busted the law once. They're after me. They might as well have some more reasons for hitting my trail."

"But is it fair to you?" asked Gaspar, intertwining his nervous fingers.

Sinclair heard the words and eyed the gesture with unutterable disgust. At last he could speak.

"Fair?" he asked in scorn. "Since when have you been interested in playing fair? Takes a man with some nerve to play fair. You've spoiled my game, Gaspar. You've blocked me every way from the start, Cold Feet. I killed Quade, and they's another in Sour Creek that needs killing. That's something you can do. Go down and tell the sheriff when he happens along and show him my confession. Go down and tell him that I ain't running away—that I'm staying close, and that I'm going to nab my second man right under his nose. That'll give him something to think about."

He favored the schoolteacher with another black look and then swung out of the saddle, throwing his reins. He sat down with his back to a stunted tree. Gaspar dismounted likewise and hovered near, after the fashion of a man who is greatly worried. He watched while Sinclair deliberately took out an old stained envelope and the stub of a pencil and started to write. His brows knitted in pain with the effort. Suddenly Gaspar cried: "Don't do it, Mr. Sinclair!"

A slight lifting of Sinclair's heavy brows showed that he had heard, but he did not raise his head.

"Don't do what?"

"Don't try to kill that second man. Don't do it!"

Gaspar was rewarded with a sneer.

"Why not?"

The schoolteacher was desperately eager. His glance roved from the set face of the cowpuncher and through the scragged branches of the tree.

"You'll be damned for it—in your own mind. At heart you're a good man; I swear you are. And now you throw yourself away. "Won't you try to open your mind and see this another way?"

"Not an inch. Kid, I gave my word for this to a dead man. I told you about a friend of mine?"

"I'll never forget."

"I gave my word to him, though he never heard it. If I have to wait fifty years I'll live long enough to kill the gent that's in Sour Creek now. The other day I had him under my gun. Think of it! I let him go!"

"And you'll let him go again. Sinclair, murder isn't in your nature. You're better than you think."

"Close up," growled the cowpuncher. "It ain't no Saturday night party for me to write. Keep still till I finish."

He resumed his labor of writing, drawing out each letter carefully. He had reached his signature when a low call from John Gaspar alarmed him. He looked up to find the little man pointing and staring up the trail. A horseman had just dropped over the crest and was winding leisurely down toward the plain below.

"We can get behind that knoll, perhaps, before he sees us," suggested Jig in a whisper. His suggestion met with no favor.

"You hear me talk, son," said Sinclair dryly. "That gent ain't carrying no guns, which means that he ain't on our trail, we being figured particularly desperate." He pointed this remark with a cold survey of the "desperate" Jig.

"But the best way to make danger follow you, Jig, is to run away from it. We stay put!"

He emphasized the remark by stretching luxuriously.

Gaspar, however, did not seem to hear the last words. Something about the strange horseman had apparently riveted his interest. His last gesture was arrested halfway, and his color changed perceptibly.

"You stay, then, Mr. Sinclair," he said hurriedly. "I'm going to slip down the hill and—"

"You stay where you are!" cut in Sinclair.

"But I have a reason."

"Your reasons ain't no good. You stay put. You hear?"

It seemed that a torrent of explanation was about to pour from the lips of Jig, but he restrained himself, white of face, and sank down in the shade of the tree. There he stretched himself out hastily, with his hands cupped behind his head and his hat tilted so far down over his face that his entire head was hidden.

Sinclair followed these proceedings with a lackluster eye.

"When you *do* move, Jig," he said, "you ain't so slow about it. That's pretty good faking, take it all in all. But why don't you want this strange gent to see your face?"

A slight shudder was the only reply; then Jig lay deadly still. In the meantime, before Sinclair could pursue his questions, the horseman was almost upon them. The cowpuncher regarded him with distinct approval. He was a man of the country, and he showed it. As his pony slouched down the slope, picking its way dexterously among the rocks, the rider met each jolt on the way with an easy swing of his shoulders, riding "straight up," just enough of his weight falling into his stirrups to break the jar on the back of the mustang.

The stranger drew up on the trail and swung the head of his horse in toward the tree, raising his hand in cavalier greeting. He was a sunbrowned fellow, as tall as Sinclair and more heavily built; as for his age, he seemed in that joyous prime of physical life, twenty-five. Sinclair nodded amiably.

"Might that be Sour Creek yonder?" asked the brown man.

"It might be. I reckon it is. Get down and rest your hoss."

"Thanks. Maybe I will."

He dropped to the ground and eased and stiffened his knees to get out the cramp of long riding. Off the horse he seemed even bigger and more capable than before, and now that he had come sufficiently close, so that the shadow from his sombrero's brim did not partially mask the upper part of his face, it seemed to Sinclair that about the eyes he was not nearly so prepossessing as around the clean-cut fighter's mouth and chin. The eyes were just a trifle too small, a trifle too close together. Yet on the whole he was a handsome fellow, as he pushed back his hat and wiped his forehead dry with a gay silk handkerchief.

Sinclair noted, furthermore, that the other had a proper cowpuncher's pride in his dress. His bench-made boots molded his long and slender feet to a nicety and fitted like gloves around the high instep. The polished spurs, with their spoon-handle curve, gleamed and flashed, as he stepped with a faint jingling. The braid about his sombrero was a thing of price. These details Sinclair noted. The rest did not matter.

"The kid's asleep?" asked the stranger, casting a careless glance at the slim form of Jig.

"I reckon so."

"He done it almighty sudden. Thought I seen him up and walking around when I come over the hill."

"You got good eyes," said Sinclair, but he was instantly put on the defensive. He was heartily tired of Cold Feet Gaspar, his peculiarities, his whims, his weaknesses. But Cold Feet was his riding companion, and this was a stranger. He was thrown suddenly in the position of a defender of the helpless. "That's the way with these kids," he confided carelessly to the stranger. "They get out and ride fast for a couple of hours. Full of ambition, they are. But just when a growed man gets warmed up to his work, they're through. The kid's tired out."

"Come far?" asked the stranger.

"Tolerable long ways."

Sinclair disliked questions, and for each interrogation his opinion of the newcomer descended lower and lower. His own father had raised him on a stern pattern. "What you mean by questions, Riley? What you can't figure out with your own eyes and ears and good, common hoss sense, most likely the other gent don't want you to know." Thereafter he had schooled himself in this particular point. He could suppress all curiosity and go six months without knowing more than the nickname of a boon companion.

"You come from Sour Creek, maybe?" went on the other.

"Sort of," replied Sinclair dryly.

His companion proceeded to dispense information on his own part so as to break the ice.

"I'm Jude Cartwright."

He paused significantly, but Sinclair's face was a blank.

"Glad to know you, Mr. Cartwright. Mostly they call me Long Riley."

"How are you, Riley?"

They shook hands heartily. Cartwright took a place on the ground, cross-legged and not far from Sinclair.

"I guess you don't know me?" he asked pointedly.

"I guess not."

"I'm of the Jesse Cartwright family."

Sinclair smiled blankly.

"Lucky Cartwright was my dad's name."

"That so?"

"I guess you ain't ever been up Montana way," said the stranger in disgust which he hardly veiled.

"Not much," said Sinclair blandly.

"I wished that I was back up there. This is a hole of a country down here."

"Hossflesh and time will take you back, I reckon."

"I reckon they will, when my job's done."

He turned a disparaging eye upon Sour Creek and its vicinity.

"Now, who would want to live in a town like that, can you tell me?"

It occurred very strongly to Riley Sinclair that Cartwright had not yet fully ascertained whether or not his companion came from that very town. And, although the day before, he had decided that Sour Creek was most undesirable and all that pertained to it, this unasked confirmation of his own opinion grated on his nerves.

"Well, they seems to be a few that gets along tolerable well in that town, partner."

"They's ten fools for one wise man," declared Cartwright sententiously.

Sinclair veiled his eyes with a downward glance. He dared not let the other see the cold gleam which he knew was coming into them. "I guess them's true words."

"Tolerable true," admitted Cartwright. "But I've rode a long ways, and this ain't much to find at the end of the trail."

"Maybe it'll pan out pretty well after all."

"If Sour Creek holds the person I'm after, I'll call it a good-paying game."

"I hope you find your friend," remarked Riley, with his deceptive softness of tone.

"Friend? Hell! And that's where this friend will wish me when I heave in sight. You can lay to that, and long odds!"

Sinclair waited, but the other changed his tack at once.

"If you ain't from Sour Creek, I guess you can't tell me what I want to know."

"Maybe not."

The brown man looked about him for diversion. Presently his eyes rested on Cold Feet, who had not stirred during all this interval.

"Son?"

"Nope."

"Kid brother?"

"Nope."

Cartwright frowned. "Not much of nothing, I figure," he said with marked insolence.

"Maybe not," replied Sinclair, and again he glanced down.

"He's slept long enough, I reckon," declared the brown man. "Let's have a look at him. Hey, kid!"

Cold Feet quivered, but seemed lost in a profound sleep. Cartwright reached for a small stone and juggled it in the palm of his hand.

"This'll surprise him," he chuckled.

"Better not," murmured Sinclair.

"Why not?"

"Might land on his face and hurt him."

"It won't hurt him bad. Besides, kids ought to learn not to sleep in the daytime. Ain't a good idea any way you look at it. Puts fog in the head."

He poised the stone.

"You might hit his eye, you see," said Sinclair.

"Leave that to me!"

But, as his arm twisted back for the throw, the hand of Sinclair flashed out and lean fingers crushed the wrist of Cartwright. Yet Sinclair's voice was still soft.

"Better not," he said.

They sat confronting each other for a moment. The stone dropped from the numbed fingers of Cartwright, and Sinclair released his wrist. Their characters were more easily read in the crisis. Cartwright's face flushed, and a purple vein ran down his forehead between the eyes. Sinclair turned pale. He seemed, indeed, almost afraid, and apparently Cartwright took his cue from the pallor.

"I see," he said sneeringly. "You got your guns on. Is that it?"

Sinclair slipped off the cartridge belt.

"Do I look better to you now?"

"A pile better," said Cartwright.

They rose, still confronting each other. It was strange how swiftly they had plunged into strife.

"I guess you'll be rolling along, Cartwright."

"Nope. I guess I like it tolerable well under this here tree."

"Except that I come here first, partner."

"And maybe you'll be the first to leave."

"I'd have to be persuaded a pile."

"How's this to start you along?"

He flicked the back of his hand across the lips of Sinclair, and then sprang back as far as his long legs would carry him. So doing, the first leap of Sinclair missed him, and when the cowpuncher turned he was met with a stunning blow on the side of the head.

At once the blind anger faded from the eyes of Riley. By the weight of that first blow he knew that he had encountered a worthy foeman, and by the position of Cartwright he could tell that he had met a confident one. The big fellow was perfectly poised, with his weight well back on his right foot, his left foot feeling his way over the rough ground as he advanced, always collected for a heavy blow, or for a leap in any direction. He carried his guard high, with apparent contempt for an attack on his body, after the manner of a practiced boxer.

As for Riley Sinclair, boxing was Greek to him. His battles had been those of bullets and sharp steel, or sudden, brutal fracas, where the rule was to strike with the first weapon that came to hand. This single encounter, hand to hand, was more or less of a novelty to him, but instead of abashing or cowing him, it merely brought to the surface all his coldness of mind, all of his cunning.

He circled Cartwright, his long arms dangling low, his step soft and quick as the stride of a great cat, and always there was thought in his face. One gained an impression that if ever he closed with his enemy the battle would end.

Apparently even Cartwright gained that impression. His own brute confidence of skill and power was suddenly tinged with doubt. Instead of waiting he led suddenly with his left, a blow that tilted the head of Sinclair back, and then sprang in with a crushing right. It was poor tactics, for half of a boxer's nice skill is lost in a plunging attack. The second blow shot humming past Sinclair as the latter dodged; and, before the brown man could recover his poise, the cowpuncher had dived in under the guarding arms.

A shrill cry rose from Cold Feet, a cry so sharp and shrill that it sent a chill down the back of Sinclair. For a moment he whirled with the weight of his struggling, cursing enemy, and then his right hand shot up over the shoulder of Cartwright and clutched his chin. With that leverage one convulsive jerk threw Cartwright heavily back; he rolled on his side, with Sinclair following like a wildcat.

But Cartwright as he fell had closed his fingers on a jagged little stone. Sinclair saw the blow coming, swerved from it, and straightway went mad. The brown man became a helpless bulk; the knee of Sinclair was planted on his shoulders, the talon fingers of Sinclair were buried in his throat.

Then—he saw it only dimly through his red anger and hardly felt it at all—Jig's hands were tearing at his wrists. he looked up in dull surprise into the face of John Gaspar.

"For heaven's sake," Jig was pleading, "stop!"

But what checked Sinclair was not the schoolteacher. Cartwright had been fighting with the fury of one who sees death only inches away. Suddenly he grew limp.

"You!" he cried. "You!"

To the astonishment of Sinclair the gaze of the beaten man rested directly upon the face of Jig.

"Yes," Gaspar admitted faintly, "it is I!"

Sinclair released his grip and stood back, while Cartwright, stumbling to his feet, stood wavering, breathing harshly and fingering his injured throat.

"I knew I'd find you," he said, "but I never dreamed I'd find you like this!"

"I know what you think," said Cold Feet, utterly colorless, "but you think wrong, Jude. You think entirely wrong!"

"You lie like a devil!"

"On my honor."

"Honor? You ain't got none! Honor!"

He flung himself into his saddle. "Now that I've located you, the next time I come it'll be with a gun."

He turned a convulsed face toward Sinclair.

"And that goes for you."

"Partner," said Riley Sinclair, "that's the best thing I've heard you say. Until then, so long!"

The other wrenched his horse about and went down the trail at a reckless gallop, plunging out of view around the first shoulder of a hill.

15

Sinclair watched him out of sight. He turned to find that Jig had slumped against the tree and stood with his arm thrown across his face. It reminded him, with a curious pang of mingled pity and disgust, of the way Gaspar had faced the masked men of Sour Creek's posse the day before. There was the same unmanly abnegation of the courage to meet danger and look it in the eye. Here, again, the schoolteacher was wincing from the very memory of a crisis.

"Look here!" exclaimed Sinclair. His contempt rang in his voice. "They ain't any danger now. Turn around here and buck up. Keep your chin high and look a man in the face, will you?"

Slowly the arm descended. He found himself looking into a white and tortured face. His respect for the schoolteacher rose somewhat. The very fact that the little man could endure such pain in silence, no matter what that pain might be, was something to his credit.

"Now come out with it, Gaspar. You double-crossed this Cartwright, eh?"

"Yes," whispered Jig.

"Will you tell me? Not that I make a business of prying into the affairs of other gents, but I figure I might be able to help you straighten things out with this Cartwright."

He made a wry face and then rubbed the side of his head where a lump was slowly growing.

"Of all the gents that I ever seen," said Sinclair softly, "I ain't never seen none that made me want to tangle with 'em so powerful bad. And of all the poisoned fatheads, all the mean, sneakin' advantage-takin' skunks that ever I run up agin', this gent Cartwright is the worst. If his hide was worth a million an inch, I would have it. If he was to pay me a hundred thousand a day, I wouldn't be his pal for a minute." He paused. "Them, taking 'em by and large, is my sentiments about this here Cartwright. So open up and tell me what you done to him."

To his very real surprise the schoolteacher shook his head. "I can't do it."

"H'm," said Sinclair, cut to the quick. "Can't you trust me with it, eh?"

"Ah," murmured Gaspar, "of all the men in the world, you're the one I'd tell it to most easily. But I can't—I can't."

"I don't care whether you tell me or not. Whatever you done, it must have been plumb bad if you can't even tell it to a gent that likes Cartwright like he likes poison."

"It was bad," said Jig slowly. "It was very bad—it was a

sin. Until I die I can never repay him for what I have done."

Sinclair recovered some of his good nature at this outburst of self-accusation.

"I'll be hanged if I believe it," he declared bluntly. "Not a word of it! When you come right down to the point you'll find out that you ain't been half so bad as you think. The way I figure you is this, Jig. You ain't so bad, except that you ain't got no nerve. Was it a matter of losing your nerve that made Cartwright mad at you?"

"Yes. It was altogether that."

Sinclair sighed. "Too bad! I don't blame you for not wanting to talk about it. They's a flaw in everything, Jig, and this is yours. If I was to be around you much, d'you know what I'd do?"

"What?"

"I'd try to plumb forget about this flaw of yours. That's a fact. But as far as Cartwright goes, to blazes with him! And that's where he's apt to wind up pronto if he's as good as his word and comes after me with a gun. In the meantime you grab your hoss, kid, and slide back into Sour Creek and show the boys this here confession I've written. You can add one thing. I didn't put it in because I knowed they wouldn't believe me. I killed Quade fair and square. I give him the first move for his gun, and then I beat him to the draw and killed him on an even break. That's the straight of it. I know they won't believe it. Matter of fact I'm saying it for you, Jig, more'n I am for them!"

It was an amazing thing to see the sudden light that flooded the face of the schoolteacher.

"And I do believe you, Sinclair," he said. "With all my heart I believe you and know you couldn't have taken an unfair advantage!"

"H'm," muttered Riley. "It ain't bad to hear you say that. And now trot along, son."

Cold Feet made no move to obey.

"Not that I wouldn't like to have you along, but where I

got to go, you'd be a weight around my neck. Besides, your game is to show the folks down yonder that you ain't a murderer, and that paper I've give you will prove it. We'll drift together along the trail part way, and down yonder I turn up for the tall timber."

To all this Jig returned no answer, but in a peculiarly lifeless manner went to his horse and climbed in his awkward way into the saddle. They went down the trail slowly.

"Because," explained the cowpuncher, "if I save my hoss's wind I may be saving my own life."

Where the trail bent like an elbow and shot sheer down for the plain and Sour Creek, Riley Sinclair pointed his horse's nose up to the taller mountains, but Jig sat his horse in melancholy silence and looked mournfully up at his companion.

"So long," said Sinclair cheerily. "And when you get down yonder, it'll happen most likely that pretty soon you'll hear a lot of hard things about Riley Sinclair."

"If I do—if I hear a syllable against you," cried the schoolteacher with a flare of color, "I'll—I'll drive the words back into their teeth!"

He shook with his emotion; Riley Sinclair shook with controlled laughter.

"Would you do all of that, partner? Well, I believe you'd try. What I mean to say is this: No matter what they say, you can lay to it that Sinclair has tried to play square and clean according to his own lights, which ain't always the best in the world. So long!"

There was no answer. He found himself looking down into the quivering face of the schoolteacher.

"Why, kid, you look all busted up!"

"Riley," gasped Jig very faintly, "I can't go!"

"And why not?"

"Because I can't meet Jude."

"Cartwright, eh? But you got to, sooner or later."

"I'll die first."

"Would your nerve hold you up through that?"

"So easily," said Jig. There was such a simple gravity and despair in his expression that Sinclair believed it. He grunted and stared hard.

"This Cartwright gent is worse'n death to you?"

"A thousand, thousand times!"

"How come?"

"I can't tell you."

"I kind of wish," said Sinclair thoughtfully, "that I'd kept my grip a mite longer."

"No, no!"

"You don't wish him dead?"

Jig shuddered.

"You plumb beat me, partner. And now you want to come along with me?" Sinclair grinned. "An outlaw's life ain't what it's cracked up to be, son. You'd last about a day doing what I have to do."

"You'll find," said the schoolteacher eagerly, "that I can stand it amazingly well. I'll—I'll be far, far stronger than you expect!"

"Somehow I kind of believe it. But it's for your own fool sake, son, that I don't want you along."

"Let me try," pleaded Jig eagerly.

The other shook his head and seemed to change his mind in the very midst of the gesture.

"Why not?" he asked himself. "You'll get enough of it inside of a day. And then you'll find out that they's some things about as bad as death—or Cartwright. Come on, kid!"

16

It was a weary ride that brought them to the end of that day and to a camping place. It seemed to Jig that the world was made up of nothing but the ups and downs of that mountain trail. Now, as the sun went down, they came out on a flat shoulder of the mountain. Far below them lay Sour Creek, long lost in the shadow of premature night which filled the valley.

"Here we are, fixed up as comfortable as can be," said Sinclair cheerily. "There's water, and there's wood aplenty. What could a gent ask for more? And here's my country!"

For a moment his expression softened as he looked over the black peaks stepping away to the north. Now he pointed out a grove of trees, and on the other side of the little plateau was heard the murmur of a feeble spring.

Riley swung down easily from the saddle, but when Jig dismounted his knees buckled with weariness, and he slumped down on a rock. He was unheeded for a moment by the cowpuncher, who was removing from his saddle the quarters of a deer which he had shot at the foot of the mountain. When this task was ended, a stern voice brought Jig to his feet.

"What's all this? How come? Going to let that hoss stand there all night with his saddle on? Hurry up!"

"All right," replied the schoolteacher, but his voice quaked with weariness, and the cinch knot, drawn taut by the powerful hand of Jerry Bent, refused to loosen. He struggled with it until his fingers ached, and his panicky breath came in gasps of nervous excitement.

Presently he was aware of the tall, dark form of Sinclair behind him, his saddle slung across his arm.

"By guns," muttered Sinclair, "it ain't possible! Not enough muscle to untie a knot? It's a good thing that your father can't see the sort of a son that he turned out. Lemme at that!"

Under his strong fingers the knot gave by magic.

"Now yank that saddle off and put it yonder with mine."

Jig pulled back the saddle, but when the full weight jerked down on him he staggered, and he began to drag the heavy load.

"Hey," cut in the voice of the tyrant, "want to spoil that saddle, kid? Lift it, can't you?"

Gaspar obeyed with a start and, having placed it in the required position, turned and waited guiltily.

"Time you was learning something about camping out," declared the cowpuncher, "and I'll teach you. Take this ax and gimme some wood, pronto!"

He handed over a short ax, heavy-headed and small of haft.

"That bush yonder! That's dead, or dead enough for us."

Plainly Jig was in awe of that ax. He carried it well out from his side, as if he feared the least touch against his leg might mean a cut. Of all this, Riley Sinclair was aware with a gradually darkening expression. He had been partly won to Jig that day, but his better opinion of the schoolteacher was being fast undermined.

With a gloomy eye he watched John Gaspar drop on his knees at the base of the designated shrub and raise the ax slowly—in both hands! Not only that, but the head remained poised, hung over the schoolteacher's shoulder. When the blow fell, instead of striking solidly on the trunk of the bush, it crashed futilely through a branch. Riley Sinclair drew closer to watch. It was excusable, perhaps, for a man to be unable to ride or to shoot or to face other men. But it was inconceivable that any living creature should be so clumsy with a common ax.

To his consummate disgust the work of Jig became

worse and worse. No two blows fell on the same spot. The trunk of the little tree became bruised, but even when the edge of the ax did not strike on a branch, at most it merely sliced into the outer surface of the wood and left the heart untouched. It was a process of gnawing, not of chopping. To crown the terrible exhibition, Jig now rested from his labors and examined the palms of his hands, which had become a bright red.

"Gimme the ax," said Sinclair shortly. He dared not trust himself to more speech and, snatching it from the hands of Cold Feet, buried the blade into the very heart of the trunk. Another blow, driven home with equal power and precision on the opposite side, made the tree shudder to its top, and the third blow sent it swishing to the earth.

This brought a short cry of admiration and wonder from the schoolteacher, for which Sinclair rewarded him with one glance of contempt. With sweeping strokes he cleared away the half-dead branches. Presently the trunk was naked. On it Riley now concentrated his attack, making the short ax whistle over his shoulders. The trunk of the shrub was divided into handy portions as if by magic.

Still John Gaspar stood by, gaping, apparently finding nothing to do. And this with a camp barely started!

It was easier to do oneself, however, than to give directions to such stupidity. Sinclair swept up an armful of wood and strode off to the spot he had selected for the campfire, near the place where the spring water ran into a small pool. A couple of big rocks thrown in place furnished a windbreak. Between them he heaped dead twigs, and in a moment the flame was leaping.

As soon as the fire was lighted they became aware that the night was well nigh upon them. Hitherto the day had seemed some distance from its final end, for there was still color in the sky, and the tops of the western mountains were still bright. But with the presence of fire brightness, the rest of the world became dim. The western peaks were ghostly; the sky faded to the ashes of its former splendor; and Jig found himself looking down upon thick night in the lower valleys. He saw the eyes of the horses glistening, as they raised their heads to watch. The gaunt form of Sinclair seemed enormous. Stooping about the fire, enormous shadows drifted above and behind him. Sometimes the light flushed over his lean face and glinted in his eyes. Again his head was lost in shadow, and perhaps only the active, reaching hands were illuminated brightly.

He prepared the deer meat with incomprehensible swiftness, at the same time arranging the fire so that it rapidly burned down to a firm, strong, level bed of coals, and by the time the bed of coals were ready, the meat was prepared in thick steaks to broil over it.

In a little time the rich brown of the cooking venison streaked across to Jig. He had kept at a distance up to this time, realizing that he was in disgrace. Now he drifted near. He was rewarded by an amiable grin from Riley Sinclair, whose ugly humor seemed to have vanished at the odor of the broiling meat.

"Watch this meat cook, kid, will you? There's something you can do that don't take no muscle and don't take no knowledge. All you got to do is to keep listening with your *nose,* and if you smell it burning, yank her off. Understand? And don't let the fire blaze. She's apt to flare up at the corners, you see? And these here twigs is apt to burn through—these ones that keep the meat off'n the coals. Watch them, too. And that's all you got to do. Can you manage all them things at once?"

Jig nodded gravely, as though he failed to see the contempt.

"I seen a fine patch of grass down the hill a bit. I'm going to take the hosses down there and hobble 'em out." Whistling, Sinclair strode off down the hill, leading the horses after him.

The schoolteacher watched him go, and when the forms

had vanished, and only the echo of the whistling blew back, he looked up. The last life was gone from the sunset. The last time he glanced up, there had been only a few dim stars; now they had come down in multitudes, great yellow planets and whole rifts of steel-blue stars.

He took from his pocket the old envelope which Sinclair had given him, examined the scribbled confession, chuckling at the crude labor with which the writing had been drawn out, and then deliberately stuffed the paper into a corner of the fire. It flamed up, singeing the cooking meat, but John Gaspar paid no heed. He was staring off down the hill to make sure that Sinclair should not return in time to see that little act of destruction. An act of self-destruction, too, it well might turn out to be.

As for Sinclair, having found his pastureland, where the grass grew thick and tall, he was in no hurry to return to his clumsy companion. He listened for a time to the sound of the horses, ripping away the grass close to the ground, and to the grating as they chewed. Then he turned his attention to the mountains. His spirit was easier in this place. He breathed more easily. There was a sense of freedom at once and companionship. He lingered so long, indeed, that he suddenly became aware that time had slipped away from him, and that the venison must be long since done. At that he hurried back up the slope.

He was hungry, ravenously hungry, but the first thing that greeted him was the scent of burning meat. It stopped him short, and his hands gripped involuntarily. In that first burst of passion he wanted literally to wring the neck of the schoolteacher. He strode closer. It was as he thought. The twigs had burned away from beneath the steak and allowed it to drop into the cinders, and beside the dying fire, barely illumined by it, sat Jig, sound asleep, with his head resting on his knees.

For a moment Sinclair had to fight with himself for control. All his murderous evil temper had flared up into his brain and set his teeth gritting. At length he could trust himself enough to reach down and set his heavy grip on the shoulder of the sleeper.

Even in sleep Jig must have been pursued by a burdened consciousness of guilt. Now he jerked up his head and stammered up to the shadowy face of Sinclair.

"I—I don't know—all at once it happened. You see the fire—"

But the telltale odor of the charring meat struck his nostrils, and his speech died away. He was panting with fear of consequences. Now a new turn came to the fear of Cold Feet. It seemed that Riley Sinclair's hand had frozen at the touch of the soft flesh of Jig's shoulder. He remained for a long moment without stirring. When his hand moved it was to take Jig under the chin with marvelous firmness and gentleness at once and lift the face of the schoolteacher. He seemed to find much to read there, much to study and know. Whatever it was, it set Jig trembling until suddenly he shrank away, cowering against the rock behind.

"You don't think—"

But the voice of Sinclair broke in with a note in it that Jig had never heard before.

"Guns and glory—a woman!"

It came over him with a rush, that revelation which explained so many things—everything in fact; all that strange cowardice, and all that stranger grace; that unmanly shrinking, that more than manly contempt for death. Now the firelight was too feeble to show more than one thing—the haunted eyes of the girl, as she cowered away from him.

He saw her hand drop from her breast to her holster and close around the butt of her revolver.

Sinclair grew cold and sick. After all, what reason had she to trust him? He drew back and began to walk up and down with long, slow strides. The girl followed him and saw his gaunt figure brush across the stars; she saw the wind furl and unfurl the wide brim of his hat, and she heard the faint stir and clink of his spurs at every step.

There was a tumult in the brain of the cowpuncher. The stars and the sky and the mountains and wind went out. They were nothing in the electric presence of this new Jig. His mind flashed back to one picture—Cold Feet with her hands tied behind her back, praying under the cottonwood.

Shame turned the cowpuncher hot and then cold. He allowed his mind to drift back over his thousand insults, his brutal language, his cursing, his mockery, his open contempt. There was a tingle in his ears, and a chill running up and down his spine.

After all that brutality, what mysterious sense had told her to trust to him rather than to Sour Creek and its men?

Other mysteries flocked into his mind. Why had she come to the very verge of death, with the rope around her neck rather than reveal her identity, knowing, as she must know, that in the mountain desert men feel some touch of holiness in every woman?

He remembered Cartwright, tall, handsome, and narrow of eye, and the fear of the girl. Suddenly he wished with all his soul that he had fought with guns that day, and not with fists.

17

At length the continued silence of the girl made him turn. Perhaps she had slipped away. His heart was chilled at the thought; turning, he sighed with relief to find her still there.

Without a word he went back and rekindled the fire, placed new venison steaks over it, and broiled them with silent care. Not a sound from Jig, not a sound from the cowpuncher, while the meat hissed, blackened, and at length was done to a turn. He laid portions of it on broad, white, clean chips which he had already prepared, and served her. Still in silence she ate. Shame held Sinclair. He dared not look at her, and he was glad when the fire lost some of its brightness.

Now and then he looked with wonder across the mountains. All his life they had been faces to him, and the wind had been a voice. Now all this was nothing but dead stuff. There was no purpose in the march of the mountains except that they led to the place where Jig sat.

He twisted together a cup of bark and brought her water from the spring. She thanked him with words that he did not hear, he was so intent in watching her face, as the firelight played on it. Now that he held the clue, everything was as plain as day. New light played on the past.

Turning away, he put new fuel on the fire, and when he looked to her again, she had unbelted the revolver and was putting it away, as if she realized that this would not help her if she were in danger.

When at length she spoke it was the same voice, and yet how new! The quality in it made Sinclair sit a little straighter.

"You have a right to know everything that I can tell you. Do you wish to hear?"

For another moment he smoked in solemn silence. He found that he was wishing for the story not so much because of its strangeness, but because he wanted that voice to run on indefinitely. Yet he weighed the question pro and con.

"Here's the point, Jig," he said at last. "I got a good deal to make up to you. In the first place I pretty near let you get strung up for a killing I done myself. Then I been treating you pretty hard, take it all in all. You got a story, and I don't deny that I'd like to hear it; but it don't seem a story that you're fond of telling, and I ain't got no right to ask for it. All I ask to know is one thing: When you stood there under that cottonwood tree, with the rope around your neck, did you know that all you had to do was to tell us that you was a woman to get off free?"

"Of course."

"And you'd sooner have hung than tell us?"

"Yes."

Sinclair sighed. "Maybe I've said this before, but I got to say it ag'in: Jig, you plumb beat me!" He brushed his hand across his forehead. "S'pose it'd been done! S'pose I had let 'em go ahead and string you up! They'd have been a terrible bad time ahead for them seven men. We'd all have been grabbed and lynched. A woman!"

He put the word off by itself. Then he was surprised to hear her laughing softly. Now that he knew, it was all woman, that voice.

"It wasn't really courage, Riley. After you'd said half a dozen words I knew you were square, and that you knew I was innocent. So I didn't worry very much—except just after you'd sentenced me to hang!"

"Don't go back to that! I sure been a plumb fool. But why would you have gone ahead and let that hanging happen?"

"Because I had rather die than be known, except to you."

"You leave me out."

"I'd trust you to the end of everything, Riley."

"I b'lieve you would, Jig—I honest believe you would! Heaven knows why."

"Because."

"That ain't a reason."

"A very good woman's reason. For one thing you've let me come along when you know that I'm a weight, and you're in danger. But you don't know what it means if I go back. You can't know. I know it's wrong and cowardly for me to stay and imperil you, but I *am* a coward, and I'm afraid to go back!"

"Hush up," murmured Sinclair. "Hush up, girl. Is they anybody asking you to go back? But you don't really figure on hanging out here with me in the mountains, me having most of the gents in these parts out looking for my scalp?"

"If you think I won't be such an encumbrance that I'll greatly endanger you, Riley."

"H'm," muttered Sinclair. "I'll take that chance, but they's another thing."

"Well?"

"It ain't exactly nacheral and reasonable for a girl to go around in the mountains with a man."

She fired up at that, sitting straight, with the fire flaring suddenly in her face through the change of position.

"I've told you that I trust you, Riley. What do I care about the opinion of the world? Haven't they hounded me? Oh, I despise them!"

"H'm," said the cowpuncher again.

He was, indeed, so abashed by this outbreak that he merely stole a glance at her face and then studied the fire again.

"Does this gent Cartwright tie up with your story?"

All the fire left her. "Yes," she whispered.

He felt that she was searching his face, as if suddenly in doubt of him.

"Will you let me tell you—everything?"

"Shoot ahead."

"Some parts will be hard to believe."

"Lady, they won't be nothing as hard to believe as what I've seen you do with my own eyes."

Then she began to tell her story, and she found a vast comfort in seeing the ugly, stern face of Sinclair lighted by the burning end of his cigarette. He never looked at her, but always fixed his stare on the sea of blackness which was the lower valley.

"All the trouble began with a theory. My father felt that

the thing for a girl was to be educated in the East and marry in the West. He was full of maxims, you see. 'They turn out knowledge in cities; they turn out men in mountains,' was one of his maxims. He thought and argued and lived along those lines. So as soon as I was half grown—oh, I was a wild tomboy!"

"Eh?" cut in Sinclair.

"I could really do the things then that you'd like to have a woman do," she said. "I could ride anything, swim like a fish in snow water, climb, run, and do anything a boy could do. I suppose that's the sort of a woman you admire?"

"Me!" exclaimed Riley with violence. "It ain't so, Jig. I been revising my ideas on women lately. Besides, I never give 'em much thought before."

He said all this without glancing at her, so that she was able to indulge in a smile before she went on.

"Just at that point, when I was about to become a true daughter of the West, Dad snapped me off to school in the East, and then for years and years there was no West at all for me except a little trip here and there in vacation time. The rest of it was just study and play, all in the East. I still liked the West—in theory, you know."

"H'm," muttered Riley.

"And then, I think it was a year ago, I had a letter from Dad with important news in it. He had just come back from a hunting trip with a young fellow who he thought represented everything fine in the West. He was big, good-looking, steady, had a large estate. Dad set his mind on having me marry him, and he told me so in the letter. Of course I was upset at the idea of marrying a man I did not know, but Dad always had a very controlling way with him. I had lost any habit of thinking for myself in important matters.

"Besides, there was a consolation. Dad sent the picture of his man along with his letter. The picture was in profile, and it showed me a fine-looking fellow, with a glorious carriage, a high head, and oceans of strength and manliness.

"I really fell in love with that picture. To begin with, I thought that it was destiny for me, and that I had to love that man whether I wished to or not. I admitted that picture into my inmost life, dreamed about it, kept it near me in my room.

"And just about that time came news that my father was seriously ill, and then that he had died, and that his last wish was for me to come West at once and marry my chosen husband.

"Of course I came at once. I was too sick and sad for Dad to think much about my own future, and when I stepped off the train I met the first shock. My husband to be was waiting for me. He was enough like the picture for me to recognize him, and that was all. He was tall and strong enough and manly enough. But in full face I thought he was narrow between the eyes. And—"

"It was Cartwright!"

"Yes, yes. How did you guess that?"

"I dunno," said Sinclair softly, "but when that gent rode off today, something told me that I was going to tangle with him later on. Go on!"

"He was very kind to me. After the first moment of disappointment—you see, I had been dreaming about him for a good many weeks—I grew to like him and accept him again. He did all that he could to make the trip home agreeable. He didn't press himself on me. He did nothing to make me feel that he understood Dad's wishes about our marriage and expected me to live up to them.

"After the funeral it was the same way. He came to see me only now and then. He was courteous and attentive, and he seemed to be fond of me."

"A fox," snarled Sinclair, growing more and more excited, as this narrative continued. "That's the way with one of them kind. They play a game. Never out in the open.

Waiting till they win, and then acting the devil. Go on!"

"Perhaps you're right. His visits became more and more frequent. Finally he asked me to marry him. That brought the truth of my position home to me, and I found all at once that, though I had rather liked him as a friend, I had to quake at the idea of him as a husband."

Sinclair snapped his cigarette into the coals of the fire and set his jaw. She liked him in his anger.

"But what could I do? All of the last part of Dad's life had been pointed toward this one thing. I felt that he would come out of his grave and haunt me. I asked for one more day to think it over. He told me to take a month or a year, as I pleased, and that made me ashamed. I told him on the spot that I would marry him, but that I didn't love him."

"I'll tell you what he answered—curse him!" exclaimed Sinclair.

"What?"

"Through the years that was comin', he'd teach you to love him."

"That was exactly what he said in those very words! How did you guess that?"

"I'll tell you I got a sort of a second sight for the ways of a snake, or an ornery hoss, or a sneak of a man. Go on!"

"I think you have. At any rate, after I had told him I'd marry him, he pressed me to set the date as early as possible, and I agreed. There was only a ten-day interval.

"Those ten days were filled. I kept myself busy so that I wouldn't have a chance to think about the future, though of course I didn't really know how I dreaded it. I talked to the only girl who was near enough to me to be called a friend.

"'Find a man you can respect. That's the main thing,' she always said. 'You'll learn to love him later on.'

"It was a great comfort to me. I kept thinking back to that advice all the time."

"They's nothing worse than a talky woman," declared Sinclair hotly. "Go on!"

"Then, all at once, the day came. I'll never forget how I wakened that morning and looked out at the sun. I had a queer feeling that even the sunshine would never seem the same after that day. It was like going to a death."

"So you went to this gent and told him just how you felt, and he let your promise slide?"

"No."

Sinclair groaned.

"I couldn't go to him. I didn't dare. I don't imagine that I even thought of such a thing. Then there were crowds of people around all day, giving me good wishes. And all the time I felt like death.

"Somehow I got to the church. Everything was hazy to me, and my heart was thundering all the time. In the church there was a blur of faces. All at once the blur cleared. I saw Jude Cartwright, and I knew I couldn't marry him!"

"Brave girl!" cried Sinclair, his relief coming out in almost a shout. "You stopped there at the last minute?"

"Ah, if I had! No, I didn't stop. I went on to the altar and met him there, and—"

"You weren't married to him?"

"I was!"

"Go on," Sinclair said huskily.

"The end of it came somehow. I found a flood of people calling to me and pressing around me, and all the time I was thinking of nothing but the new ring on my finger and the weight—the horrible weight of it!

"We went back to my father's house. I managed to get away from all the merrymaking and go to my room. The minute the door closed behind me and shut away their voices and singing into the distance, I felt that I had saved one last minute of freedom. I went to the window and looked out at the mountains. The stars were coming out.

"All at once my knees gave way, and I began to weep on the window sill. I heard voices coming, and I knew that I mustn't let them see me with the tears running down my face. But the tears wouldn't stop coming.

"I ran to the door and locked it. Then someone tried to open the door, and I heard the voice of my Aunt Jane calling. I gathered all my nerve and made my voice steady. I told her that I couldn't let anyone in, that I was preparing a surprise for them.

" 'Are you happy, dear?' asked Aunt Jane.

"I made myself laugh. 'So happy!' I called back to her.

"Then they went away. But as soon as they were gone I knew that I could never go out and meet them. Partly because I had no surprise for them, partly because I didn't want them to see the tear stains and my red eyes. Somehow little silly things were as big and as important as the main thing—that I could never be the real wife of Jude Cartwright. Can you understand?"

"Jig, once when I had a deer under my trigger I let him go because he had a funny-shaped horn. Sure, it's the little things that run a gent's life. Go on!"

"I knew that I had to escape. But how could I escape in a place where everybody knew me? First I thought of changing my clothes. Then another thing—man's clothes! The moment that idea came, I was sure it was the thing. I opened the door very softly. There was no one upstairs just then. I ran into my cousin's room—he's a youngster of fifteen—and snatched the first boots and clothes that I could find and rushed back to my own room.

"I jumped into them, hardly knowing what I was doing. For they were beginning to call to me from downstairs. I opened the door and called back to them, and I heard Jude Cartwright answer in a big voice.

"I turned around and saw myself in the mirror in boy's clothes, with my face as white as a sheet, my eyes staring, my hair pouring down over my shoulders. I ran to the bureau and found a scissors. Then I hesitated a moment. You don't dream how hard it was to do. My hair was long, you see, below my waist. And I had always been proud of it.

"But I closed my eyes and gritted my teeth and cut it off with great slashes, close to my head. Then I stood with all that mass of hair shining in my hand and a queer, light feeling in my head.

"But I felt that I was free. I clamped on my cousin's hat—how queer it felt with all that hair cut off! I bundled the hair into my pocket, because they mustn't dream what I had done. Then someone beat on the door.

"'Coming!' I called to them.

"I ran to the window. The house was built on a slope, and it was not a very long drop to the ground, I suppose. But to me it seemed neck-breaking, that distance. It was dark, and I climbed out and hung by my hands, but I couldn't find courage to let go. Then I tried to climb back, but there wasn't any strength in my arms.

"I cried out for help, but the singing downstairs must have muffled the sound. My fingers grew numb—they slipped on the sill—and then I fell.

"The fall stunned me, I guess, for a moment. When I opened my eyes, I saw the stars and knew that I was free. I started up then and struck straight across country. At first I didn't care where I went, so long as it was away, but when I got over the first hill I made up a plan. That was to go for the railroad and take a train. I did it.

"There was a long walk ahead of me before I reached the station, and with my cousin's big boots wobbling on my feet I was very tired when I reached it. There were some freight cars on the siding, and there was hay on the floor of one of them. I crawled into the open door and went to sleep.

"After a while I woke up with a great jarring and jolting and noise. I found the car pitch dark. The door was closed, and pretty soon, by the roar of the wheels under me and the swing of the floor of the car, I knew that an engine had picked up the empty cars.

"It was a terrible time for me. I had heard stories of tramps locked into cars and starving there before the door was opened. Before the morning shone through the cracks of the boards, I went through all the pain of a death from thirst. But before noon the train stopped, and the car was dropped at a siding. I climbed out when they opened the door.

"The man who saw me only laughed. I suppose he could have arrested me.

"'All right, kid, but you're hitting the road early in life, eh!'

"Those were the first words that were spoken to me as a man.

"I didn't know where I should go, but the train had taken me south, and that made me remember a town where my father had lived for a long time—Sour Creek. I started to get to this place.

"The hardest thing I had to do was the very first thing, and that was to take my ragged head of hair into a barber shop and get it trimmed. I was sure that the barber would know I was a girl, but he didn't suspect.

"'Been a long time in the wilds, youngster, eh?' was all he said.

"And then I knew that I was safe, because people here in the West are not suspicious. They let a stranger go with one look. By the time I reached Sour Creek I was nearly over being ashamed of my clothes. And then I found this place and work as a schoolteacher. I think you know the rest." She leaned close to Sinclair. "Was I wrong to leave him?"

Sinclair rubbed his chin. "You'd ought to have told him straight off," he said firmly. "But seeing you went through with the wedding—well, take it all in all, your leaving of him was about the rightest thing I ever heard of."

Quiet fell between them.

"But what am I going to do? And where is it all going to end?" a small voice inquired of Sinclair at last.

"Roll up in them blankets and go to sleep," he advised her curtly. "I'm figuring steady on this here thing, Jig."

Jig followed that advice. Sinclair had left the fire and was walking up and down from one end of the little plateau to the other, with a strong, long step. As for the girl, she felt that an incalculable burden had been shifted from her shoulders by the telling of this tale. That burden, she knew, must have fallen on another person, and it was not unpleasant to know that Riley Sinclair was the man.

Gradually the sense of strangeness faded. As she grew drowsy, it seemed the most natural thing in the world for her to be up here at the top of the world with a man she had known two days. And, before she slept, the last thing of which she was conscious was the head of Sinclair in the broad sombrero, brushing to and fro across the stars.

18

With a bang the screen door of Sheriff Kern's office had creaked open and shut four times at intervals, and each man, entering in turn with a "Howdy" to the sheriff, had stamped the dust out of the wrinkles of his riding boots, hitched up his trousers carefully, and slumped into a chair. Not until the last of his handpicked posse had taken his place did the sheriff begin his speech.

"Gents," he said, "how long have I been a sheriff?"

"Eighteen to twenty years," said Bill Wood. "And it's been twenty years of bad times for the safecrackers and gunmen of these parts."

"Thanks," said the sheriff hastily. "And how many that I've once put my hands on have got loose?"

Again Bill Wood answered, being the senior member.

"None. Your score is exactly one hundred percent, sheriff."

Kern sighed. "Gents," he said, "the average is plumb spoiled."

It caused a general lifting of heads and then a respectful silence. To have offered sympathy would have been insulting; to ask questions was beneath their dignity, but four pairs of eyes burned with curiosity. The least curious was Arizona. He was a fat, oily man from the southland, whose past was unknown in the vicinity of Woodville, and Arizona happened to be by no means desirous of rescuing that past from oblivion. He held the southlander's contempt for the men and ways of the north. His presence in the office was explained by the fact that he had long before discovered it to be an excellent thing to stand in with the sheriff. After this statement from Kern, therefore, he first glanced at his three companions, and, observing their agitation, he became somewhat stirred himself and puckered his fat brows above his eyes, as he glanced back at Kern.

"You've heard of the killing of Quade?" asked the sheriff.

"Yesterday," said Red Chalmers.

"And that they got the killer?"

"Nope."

"It was a gent you'd never have suspected—that skinny little schoolteacher, Gaspar."

"I never liked the looks of him," said Red Chalmers gloomily. "I always got to have a second thought about a gent that's too smooth with the ladies. And that was this here Jig. So he done the shooting?"

"It was a fight over Sally Bent," explained the sheriff. "Sandersen and some of the rest in Sour Creek fixed up a posse and went out and grabbed Gaspar. They gave him a lynch trial and was about to string him up when a stranger named Sinclair, a man who had joined up with the posse, steps out and holds for keeping Gaspar and turning him over to me, to be hung all proper and legal. I heard about all this and went out to the Bent house, first thing this morning, to get Gaspar, who was left there in charge of this Sinclair. Any of you ever heard about him?"

A general bowing of heads followed, as the men began to consider, all save Arizona, who never thought when he could avoid it, and positively never used his memory. He habitually allowed the dead past to bury its dead.

"It appears to me like I've heard of a Sinclair up to Colma," murmured Bill Wood. "That was four or five years back, and I b'lieve he was called a sure man in a fight."

"That's him," muttered the sheriff. He was greatly relieved to know that his antagonist had already achieved so comfortable a reputation. "A big, lean, hungry-eyed gent, with a restless pair of hands. He come along with me while I was bringing Gaspar, but I didn't think nothing about it, most nacheral. I leave it to you, boys!"

Settling themselves they leaned forward in their chairs.

"We was talking about hosses and suchlike, which Sinclair talked uncommon slick. He seemed a knowing gent, and I opened up to him, but in the middle of things he paws out his Colt, as smooth as you ever see, and he shoves it under my nose."

Sheriff Kern paused. He was wearing gloves in spite of the fact that he was in his office. Those gloves seemed to have a peculiarly businesslike meaning for the others, and now they watched, fascinated, while the sheriff tugged his fingers deeper into the gloves, as if he were getting ready for action. He cleared his throat and managed to snap out the rest of the shameful statement.

"He stuck me up, boys, and he told Jig to beat it up the trail. Then he backed off, keeping me covered all the time, until he was around the hill. The minute he was out of sight I follered him, but when it come into view, him and

Gaspar was high-tailing through the hills. I didn't have no rifle, and it was plumb foolish to chase two killers with nothing but a Colt. Which I leave it to you gents!"

"Would have been crazy, sheriff," asserted Red Chalmers.

"I dunno," sighed Arizona, patting his fat stomach reminiscently. "I dunno. I guess you was right, Kern."

The others glared at him, and the sheriff became purple.

"So I come back and figured that I'd best get together the handiest little bunch of fighting men I could lay hands on. That's why I sent for you four."

Clumsily they made their acknowledgements.

"Because," said Kern, "it don't take no senator to see that something has got to be done. Sour Creek is after Gaspar, and now it'll be after Sinclair, too. But they got clear of me, and I'm the sheriff of Woodville. It's up to Woodville to get 'em back. Am I right?"

Again they nodded, and the sheriff, growing warmer as he talked, snatched off a glove and mopped his forehead. As his arm fell, he noted that Arizona had seen something which fascinated him. His eyes followed every gesture of the sheriff's hand.

"Is that the whole story?" asked Arizona.

"The whole thing," declared Kern stoutly, and he glared at the man from the southland.

"Because if it's anything worse," said Arizona innocently, "we'd ought to know it. The honor of Woodville is at stake."

"Oh, it's bad enough this way," grumbled Joe Stockton, and the sheriff, hastily restoring his glove, grunted assent.

"Now, boys, let's hear some plans."

"First thing," said Red Chalmers, rising, "is for each of us to pick out the best hoss in his string, and then we'll all ride over to the place where they left and pick up the trail."

"Not a bad idea," approved Kern.

There was a general rising.

"Sit down," said Arizona, who alone had not budged in his chair.

Without obeying, they turned to him.

"Was that the Morris trail, Kern?" asked Arizona.

"Sure."

"Well, you ain't got a chance of picking up the trail of two hosses out of two hundred."

In silence they received the truth of this assertion. Then Joe Stockton spoke. He was not exactly a troublemaker, but he took advantage of every disturbance that came his way and improved it to the last scruple.

"Sinclair comes from Colma, according to Bill, and Colma is north. Ride north, Kern, and the north trail will keep us tolerable close to Sinclair. We can tend to Gaspar later on—unless he's a pile more dangerous'n he looks."

"Yes, Sinclair is the main one," said the sheriff. "He's more'n a hundred Gaspars. Boys, the north trail looks good to me. We can pick up Gaspar later on, as Joe Stockton says. Straight for Colma, that's where we'll strike."

"Hold on," cut in Arizona.

Patently they regarded him with disfavor. There was something blandly superior in Arizona's demeanor. He had a way of putting forth his opinions as though it were not the slightest effort for him to penetrate truths which were securely veiled from the eyes of ordinary men.

Now he looked calmly, almost contemptuously upon the sheriff and the rest of the posse.

"Gents, has any of you ever seen this Jig you talk about ride a hoss?"

"Me, of course," said the sheriff.

"Anything about him strike you when he was in a saddle?"

"Sure! Got a funny arm motion."

"Like he was fanning his ribs with his elbows to keep cool?" went on Arizona, grinning.

The sheriff chuckled.

"Would you pick him for a good hand on a long trail?"
"Never in a million years," said the sheriff. "Is he?"
Kern seemed to admit his inferiority by asking this question. He bit his lip and was about to go on and answer himself when Arizona cut in with: "Never in a million years, sheriff. He couldn't do twenty miles in a day without being laid up."
"What's the point of all this, Arizona?"
"I'll show you pronto. Let's go back to Sinclair. The other day he was one of a bunch that pretty near got Gaspar hung, eh?"
"Yep."
"But at the last minute he saved Jig?"
"Sure. I just been telling you that."
Their inability to follow Arizona's train of thought irritated the others. He literally held them in the palm of his hand as he developed his argument.
"Why did he save Jig?" he went on. "Because when Gaspar was about to swing, they was something about him that struck Sinclair. What was it? I dunno, except that Jig is tolerable young looking and pretty helpless, even though you say he killed Quade."
"*Say* he killed him?" burst out the sheriff. "It was plumb proved on him."
"I'd sure like to see that proof," said the man from the southland. "The point is that Sinclair took pity on him and kept him from the noose. Then he stays that night guarding him and gets more and more interested. This Jig has got a pile of education. I've heard him talk. Today you come over the hills. Sinclair sees Woodville, figures that's the place where Jig'll be hung, and he loses his nerve. He sticks you up and gets Jig free. All right! D'you think he'll stop at that? Don't he know that Jig's plumb helpless on the trail? And knowing that, d'you think he'll split with Jig and leave the schoolteacher to be picked up the first thing? No, sir, he'll stick with Jig and see him through.
"Well, all the better," snapped the sheriff. "That's going

to make our trail shorter—if what you say turns out true."

"It's true, well enough. Sinclair right now is camping somewhere in the hills near Sour Creek, waiting for things to quiet down before he hits the out-trail with this Gaspar."

"He wouldn't be fool enough for that," grumbled the sheriff.

"Fool? Has any one of you professional man hunters figured yet on hunting for 'em near Sour Creek? Ain't you-all been talking long trails—Colma, and what not?"

They were crushed.

"All you say is true, if Sinclair saddles himself with the tenderfoot. Might as well tie so much lead around his neck."

"He'll do it, though," said Arizona carelessly. "I know him."

It caused a new focusing of attention upon him, and this time Arizona seemed to regret that he stood in the limelight.

"You *know* him?" asked Joe Stockton softly.

The bright black eyes of the fat man glittered and flickered from face to face. He seemed to be gauging them and deciding how much he could say—or how little.

"Sure, I drifted up to this country one season and rode there. I heard a pile about this Sinclair and seen him a couple of times."

"How good a man d'you figure him to be with a gun?" asked the sheriff without apparent interest.

"Good enough," sighed Arizona. "Good enough, partner!"

Presently the sheriff showed that he was a man capable of taking good advice, even though he could not stamp it as his own original device.

"Boys," he said, "I figure that what Arizona has said is tolerable sound. Arizona, what d'you advise next?"

"That we go to Sour Creek pronto—and sit down and wait!"

A chorus of exclamations arose.

Arizona grew impatient with such stupidity. "Sinclair come to Sour Creek to do something. I dunno what he wants, but what he wants he ain't got yet, and he's the sort that'll stay till he does his work."

"I've got in touch with the authorities higher up, boys," declared Kern. "Sinclair and Gaspar is both outlawed, with a price on their heads. Won't that change Sinclair's mind and make him move on?"

"You don't know Sinclair," persisted Arizona. "You don't know him at all, sheriff."

"Grab your hosses, boys. I'm following Arizona's lead."

Pouring out of the door in silence, the omniscience of Arizona lay heavily upon their minds. Inside, the sheriff lingered with the wise man from the southland.

"If I was to get in touch with Colma, Fatty, what d'you think they'd be able to tell me about your record up there?"

The olive skin of Arizona became a bleached drab.

"I dunno," he said rather thickly, and all the while his little black eyes were glittering and shifting. "Nothing much, Kern."

His glance steadied. "By the way, when you had your glove off a while ago I seen something on your wrist that looked like a rope gall, Kern. If I was to tell the boys that, what d'you figure they'd think about their sheriff?"

It was Kern's turn to change color. For a moment he hesitated, and then he dropped a hand lightly on Arizona's shoulder.

"Look here, Arizona," he muttered in the ear of the fat man, "what you been before you hit Woodville I dunno, and I don't care. I figure we come to a place where we'd both best keep our mouths shut. Eh?"

"Shake," said Arizona, and they went out the door, almost arm in arm.

19

For Jude Cartwright the world was gone mad, as he spurred down the hills away from Sinclair and the girl. It was really only the second time in his life that he had been thwarted in an important matter. To be sure he had been raised roughly among rough men, but among the roughest of them, the repute of his family and the awe of his father's wide authority had served him as a shield in more ways than Jude himself could realize. He had grown very much accustomed to having his way.

All things were made smooth for him; and when he reached the age when he began to think of marriage, and was tentatively courting half a dozen girls of the district, unhoped-for great fortune had fairly dropped into his path.

The close acquaintance with old Mervin in that hunting trip had been entirely accidental, and he had been astounded by the marriage contract which Mervin shortly after proposed between the two families. Ordinarily even Jude Cartwright, with all his self-esteem, would never have aspired to a star so remote as Mervin's daughter. The miracle, however happened. He saw himself in the way to be the richest man on the range, the possessor of the most lovely wife.

That dream was first pricked by the inexplicable disappearance of the girl on their marriage day. He had laid that disappearance to foul play. That she could have left him through any personal aversion never entered his complacent young head.

He went out on the quest after the neighboring district

had been combed for his wife, and he had spent the intervening months in a ceaseless search, which grew more and more disheartening. It was only by chance that he remembered that Mervin had lived for some time in Sour Creek, and only with the faintest hope of finding a clue that he decided to visit that place. In his heart he was convinced that the girl was dead, but if she were really hiding it was quite possible that she might have remembered the town where her father had made his first success with cattle.

Now the coincidence that had brought him face to face with her, stunned him. He was still only gradually recovering from it. It was totally incredible that she should have fled at all. And it was entirely beyond the range of credence that modest Elizabeth Mervin should have donned the clothes of a man and should be wandering through the hills with a male companion.

But when his wonder died away, he felt little or no pity for his wife. The pang that he felt was the torture of offended pride. Indeed, the fact that he had lost his wife meant less to him than that his wife had seen him physically beaten by another man. He writhed in his saddle at the memory.

Instantly his mind flashed back to the details of the scene. He rehearsed it with himself in a different role, beating the cowpuncher to a helpless pulp of bruised muscle, snatching away his wife. But even if he had been able to do that, what would the outcome be? He could not let the world know the truth—that his wife had fled from him in horror on their marriage day, that she had wandered about in the clothes of a man, that she was the companion of another man. And if he brought her back, certainly all these facts would come to light. The close-cropped hair alone would be damning evidence.

He framed a wild tale of abduction by villains, of an injury, a sickness, a fever that forced a doctor to cut her hair short. He had no sooner framed the story than he threw it away as useless. With all his soul he began to wish for the only possible solution which would save the remnants of his ruined self-respect and keep him from the peril of discovery. The girl must indubitably die!

By the time he came to this conclusion, he had struck out of the hills, and, as his horse hit the level going and picked up speed, the heart of Jude Cartwright became lighter. He would get weapons and the finest horse money could buy in Sour Creek, trail the pair, take them by surprise, and kill them both. Then back to the homeland and a new life!

Already he saw himself in it, his name surrounded with a glamour of pathetic romance, as the sad widower with a mystery darkening his past and future. It was an agreeable gloom into which he fell. Self-pity warmed him and loosened his fierceness. He sighed with regret for his own misfortunes.

In this frame of mind he reached Sour Creek and its hotel. While he wrote his name in the yellowed register he overheard loud conversation in the farther end of the room. Two men had been outlawed that day—John Gaspar, the schoolteacher who killed Quade, and Riley Sinclair, a stranger from the North.

Paying no further attention to the talk, he passed on into the general merchandise store which filled most of the lower story of the hotel. There he found the hardware department, and prominent among the hardware were the gun racks. He went over the Colts and with an expert hand took up the guns, while the gray-headed storekeeper advanced an eulogium upon each weapon. His attention was distracted by the entrance of a tall, painfully thin man who seemed in great haste.

"What's all this about Cold Feet, Whitey?" he asked. "Cold Feet and Sinclair?"

"I dunno, Sandersen, except that word come in from Woodville that Sinclair stuck up the sheriff on his way in with Jig, and Sinclair got clean away. What could have been in his head to grab Jig?"

"I dunno," said Sandersen, apparently much perturbed. "They outlawed 'em both, Whitey?"

There was an eagerness in this question so poorly concealed that Cartwright jerked up his head and regarded Sandersen with interest.

"Both," replied Whitey. "You seem sort of pleased, Sandersen?"

"I knowed that Sinclair would come to a bad end," said Sandersen more soberly.

"Why, I thought they said you cottoned to him when the boys was figuring he might have had something to do with Quade?"

"Me? Well, yes, for a minute. But out at the necktie party, Whitey, I kept watching him. Thinks a lot more'n he says, and gents like that is always dangerous."

"Always," replied Whitey.

"But it's the last time Sinclair'll show his face in Sour Creek—alive," said Sandersen.

"If he does show his face alive, it'll be a dead face pronto. You can lay to that."

Sandersen seemed to turn this fact over and over in his mind, with immense satisfaction.

"And yet," pursued the storekeeper, "think of a full-grown man breaking the law to save such a skinny little shrimp of a gent as Jig? Eh? More like a pretty girl than a boy, Jig is."

Cartwright exclaimed, and both of the others turned toward him.

"Here's the gun for me," he said huskily, "and that gun belt—filled—and this holster. They'll all do."

"And a handy outfit," said Whitey. "That gun'll be a friend in need!"

"What makes you think they'll be a need?" asked Cartwright, with such unnecessary violence that the others both stared. He went on more smoothly: "What was you saying about a girl-faced gent?"

"The schoolteacher—he plugged a feller named Quade. Sinclair got him clean away from Sheriff Kern."

"And what sort of a looking gent is Sinclair? Long, brown, and pretty husky-looking, with a mean eye?"

"You've named him! Where'd you meet up with him?"

"Over in the hills yonder, just where the north trail comes over the rise. They was sitting down under a tree resting their hosses when I come along. I got into an argument with this Sinclair—Long Riley, he called himself."

"Riley's his first name."

"We passed some words. Pretty soon I give him the lie! He made a reach for his gun. I told him I wasn't armed and dared him to try his fists. He takes off his belt, and we went at it. A strong man, but he don't know nothing about hand fighting. I had him about ready to give up and begging me to quit when this Jig, this girl-faced man you talk about—he pulls a gun and slugs me in the back of the head with it."

Removing his sombrero he showed on the back of his head the great welt which had been made when he struck the ground with the weight of Sinclair on top of him. It was examined with intense interest by the other two.

"Dirty work!" said Sandersen sympathetically.

The storekeeper said nothing at all, but began to fold up a bolt of cloth which lay half unrolled on the counter.

"It knocked me cold," continued Cartwright, "and when I come to, they wasn't no sign nor trace of 'em."

Buckling on the belt, he shoved the revolver viciously home in the holster.

"I'll land that pair before the posse gets to 'em, and when I land 'em I won't do no arguing with fists!"

"Say, I call that nerve," put in the storekeeper, with patent admiration in his eyes, while he smoothed a fold of the cloth. "Running agin' one gent like Sinclair is bad enough—let alone tackling two at once. But you'd ought to take out a big insurance on your life, friend, before you take that trail. It's liable to be all out-trail and no coming back."

A great deal of enthusiasm faded from Cartwright's face.

"How come?" he asked briefly.

"Nothing much. But they say this Sinclair is quite a gunfighter, my friend. Up in his home town they scare the babies by talk about Sinclair."

"H'm," murmured Cartwright. "He can't win always, and maybe I'll be the lucky man."

But he went out of the store with his head thoughtfully inclined.

"Think of meeting up with them two all alone and not knowing what they was!" sighed Sandersen. "He's lucky to be alive, I'll tell a man."

Whitey grinned.

"Plenty of nerve in a gent like that," went on Sandersen, his pale blue eyes becoming dreamy.

"Get your gat out, will you, Bill?"

Bill Sandersen obliged.

"Look at the butt. D'you see any point on it?"

"Nope."

"Did you look at that welt on the stranger's head?"

"Sure."

"Did you see a little cut in the middle of the welt?"

"Come to think of it, I sure did."

"Well, Sandersen, how d'you make out that a gun butt would make a cut like that?"

"What are you driving at, Whitey?"

"I'm just discounting the stranger," said Whitey. "I dunno what other talents he's got, but he's sure a fine nacheral liar."

20

It was some time before Riley Sinclair interrupted his pacing and, turning, strode over to the dim outlines of the sleeping girl. She did not speak, and, leaning close above her, he heard her regular breathing.

Waiting until he was satisfied that she slept, he began to move rapidly. First, with long, soft steps he went to his saddle, which was perched on a ridge of rock. This he raised with infinite care, gathering up the stirrups and the cinches so that nothing might drag or strike. With this bundle secured, he once more went close to the figure of the sleeper and this time dropped on one knee beside her. He could see nothing distinctly by the starlight, but her forehead gleamed with one faint highlight, and there was the pale glimmer of one hand above the blankets.

For the moment he almost abandoned the plan on which he had resolved, which was no less than to attempt to ride into Sour Creek and return to the girl before she wakened in the dawn. But suppose that he failed, and that she wakened to find herself alone in that mountain wilderness? He shuddered at the idea, yet he saw no other issue for her than to attempt the execution of his plan.

He rose hastily and walked off, letting his weight fall on his toes altogether, so that the spurs might not jingle.

Even that brief rest had so far refreshed his mustang that he was greeted with flattened ears and flying heels. These efforts Sinclair met with a smile and terrible whispered curses, whose familiar sound seemed to soothe the horse. He saddled at once, still using care to avoid noise, and swung steeply down the side of the mountain. On the descending trail, he could cut by one half the miles they had traversed winding up the slope.

Recklessly he rode, giving the wise pony its head most of the time, and only seeing that it did not exceed a certain speed, for when a horse passes a certain rate of going it becomes as reckless as a drunken man. Once or twice they floundered onto sheer gravel slides which the broncho took by flinging back on its haunches and going down with stiffly braced forelegs. But on the whole the mustang took care of itself admirably.

In an amazingly short time they struck the more placid footing of the valley, and Sinclair, looking up, could not believe that he had been so short a time ago at the top of the flat-crested mountain.

He gave little time to wondering, however, but cut across the valley floor at a steady lope. From the top of the mountain the lights of Sour Creek were a close-gathered patch. From the level they appeared as a scattering line. Sinclair held straight toward them, keeping away to the left so as to come onto the well-beaten trail which he knew ran in that direction. He found it and let the mustang drop back to a steady dogtrot; for, if the journey to Sour Creek was now a short distance, there would be a hard ride back to the flat-topped mountain if he wished to accomplish his business and return before the full dawn. He must be there by that time, for who could tell what the girl might do when she found herself alone. Therefore he saved the cattle pony as much as possible.

He was fairly close to Sour Creek, the lights fanning out broader and broader as he approached. Suddenly two figures loomed up before him in the night. He came near and made out a barelegged boy, riding without a saddle and driving a cow before him. He was a very angry herdsman, this boy. He kept up a continual monologue directed at the cow and his horse, and so he did not hear the approach of Riley Sinclair until the outlaw was close upon him. Then he hitched himself around, with his hand on the hip of his old horse, swaying violently with the jerk of the gait. He was glad of the company, it seemed.

"Evening, mister. You ain't Hi Corson, are you?"

"Nope, I ain't Hi. Kind of late driving that cow, ain't you?"

The boy swore with shrill fluency.

"We bought old Spot over at the Apwell place, and the darned old fool keeps breaking down fences and running back every time she gets a chance. Ain't nothing so foolish as a cow."

"Why don't your dad sell her for beef?"

"Beef?" The boy laughed. "Say, mister, I'd as soon try to chew leather. They ain't nothing but bones and skin and meanness to old Spot. But she's a good milker. When she comes in fresh she gives pretty nigh onto four gallons a milking."

"Is that so!"

"Sure is! Hard to milk, though. Kick the hat right off'n your head if you don't watch her. Never see such a fool cow as old Spot! Hey!"

Taking advantage of this diversion in the attention of her guardian, Spot had ambled off to the side of the road. The boy darted his horse after her and sent her trotting down the trail, with clicking hoofs and long, sweeping steps that scuffed up a stifling dust.

"Ain't very good to heat a milker up by running 'em, son," reproved Sinclair.

"I know it ain't. But it wouldn't make me sorry if old Spot just nacherally dropped down dead—she gives me that much trouble. Look at her now, doggone her!"

Spot had turned broadside to them and waited for the boy to catch up before she would take another forward step.

"You just coming in to Sour Creek?"

"Yep, I'm strange to this town."

"Well, you sure couldn't have picked a more fussed-up time."

"How come?"

"Well, you hear about the killing of Quade, I reckon?"

"Not a word."

"You ain't? Where you been these days?"

"Oh, yonder in the hills."

"Chipping rocks, eh? Well, Quade was a gent that lived out the north trail, and he had a fuss with the schoolteacher over Sally Bent, and the schoolteacher up and murders Quade, and they raise a posse and go out to hang Gaspar, the teacher, and they're kept from it by a stranger called Sinclair; when the sheriff comes to get Gaspar and hang him legal and all, that Sinclair sticks up the sheriff and takes Gaspar away, and now they're both outlawed, I hear tell, and they's a price on their heads."

The lad brought it out in one huge sentence, sputtering over the words in his haste.

"How much of a price?"

"I dunno. It keeps growing. Everybody around Woodville and Sour Creek is chipping in to raise that price. They sure want to get Gaspar and Sinclair bad. Gaspar ain't much. He's a kind of a sissy, but Sinclair is a killer—and then some."

Sinclair raised his head to the black, solemn mountains. Then he looked back to his companion.

"Why, has he killed anybody lately?"

"He left one for dead right today!"

"You don't mean it! He sure must be bad."

"Oh, he's bad, right enough. They was a gent named Cartwright come into town today with his head all banged up. He'd met up with Gaspar and Sinclair in the hills, not knowing nothing about them. Got into an argument with Sinclair, and, not being armed, he had it out with fists. He was beating up Sinclair pretty bad—him being a good deal of a man—when Gaspar sneaks up and whangs him on the back of the head with the butt of his Colt. They rode off and left him for dead. But pretty soon he wakes up. He comes on into Sour Creek, rarin' and tearin' and huntin' for revenge. Sure will be a bad mess if he meets up with Sinclair ag'in!"

"Reckon it had ought to be," replied Sinclair. "Like to see this gent that waded into two outlaws with his bare fists."

"He's a man, right enough. Got a room up in the hotel. Must have a pile of money, because he took the big room onto the north end of the hotel, the room that's as big as a house. Nothin' else suited him at all. Dad told me."

"I ain't got nothing particular on hand," murmured Sinclair. "Maybe I can get in on this manhunt—if they ain't started already."

The boy laughed. "Everybody in town has been trying to get in on that manhunt, but it ain't any use. Sheriff Kern has got a handpicked posse—every one a fightin' fool, Dad says. Wish you luck, though. They ain't starting till the morning. Well, here's where I branch off. S'long! Hey, Spot, you old fool, git along, will you?"

Sinclair watched the youngster fade into the gloom behind the ambling cow, then he struck on toward Sour Creek; but, before he reached the main street, he wound off to the left and let his horse drift slowly beyond the outlying houses.

His problem had become greatly complicated by the information from the boy. He had a double purpose, which was to see Cartwright in the first place, and then Sandersen, for these were the separate stumbling blocks for Jig and for himself. For Cartwright he saw a solution, through which he could avoid a killing, but Sandersen must die.

He skirted behind the most northerly outlying shed of the hotel, dismounted there, and threw the reins. Then he slipped back into the shadow of the main building. Directly above him he saw three dark windows bunched together. This must be Cartwright's room.

21

It seemed patent to Bill Sandersen, earlier that afternoon, that fate had stacked the cards against Riley Sinclair. Bill Sandersen, indeed, believed in fate. He felt that great hidden forces had always controlled his life, moving him hither and yon according to their pleasure.

To the dreamy mind of the mystic, men are accidents, and all they perform are the dictates of the power and the brain of the other world.

Sandersen could tell at what definite moments hunches had seized him. He had looked at the side of a mountain and suddenly felt, without any reason or volition on his part, that he was impelled to search that mountainside for gold-bearing ore. He had never fallen into the habit of using his reason. He was a wonderful gambler, playing with singular abandon, and usually winning. It mattered not what he held in his hand.

If the urge came to him, and the surety that he was going to bet, he would wager everything in his wallet, all that he could borrow, on a pair of treys. And when such a fit was on him, the overwhelming confidence that shone in his face usually overpowered the other men sitting in at the game. More than once a full house had been laid down to his wretched pair. There were other occasions when he had lost the very boots he wore, but the times of winning naturally overbalanced the losses in the mind of Bill. It was not he who won, and it was not he who lost. It was fate which ruled him. And that fate, he felt at present, had sided against Riley Sinclair.

A sort of pity for the big cowpuncher moved him. He knew that he and Quade and Lowrie deserved death in its most terrible form for their betrayal of Hal Sinclair in the desert; and nothing but fate, he was sure, could save him from the avenger. Fate, however, had definitely intervened. What save blind fate could have stepped into the mind of Sinclair and made him keep Cold Feet from the rope, when that hanging would have removed forever all suspicion that Sinclair himself had killed Quade?

Another man would have attributed both of those actions to common decency in Sinclair, but Sandersen always hunted out more profound reasons. In order to let the fact of his own salvation from Sinclair's gun sink more definitely into his brain, he trotted his horse into the hills that afternoon. When he came back he heard that the posse was in town.

To another it might have seemed odd that the posse was there instead of on the trail of the outlaws. But Sandersen never thought of so practical a question. To him it was as clear as day. The posse had been brought to Sour Creek by fate in order that he, Sandersen, might enlist in its ranks and help in the great work of running down Sinclair, for, after all, it was work primarily to his own interest. There was something ironically absurd about it. He, Sandersen, having committed the mortal crime of abandoning Hal Sinclair in the desert, was now given the support of legal society to destroy the just avenger of that original crime. It was hardly any wonder that Sandersen saw in all this the hand of fate.

He went straight to the hotel and up to the room which the sheriff had engaged. Cartwright was coming out with a black face, as Sandersen entered. The former turned at the door and faced Kern and the four assistants of the sheriff.

"I'll tell you what you'll do, you wise gents," he growled. "You'll miss him altogether. You hear?"

And then he stamped down the hall.

Sandersen carefully removed his hat as he went in. He was quite aware that Cartwright must have been just refused a place on the posse, and he did not wish to appear too confident. He paid his compliments to the bunch, except Arizona, to whom he was introduced. The sheriff forestalled his request.

"You've come for a job in the posse, Bill?"

Hastily Sandersen cut in before the other should pronounce a final judgment.

"I don't blame you for turning down Cartwright," he said. "A gent like that who don't know the country ain't much use on the trail, eh?"

"The point is, Bill, that I got all the men I need. I don't want a whole gang."

"But I got a special reason, sheriff. Besides a tolerable fast hoss that might come in handy for a chase, I sling a tolerable fast gun, sheriff. But beyond all that, I got a grudge."

"A grudge?" asked the sheriff, pricking his ears.

"So did Cartwright have a grudge," cut in Arizona dryly.

Perhaps after all, Sandersen felt, fate might not be with him in this quest for Sinclair. He said earnestly: "You see, boys, it was me that raised the posse that run down Cold Feet in the first place. It was me that backed up Sinclair all the way through the trail, and I feel like some of the blame for what happened is coming to me. I want to square things up and get a chance at Sinclair. I want it mighty bad. You know me, Kern. Gimme a chance, will you?"

"Well, that sounds like reason," admitted the sheriff. "Eh, boys?"

The posse nodded its general head, with the usual exception of Arizona, who seemed to take a particular pleasure in diverging from the judgments of the others.

"Just a minute, gents," he said. "Don't it strike you that they's something the same with Cartwright and Sandersen? Both of 'em is particular anxious to cut in on this party; both of 'em has grudges. Cartwright said he didn't want no share of the money if you caught Gaspar and Sinclair. Is that right for you, too, Sandersen?"

"It sure is. I want the fun, not the coin," said Sandersen.

"Boys," resumed Arizona, "it rounds up to this: Sinclair came down here to Sour Creek for a purpose."

Sandersen began to listen intently. He even dreaded this fat man from the southland.

"I dunno what this purpose was," went on Arizona, "but mostly when a gent like Sinclair makes a trip they's a man at the far end of it—because this ain't his range. Now, if it's a man, why shouldn't it be one of these two, Cartwright or Sandersen, who both pack a grudge against Sinclair? Sinclair is resting somewhere up yonder in them hills. I'm sure of that. He's waiting there to get a chance to finish his business in Sour Creek, and that business is Cartwright or Sandersen, I dunno which. Now, I'm agin' taking in Sandersen. When we're private I'll tell you my reason why."

There was something of an insult in this speech and the tall man took instant offense.

"Partner," he drawled, "it looks to me like them reasons could be spoke personal to me. Suppose you step outside and we talk shop?"

Arizona smiled. It took a man of some courage and standing to refuse such an invitation without losing caste. But for some reason Arizona was the last man in the world whom one would accuse of being a coward.

"Sandersen," he said coldly, "I don't mean to step on your toes. You may be as good a man as the next. The reasons that I got agin' you ain't personal whatever, which they're things I got a right to think, me being an officer of the law for the time being. If you hold a grudge agin' me for what I've said, you and me can talk it over after this here job's done. Is that square?"

"I s'pose it's got to be," replied Sandersen. "Gents, does the word of your fat friend go here?"

Left to themselves, the posse probably would have refused Arizona's advice on general principles, but Arizona did not leave them to themselves.

"Sure, my word goes," he hastened to put in. "The

sheriff and all of us work like a closed hand—all together!"

There was a subtle flattery about this that pleased the sheriff and the others.

"Reckoning it all in all," said sheriff, "I think we better figure you out, Sandersen. Besides they ain't anything to keep you and Cartwright and the rest from rigging up a little posse of your own. Sinclair is up yonder in the hill waiting—"

Suddenly he stopped. Sandersen was shaken as if by a violent ague, and his face lost all color, becoming a sickly white.

"And we're going to find him by ourselves. S'long Sandersen, and thanks for dropping in. No hard feelings, mind!"

To this friendly dismissal Sandersen returned no answer. He turned away with a wide, staring eye, and went through the doorway like a man walking in a dream. Arizona was instantly on his feet.

"You see, boys?" he asked exultantly. "I was right. When you said Sinclair was waiting up there in the hills, Sandersen was scared. I was right. He's one of them that Sinclair is after, and that's why he wanted to throw in with us!"

"And why the devil shouldn't he?" asked the sheriff.

"For a good reason, sheriff, reason that'll save us a pile of riding. We'll sit tight here in Sour Creek for a while and catch Sinclair right here. D'you know how? By watching Cartwright and Sandersen. As sure as they's a sky over us, Sinclair is going to make a try at one of 'em. They both hate him. Well, you can lay to it that he hates 'em back. And a man that Sinclair hates he's going to get sooner or later—chiefly sooner. Sheriff, keep an eye on them two tonight, and you'll have Sinclair playing right into your hands!"

"Looks to me," muttered Red Chalmers, "like you had a grudge agin' Cartwright and Sandersen, using them for live bait and us for a trap."

"Why not?" asked Arizona, sitting down and rubbing his fat hands, much pleased with himself. "Why not, I'd like to know?"

In the meantime Bill Sandersen had gone down to the street, still with the staring eyes of a sleep walker. It was evening, and from the open street he looked out and up to the mountains, growing blue and purple against the sky. He had heard Hal Sinclair talk about Riley and Riley's love for the higher mountains. They were "his country." And a great surety dropped upon him that the fat man of the posse had been right. Somewhere in those mountains Sinclair was lurking, ready for a descent upon Sour Creek.

Now Sandersen grew cold. All that was superstitious in his nature took him by the throat. The fate, which he had felt to be fighting with him, he now was equally sure was aligned against him. Otherwise, why had the posse refused to accept him as a member? For only one reason: He was doomed to die by the hand of Riley Sinclair, and then, no doubt, Riley Sinclair would fall in turn by the bullets of the posse.

The shadows were pouring out of the gorges of the western mountains, and night began to invade the hollow of Sour Creek. Every downward step of those shadows was to the feverish imagination of Sandersen a forecast of the coming of Sinclair—Sinclair coming in spite of the posse, in spite of the price upon his head.

In the few moments during which Sandersen remained in the street watching, the tumult grew in his mind. He was afraid. He was mortally in terror of something more than physical death, and, like the cornered rat, he felt a sudden urge to go out and meet the danger halfway. A dozen pictures came to him of Sinclair slipping into the town under cover of the night, of the stealthy approach, of the gunplay that would follow. Why not take the desperate chance of going out to find the assailant and take *him* by surprise instead?

The mountains—that was the country of Sinclair. Instinctively his eye fell and clung on the greatest height he could see, a flat-topped mountain due west of Sour Creek. Sandersen swung into his saddle and drove out of Sour Creek toward the goal and into the deepening gloom of the evening.

22

In the darkness beneath the north windows of the hotel, Sinclair consulted his watch, holding it close until he could make out the dim position of the hands against the white dial. It was too early for Cartwright to be in bed, unless he were a very long sleeper. So Sinclair waited.

A continual danger lay beside him. The kitchen door constantly banged open and shut, as the Chinese cook trotted out and back, carrying scraps to the waste barrel, or bringing his new-washing tins to hang on a rack in the open air, a resource on which he was forced to fall back on account of his cramped quarters.

But the cook never left the bright shaft of light which fell through the doorway behind and above him, and consequently he could not see into the thick darkness where Sinclair crouched only a few yards away; and the cowpuncher remained moveless. From time to time he looked up, and still the windows were black.

After what seemed an eternity, there was a flicker, as when the wick of a lamp is lighted, and then a steady glow as the chimney was put on again. That glow brightened, decreased, became an unchanging light. The wick had been trimmed, and Cartwright was in for the evening.

However, the cook had not ceased his pilgrimages. At

the very moment when Sinclair had straightened to attempt the climb up the side of the house, the cook came out and crouched on the upper step, humming a jangling tune and sucking audibly a long-stemmed pipe. The queer-smelling smoke drifted across to Sinclair; for a moment he was on the verge of attempting a quick leap and a tying and gagging of the Oriental, but he desisted.

Instead, Sinclair flattened himself against the wall and waited. Providence came to his assistance at that crisis. Someone called from the interior of the house. There was an odd-sounding exclamation from the cook, and then the latter jumped up and scurried inside, slamming the screen door behind him with a great racket.

Sinclair raised his head and surveyed the side of the wall for the last time. The sill of the window of the first floor was no higher than his shoulders. The eaves above that window projected well out, and they would afford an excellent hold by which he could swing himself up. But having swung up, the great problem was to obtain sufficient purchase for his knee to keep from sliding off before he had a chance to steady himself. Once on the ledge of those eaves, he could stand up and look through any one of the three windows into the room which, according to the boy, Cartwright occupied.

He lifted himself onto the sill of the first window, bumping his nose sharply against the pane of the glass.

Then began the more difficult task. He straightened and fixed his fingers firmly on the ledge above him, waiting until his palm and the fingertips had sweated into a steady grip. Then he stepped as far as possible to one side and sprang up with a great heave of the shoulders.

But the effort was too great. He not only flung himself far enough up, but too far, and his descending knee, striving for a hold, slipped off as if from an oiled surface. He came down with a jar, the full length of his arms, a fall that flung him down on his back on the ground.

With a stifled curse he leaped up again. It seemed that

the noise of that fall must have resounded for a great distance, but, as he stood there listening, no one drew near. Someone came out of the front door of the hotel, laughing.

The cowpuncher tried again. He managed the first stage of the ascent, as before, very easily, but, making the second effort he exceeded too much in caution and fell short. However, the fall did not include a toppling all the way to the ground. His feet landed softly on the sill, and, at the same time, voices turned the corner of the building beside him. Sinclair flattened himself against the pane of the lower window and held his breath. Two men were beneath him. Their heads were level with his feet. He could have kicked the hats off their heads, without the slightest trouble.

It was a mystery that they did not see him, he thought, until he recalled that all men, at night, naturally face outward from a wall. It is an instinct. They stood close together, talking rather low. The one was fairly tall, and the other squat. The shorter man lighted a cigarette. The match light glinted on an oily, olive skin, and so much of the profile as he could see was faintly familiar. He sent his memory lurching back into far places and old times, but he had no nerve for reminiscence. He recalled himself to the danger of the moment and listened to them talking.

"What's happened?" the taller man was saying.

"So far, nothing," grunted the other.

"And how long do you feel we'd ought to keep it up?"

"I dunno. I'll tell you when I get tired."

"Speaking personal, Fatty, I'm kind of tired of it right now. I want to hit the hay."

"Buck up, buck up, partner. We'll get him yet!"

Now it flashed into the mind of Sinclair that it must be a pair of crooked gamblers working on some fat purse in the hotel, come out here to arrange plans because they failed to extract the bank roll as quickly as they desired. Otherwise, there could be no meaning to this talk of "getting" someone.

"But between you and me," grumbled the big man, "it looked from the first like a bum game, Fatty."

"That's the trouble with you, Red. You ain't got any patience. How does a cat catch a mouse? By sitting down and waiting—maybe three hours. And the hungrier she gets, the longer she'll wait and the stiller she'll sit. A man could take a good lesson out'n that."

"You always got a pile of fancy words," protested the big man.

Sinclair saw Fatty put his hand on the shoulder of his companion. Plainly he was the dominant force of the two, in spite of his lack of height.

"Red, as sure as you're born, they's something going to happen this here night. My scars is itching, Red, and that means something."

Again the mind of Sinclair flashed back to something familiar. A man who prophesied by the itching of his scars. But once more the danger of the moment made his mind a blank to all else.

"What scars?" asked Red.

"Scratches I got when I was a kid," flashed the fat man. "That's all."

"Oh," chuckled Red, plainly unconvinced. "Well, we'll play the game a little longer."

"That's the talk, partner. I tell you we got this trap baited, and it's *got* to catch!"

Presently they drifted around the corner of the building and out of sight. For a moment Sinclair wondered what that trap could be which the fat man had baited so carefully. His mind reverted to his original picture of a card game. Cheap tricksters, sharpers with the cards, he decided, and with that decision he banished them both from his mind.

There was no other sign of life around him. All of Sour

Creek lived in the main street, or went to bed at this hour of the early night. The back of the hotel was safe from observance, except for the horse shed, and the back of the shed was turned to him. He felt safe, and now he turned, settled his fingers into a new grip on the eaves, and made his third attempt. It succeeded to a nicety, his right knee catching solidly on the ledge.

He got a fingertip hold on the boards and stood up. Straightening himself slowly, he looked into the room through a corner of the window pane.

Cartwright sat with his back to the window, a lamp beside him on the table, writing. He had thrown off his heavy outer shirt, and he wore only a cotton undershirt. His heavy shoulders and big-muscled arms showed to great advantage, with the light and sharp shadows defining each ridge. Now and then he lifted his head to think. Then he bent to his writing again.

It occurred to Sinclair to fling the window up boldly, and when Cartwright turned, cover him with a gun. But the chances, including his position on the ledge, were very much against him. Cartwright would probably snatch at his own gun which lay before him in its holster on the table, and whirling he would try a snap shot.

The only other alternative was to raise the window—and that with Cartwright four paces away!

First Sinclair took stock of the interior of the room. It was larger than most parlors he had seen. There was a big double bed on each side of it. Plainly it was intended to accommodate a whole party, and Sinclair smiled at the vanity of the man who had insisted on taking "the best you have." No wonder Sour Creek knew the room he had rented.

In the corner was a great fireplace capable of taking a six-foot log, at least. He admired the massive andirons, palpably of home manufacture in Sour Creek's blacksmith shop. It proved the age of the building. No one would waste money on such a fireplace in these days. A little stove would do twice the work of that great, hungry chimney. There were two great chests of drawers, also, each looking as if it were built up from the floor and made immovable, such was its weight. The beds, also, were of an ancient and solid school of furniture making.

To be sure, everything was sadly run down. On the floor the thin old carpet was worn completely through at the sides of the beds. Both mirrors above the chests of drawers were sadly cracked, and the table at which Cartwright sat, leaned to the right under the weight of the arm he rested on it.

Having thus taken in the details of the battle ground, Sinclair made ready for the attack. He made sure of his footing on the ledge, gave a last glance over his shoulder to see that no one was in sight, and then began to work at the window, moving it fractions of an inch at a time.

23

When the window was half raised—the work of a full ten minutes—Sinclair drew his revolver and rested the barrel on the sill. He continued to lift the sash, but now he used his left hand alone, and thereby the noises became louder and more frequent. Cartwright occasionally raised his head, but probably he was becoming accustomed to the sounds.

Now the window was raised to its full height, and Sinclair prepared for the command which would jerk Cartwright's hands above his head and make him turn slowly to look into the mouth of the gun. Weight which he could have handled easily with a lurch, became tenfold heavier with the slowness of the lift; eventually both shoulders were in the room, and he was kneeling on the sill.

Cartwright raised his hands slowly, luxuriously, and stretched. It was a movement so opportune that Sinclair almost laughed aloud. He twisted his legs over the sill and dropped lightly on the floor.

"No noise!" he called softly.

The arms of Cartwright became frozen in their position above his head. He turned slowly, with little jerky movements, as though he had to fight to make himself look. And then he saw Sinclair.

"Keep 'em up!" commanded the cowpuncher, "and get out of that chair, real soft and slow. That's it!"

Without a word Cartwright obeyed. There was no need of speech, indeed, for a score of expressions flashed into his face.

"Go over and lock the door."

He obeyed, keeping his arms above his head, all the way across the room, while Sinclair jerked the new Colt out of its holster and tossed it on the farthest bed. In the meantime Cartwright lingered at the door for a moment with his hand on the key. No doubt he fought, for the split part of a second, with a wild temptation to jerk that door open and leap into the safety of the hall. Sinclair read that thought in the tremor of the big man's body. But presently discretion prevailed. Cartwright turned the key and faced about. He was a deadly gray, and his lips were working.

"Now," he began.

"Wait till I start talking," urged Sinclair. "Come over here and sit down. You're too close to the door to suit me, just now. This is a pile better."

Cartwright obeyed quietly. Sitting down, he locked his hands nervously about one knee and looked up with his eyes to Sinclair.

"I come in for a quiet talk," said Sinclair, dropping his gun into the holster.

That movement drew a sudden brightening of the eyes of Cartwright, who now straightened in his chair, as if he had regained hope.

"Don't make no mistake," said Sinclair, following the meaning of that change accurately. "I'm pretty handy with this old gun, partner. And on you, just now, they ain't any reason why I sould take my time or any chances, when it comes to shooting."

Unconsciously Cartwright moistened his white lips, and his eyes grew big again.

"Except that the minute you shoot, you're a dead one, Sinclair."

"Me? Oh, no. When a gun's heard they'll run to the room where the shot's been fired. And when they get the lock open, I'll be gone the way I come from." Sinclair smiled genially on his enemy. "Don't start raising any crop of delusions, friend. I mean business—a lot."

"Then talk business. I'll listen."

"Oh, thanks! I come here about your wife."

He watched Cartwright wince. In his heart he pitied the man. All the story of Cartwright's spoiled boyhood and viciously selfish youth were written in his face for the reading of such a man as Sinclair. The rancher's son had begun well enough. Lack of discipline had undone him; but whether his faults were fixed or changeable, Sinclair could not tell. It was largely to learn this that he took the chances for the interview.

"Go on," said Cartwright.

"In the first place, d'you know why she left you?"

An anguish came across Cartwright's face. It taught Sinclair at least one thing—that the man loved her.

"You're the reason—maybe."

"Me? I never seen her till two days ago. That's a tolerable ugly thing to say, Cartwright!"

"Well, I got tolerable ugly reasons for saying it," answered the other.

The cowpuncher sighed. "I follow the way you drift. But you're wrong, partner. Fact is, I didn't know Cold Feet was a girl till this evening."

Cartwright sneered, and Sinclair stiffened in his chair.

"Son," he said gravely, "the worst enemies I got will all tell you that Riley Sinclair don't handle his own word careless. And I give you my solemn word of honor that I didn't know she was a girl till this evening, and that, right away after I found it out, I come down here to straighten things out with you if I could. Will you believe it?"

It was a strange study to watch the working in the face of Cartwright—of hope, passion, doubt, hatred. He leaned closer to Sinclair, his big hands clutched together.

"Sinclair, I wish I could believe it!"

"Look me in the eye, man! I can stand it."

"By the Lord, it's true! But, Sinclair, have you come down to find out if I'd take her back?"

"Would you?"

The other grew instantly crafty. "She's done me a pile of wrong, Sinclair."

"She has," said the cowpuncher. He went on gently: "She must of cut into your pride a lot."

"Oh, if it was known," said Cartwright, turning pale at the thought, "she'd make me a laughing stock! Me, old Cartwright's son!"

"Yep, that'd be bad." He wondered at the frank egoism of the youth.

"I leave it to you," said Cartwright, settling back in his chair. "Something had ought to be done to punish her. Besides, she's a weight on your hands, and I can see you'd be anxious to get rid of her quick."

"How d'you aim to punish her?" asked Sinclair.

"Me?"

"Sure! Kind of a hard thing to do, wouldn't it be?"

Cartwright's eyes grew small. "Ways could be found." He swallowed hard. "I'd find a heap of ways to make her wish she'd died sooner'n shame me!"

"I s'pose you could," said Sinclair slowly. He lowered his glance for a moment to keep his scorn from standing up in his eyes. "But I've heard of men, Cartwright, that'd love a woman so hard that they'd forgive anything."

"The world's full of fools," said the rich rancher. He stabbed a stern forefinger into the palm of his other hand. "She's got to do a lot of explaining before I'll look at her. She's got to make me an accounting of every day she's spent since I last seen her at—"

"At the wedding?" asked Sinclair cruelly.

Cartwright writhed in the chair till it groaned beneath his uneasy weight. "She told you that?"

"Look here," went on Sinclair, assuming a new tone of frank inquiry. "Let's see if we can't find out why she left you?"

"They ain't any reason—just plain fool woman, that's all."

"But maybe she didn't love you, Cartwright. Did you ever think of that?"

The big man stared. "Not love me? Who *would* she love, then? Was they anybody in them parts that could bring her as much as I could? Was they anybody that had as good a house as mine, or as much land, or as much cattle? Didn't I take her over the ground and show her what it amounted to? Didn't I offer her her pick of my own string of riding horses?"

"Did you do as much as that?"

"Sure I did. She wouldn't have lacked for nothing."

"You sure must have loved her a lot," insinuated Sinclair. "Must have been plumb foolish about her."

"Oh, I dunno about that. Love is one thing that ain't bothered me none. I got important interests, Sinclair. I'm a business man. And this here marriage was a business proposition. Her dad was a business man, and he fixed it all up for us. It was to tie the two biggest bunches of land together that could be found in them parts. Anyway"—he grinned—"I got the land!"

"And why not let the girl go, then?"

"Why?" asked Cartwright eagerly. "Who wants her? You?"

"Maybe, if you'd let her go."

"Not in a thousand years! She's mine. They ain't no face but hers that I can see opposite to me at the table—not one! Besides, she's mine, and I'm going to keep her—after I've taught her a lesson or two!"

Sinclair wiped his forehead hastily. Eagerness to jump at the throat of the man consumed him. He forced a smile on his thin lips and persistently looked down.

"But think how easy it'd be, Cartwright. Think how easy you could get a divorce on the grounds of desertion."

"And drag all this shame into the courts?"

"They's ways of hushing these here things up. It'd be easy. She wouldn't put up no defense, mostlike. You'd win your case. And if anybody asked questions, they'd simply say she was crazy, and that you was lucky to get rid of her. They wouldn't blame you none. And it wouldn't be no disgrace to be deserted by a crazy woman, would it?"

Cartwright drew back into a shell of opposition. "You talk pretty hot for this."

"Because I'm telling you the way out for both of you."

"I can't see it. She's coming back to me. Nobody else is going to get her. I've set my mind on it!"

"Partner, don't you see that neither of you could ever be happy?"

"Oh, we'd be happy enough. I'd forgive her—after a while."

"Yes, but what about her?"

"About her? Why, curse her, what right has she got to be considered?"

"Cartwright, she doesn't love you."

The bulldog came into the face of Cartwright and contorted it. "Don't she belong to me by law? Ain't she sworn to—"

"Don't" said Sinclair, as if the words strangled him. "Don't say that, Cartwright, if you please!"

"Why not? You put up a good slick talk, Sinclair. But you don't win. I ain't going to give her up by no divorce. I'm going to keep her. I don't love her enough to want her back, I hate her enough. They's only one way that I'd stop caring about—stop fearing that she'd shame me. And that's by having her six feet underground. But you, Sinclair, you need coin. You're footloose. Suppose you was to take her and bring her to—"

"Don't!" cried Sinclair again. "Don't say it, Cartwright. Think it over again. Have mercy on her, man. She could make some home happy. Are you going to destroy that chance?"

"Say, what kind of talk is this?" asked the big man.

"Now," said Sinclair, "look to your own rotten soul!"

The strength of Cartwright was cut away at the root. The color was struck out of his face as by a mortal blow. "What d'you mean?" he whispered.

"You don't deserve a man's chance, but I'm going to give it to you. Go get your gun, Cartwright!"

Cartwright slunk back in his chair. "Do you mean murder, Sinclair?"

"I mean a fair fight."

"You're a gunman. You been raised and trained for gunfighting. I wouldn't have no chance!"

Sinclair controlled his scorn. "Then I'll fight left-handed. I'm a right-handed man, Cartwright, and I'll take you with my gun in my left hand. That evens us up, I guess."

"No, it don't!"

But with the cry on his lips, the glance of Cartwright flickered past Sinclair. He grew thoughtful, less flabby. He seemed to be calculating his chances as his glance rested on the window.

"All right," he whispered, a fearful eye on Sinclair, as if

he feared the latter would change his mind. "Gimme a fair break."

"I'll do it."

Sinclair shifted his gun to his left hand and turned to look at the window which Cartwright had been watching with such intense interest. He had not half turned, however, when a gun barked at his very ear, it seemed, a tongue of flame spat in from the window, there was a crash of glass, and the lamp was snuffed. Some accurate shot had cut the burning wick out of the lamp with his bullet, so nicely placed that, though the lamp reeled, it did not fall.

24

With the spurt of flame, Sinclair leaped back until his shoulders grazed the wall. He crouched beside the massive chest of drawers. It might partially shelter him from fire from the window.

There fell one of those deadly breathing spaces of silence—silence, except for the chattering of the lamp, as it steadied on the table and finally was still. There was a light crunching noise from the opposite side of the room. Cartwright had moved and put his foot on a fragment of the shattered chimney.

Sinclair studied the window. It was a rectangle of dim light, but nothing showed in that frame. He who had fired the shot must have crouched at once, or else have drawn to one side. He waited with his gun poised. Steps were sounding far away in the building, steps which approached rapidly. Voices were calling. Somewhere on the farther side of the room Cartwright must have found the best shelter he could, and Sinclair shrewdly guessed that it would be on the far side of the chest of drawers which faced him.

In the meantime he studied the blank rectangle of the window. Sooner or later the man who stood on the ledge would risk a look into the dark interior; otherwise, he would not be human. And, sure enough, presently the faintest shadow of an outline encroached on the solid rectangle of faint light. Sinclair aimed just to the right and fired. At once there was a splash of red flame and a thundering report from the other side of the room. Cartwright had fired at the flash of Sinclair's gun, and the bullet smashed into the chest beside Sinclair. As for Sinclair's own bullet, it brought only a stifled curse from the window.

"No good, Riley," sang out the voice. "This wall's too thick for a Colt."

Sinclair had flung himself softly forward on his stomach, his gun in readiness and leveled in the direction of Cartwright. There was the prime necessity. Now heavy footfalls rushed down the hall, and a storm of voices broke in upon him.

At the same time Cartwright's gun spat fire again. The bullet buzzed angrily above Sinclair's head. His own brought a yell of pain, sharp as the yelp of a coyote.

"Keep quiet, Cartwright," ordered the man at the window. "You'll get yourself killed if you keep risking it. Sheriff!"

His voice rose and rang.

"Blow the lock off'n that door. We got him!"

There was an instant reply in the explosion of a gun, the crash of broken metal, and the door swung slowly in, admitting a dim twilight into the room. The light showed Sinclair one thing—the dull outlines of Cartwright. He whipped up his gun and then hesitated. It would be murder. He had killed before, but never save in fair fight, standing in a clear light before his enemy. He knew that he could not kill this rat he detested. He thought of the wrecked life of the girl and set his teeth. Still he could not fire.

"Cartwright," he said softly, "I got you covered. Your right hand's on the floor with your gun. Don't raise that hand!"

In the shadow against the wall Cartwright moved, but he obeyed. The revolver still glimmered on the floor.

A new and desperate thought came to Sinclair—to rush straight for the window, shoot down the man on the ledge, and risk the leap to the ground.

"Scatter back!" called the man on the ledge.

That settled the last chance of Sinclair. There were guards on the ground, scattered about the house. He could never get out that way.

"Keep out of the light by the door," commanded the man at the window. "And start shooting for the chest of drawers on the left-hand side of the room—and aim low down. It may take time, but we'll get him!"

Obviously the truth of that statement was too clear for Sinclair to deny it. He reviewed his situation with the swift calm of an old gambler. He had tried his desperate coup and had failed. There was nothing to do but accept the failure, or else make a still more desperate effort to rectify his position, risking everything on a final play.

He must get out of the room. The window was hopelessly blocked. There remained the open door, but the hall beyond the door was crowded with men.

Perhaps their very numbers would work against them. Even now they could be heard cautiously maneuvering. They would shoot through the door in his general direction, unaimed shots, with the hope of a chance hit, and eventually they would strike him down. Suppose he were to steal close to the door, leap over the bed, and plunge out among them, his Colt splitting lead and fire.

That unexpected attack would cleave a passage for him. The more he thought of it, the more clearly he saw that the chances of escape to the street were at least one in three. And yet he hesitated. If he made that break two or three innocent men would go down before his bullets, as he sprang out, shooting to kill. He shrank from the thought. He was amazed at himself. Never before had he been so tender of expedients. He had always fought to win—cleanly, but to win. Why was he suddenly remembering that to these men he was an outlaw, fit meat for the first bullet they could send home? Had he been one of them, he would have taken up a position in that very hall just as they were doing.

Slowly, reluctantly, fighting himself as he did it, he shoved his revolver back into his holster and determined to take the chance of that surprise attack, with his empty hands against their guns. If they did not drop him the instant he leaped out, he would be among them, too close for gunplay unless they took the chance of killing their own men.

Keeping his gaze fixed on Cartwright across the room—for the moment he showed his intention, Cartwright would shoot—he maneuvered softly toward the bed. Cartwright turned his head, but made no move to lift his gun. There was a reason. The light from the door fell nearer to the rancher than it did to Sinclair. To Cartwright he must be no more than a shapeless blur.

A gun exploded from the doorway, with only a glint of steel, as the muzzle was shoved around the jamb. The bullet crashed harmlessly into the wall behind him. Another try. The sharp, stifling odor of burned powder began to fill the room, stinging the nostrils of Sinclair. Cartwright was coughing in a stifled fashion on the far side of the room, as if he feared a loud noise would draw a bullet his way.

All at once there was no sound in the hotel, and, as the wave of silence spread, Sinclair was aware that the whole little town was listening, waiting, watching. Not a whisper in the hall, not a stir from Cartwright across the room. The quiet made the drama seem unreal.

Then that voice outside the window, which seemed to be Sinclair's Nemesis, cried: "Steady, boys. Something's going to happen. He's getting ready. Buck up boys!"

In a moment of madness Sinclair decided to rush that window and dispose of the cool-minded speaker at all costs before he died. There, at least, was the one man he wished to kill. He followed that impulse long enough to throw himself sidling along the floor, so as not to betray his real strategic position to those at the door, and he splashed two bullets into the wall, trimming the side of the window.

Only clear, deep-throated laughter came in response.

"I told you, boys. I read his mind, and he's mad at me, eh?"

But Riley Sinclair hardly heard that mocking answer. He had glided back behind the bed, the instant the shots were fired. As he moved, two guns appeared for a flickering instant around the edge of the doorway, one on each side. Their muzzles kicked up rapidly, one, two, three, four, five, six, and each, as he fired, spread the shots carefully from side to side. Sinclair heard the bullets bite and splinter the woodwork close to the floor. The chest of drawers staggered with the impact.

He raised his own gun, watched one of the jumping muzzles for an instant, and then tried a snap shot. The report of his revolver was bitten off short by the clang of metal; there was a shouted curse from the hallway. He had blown the gun cleanly out of the sharpshooter's hand.

Before the amazed rumble from the hall died away, Sinclair had acted. He shoved his weapon back in its holster, and cleared the bed with a flying leap. From the corner of his eye, he saw Cartwright snatch up his gun and take a chance shot that whistled close to his head, and then Sinclair plunged into the hall.

One glimmering chance of success remained. On the

side of the door toward which he drove there were only three men in the hall; behind him were more, far more, but their weapons were neutralized. They could not fire without risking a miss that would be certain to lodge a bullet in the body of one of the men before Sinclair.

Those men were kneeling, for they had been reaching out and firing low around the door to rake the floor of the room. At the appearance of Sinclair they started up. He saw a gun jerk high for the snap shot, and, swerving as he leaped, he drove out with all his weight behind his fist. The knuckles bit through flesh to the bone. There was a jarring impact, and now only two men were before him. One of them dropped his gun—it was he who had just emptied his weapon into the room—and flung himself at Sinclair, with outspread arms. The cowpuncher snapped up his knee, and the blow crumpled the other back and to the side. He sprang on toward the last man who barred his way. And all this in the split part of a second.

Chance took a hand against him. In the very act of striking, his foot lodged on the first senseless body, and he catapulted forward on his hands. He struck the legs of the third man as he fell.

Down they went together, and Sinclair lurched up from under the weight only to be overtaken by many reaching hands from behind. That instant of delay had lost the battle for him; and, as he strove to whirl and fight himself clear, an arm curled around his neck, shutting off his breath. A great weight jarred between his shoulders, and he pitched down to the floor.

He stopped fighting. He felt his gun slipped from the holster. Deft, strong hands jerked his arms behind him and tied the wrists firmly together. Then he was drawn to his feet.

All this without a word spoken, only the pant and struggle of hard-drawn breaths. Not until he stood on his feet again, with a bleeding-faced fellow rising with dazed eyes, and another clambering up unsteadily, with both hands pressed against his head, did the captors give voice. And their voice was a yell of triumph that was taken up in two directions outside the hotel.

They became suddenly excited, riotously happy. In the overflowing of their joy they were good-natured. Some one caught up Sinclair's hat and jammed it on his head. Another slapped him on the shoulder.

"A fine, game fight!" said the latter. It was the man with the smeared face. He was grinning through his wounds. "Hardest punch I ever got. But I don't blame you, partner!"

Presently he saw Sheriff Kern. The latter was perfectly cool, perfectly grave. It was his arm that had coiled around the neck of Sinclair and throttled him into submission.

"You didn't come out to kill, Sinclair. Why?"

"I ain't used to slaughterhouse work," said Sinclair with equal calm, although he was panting. "Besides, it wasn't worth it. Murder never is."

"Kind of late to come to that idea, son. Now just trot along with me, will you?" He paused. "Where's Arizona?"

Cartwright lurched out of the room with his naked gun in his hand. Red dripped from the shallow wound where Sinclair's bullet had nicked him. He plunged at the captive, yelling.

"Stop that fool!" snapped the sheriff.

Half a dozen men put themselves between the outlaw and the avenger. Cartwright struggled vainly.

"Between you and me," said Sinclair coldly to the sheriff, "I think that skunk would plug me while I got my hands tied."

The sheriff flashed a knowing glance up at his tall prisoner's face.

"I dunno, Sinclair. Kind of looks that way."

Although Cartwright had been persuaded to restore his gun to its cover, he passed through the crowd until he confronted Sinclair.

"Now, the tables is turned, eh? I'll take the high hand from now on, Sinclair!"

"It's no good," said Sinclair dryly. "The gent that shot out the light had a chance to see something before he done the shooting. And what he seen must have showed that you're yaller, Cartwright—yaller as a yaller dog!"

Cartwright flung his fist with a curse into the face of the cowpuncher. The weight of the blow jarred him back against the wall, but he met the glare of Cartwright with a steady eye, a thin trickle of crimson running down his cut lips. The sheriff rushed in between and mastered Cartwright's arms.

"One more little trick like that, stranger, and I'll turn you over to the boys. They got ways of teaching gents manners. How was you raised, anyway?"

Suddenly sobered, Cartwright drew back from dark glances on every side.

"Fellows," he said, in a shaken voice, "I forgot his hands was tied. But I'm kind of wrought up. He tried to murder me!"

"It's all right, partner," drawled Red Chalmers, and he laid a strong hand on the shoulder of Cartwright. "It's all right. We all allow for one break. But don't do something like that twice—not in these parts!"

Sinclair walked beside the sheriff, while the crowd poured past him and down the hall. When they reached the head of the stairs they found the lighted room below filled with excited, upturned faces; at the sight of the sheriff and his prisoner they roared their applause. The faces were blotted and blurred by a veil of rapidly, widely waving sombreros.

The sheriff paused halfway down the stairs and held up his hand. Sinclair halted beside him looking disdainfully over the crowd. Instantly noise and movement ceased. It was a spectacular picture, the stubby little sheriff and the tall, lean, wolflike man he had captured. It seemed a vivid illustration of the power of the law over the lawbreaker.

Sinclair glanced down in wonder at Kern. It was in character for the sheriff to make a speech. A moment later the sheriff's own words had explained his reason for the impromptu address.

"Boys," he said, "I figure some of you has got an almighty big wish to see Sinclair on the end of a rope, eh?"

A deep growl answered him.

"Speaking personal," went on the sheriff smoothly, "I don't see how he's done a thing worth hanging. He took a prisoner away from me, and he's resisted arrest. That's all. Sinclair has got a name as a killer. Maybe he is. But I know he ain't done no killing around these parts that's come to light yet. I'll tell you another thing. A minute ago he could have sent three men to death and maybe come off with a free skin. But he chose to take his chance without shooting to kill. He tried to fight his way out with his hands sooner'n blow the heads off of gents that never done him no harm except to get in his way. Well, boys, that's something you don't often see. And I tell you this right now: If they's any lynch talk around this here town, you can lay to it that you'll have to shoot your way to Sinclair through me. And I'll be a dead one before you reach to him."

He paused. Someone hissed from the back of the crowd, but the majority murmured in appreciation.

"One more thing," went on the sheriff. "Some of you may think it was great guns to take Sinclair. It *was* a pretty good job, but they ain't no credit coming to me. I'm up here saying that all the praise goes to a fat friend of mine by name Arizona. If you got any free drinks, let 'em drift the way of Arizona. Hey, Arizona, step out and make a bow, will you?"

But no Arizona appeared. The crowd cheered him, and then cheered the generous sheriff. Kern had won more by his frankness than he could possibly have won in half a dozen spectacular exploits with a gun.

25

The crowd swirled out of the hotel before the sheriff and his prisoner, and then swirled back again. No use following the sheriff if they hoped for details. They knew his silence of old. Instead they picked off the members who had taken part in some phase of the fight, and drew them aside. As Sinclair went on down the street, the populace of Sour Creek was left pooled behind him. Various orators were giving accounts of how the whole thing had happened.

Sinclair had neither eye nor ear for them. But he looked back and up to the western sky, with a flat-topped mountain clearly outlined against it. There was his country, and in his country he had left Jig alone and helpless. A feeling of utter desolation and failure came over him. He had started with a double goal—Sandersen or Cartwright, or both. He had failed lamentably of reaching either one. He looked back to the sheriff, squat, insignificant, gray-headed. What a man to have blocked him!

"But who's this Arizona?" he asked.

"I dunno. Seems to have known you somewhere. Maybe a friend of yours, Sinclair?"

"H'm," said the cowpuncher. "Maybe! Tell me: Was it him that was outside the window and trimmed the light on me?"

"You got him right, Sinclair. That was the gent. Nice play he made, eh?"

"Very pretty, sheriff. I thought I knowed his voice."

"He seems to have made himself pretty infrequent. Didn't know Arizona was so darned modest."

"Maybe he's got other reasons," said Sinclair. "What's his full name?"

"Ain't that curious! I ain't heard of anybody else that knows it. He's a cool head, this Arizona. Seemed to read your mind and know jest how you'd jump, Sinclair. I would have been off combing the trails, but he seemed to know that you'd come into town."

"I'll sure keep him in mind if I ever meet up with him," murmured Sinclair. "Is this where I bunk?"

The sheriff had paused before a squat, dumpy building and was working noisily at the lock with a big key. Now that his back was necessarily toward his prisoner, two of the posse stepped up close beside Sinclair. They had none of the sheriff's nonchalance. One of them was the man whose head had made the acquaintance of Sinclair's knee, and both were ready for instant action of any description.

"I'm Rhinehart," said one softly. "Keep me in mind, Sinclair. I'm him that you smashed with your knee. Dirty work! I'll see you when you get out of the lockup—if that ever happens!"

The voice of Sinclair was not so soft. "I'll meet you in jail or out," he answered, "on foot or on horseback, with fists or knife or gun. And you can lay to this, Rhinehart: I'll remember you a pile better'n you'll remember me!"

All the repressed savagery of his nature came quivering into his voice as he spoke, and the other shrank instinctively a pace. In the meantime the sheriff had succeeded in turning the rusted lock, which squeaked back. The door grumbled on its heavy hinges. Sinclair stepped into the musty, close atmosphere within.

"Don't look like you had much use for this here outfit," he said to the sheriff.

The latter lighted a lantern.

"Nope," he said. "It sure beats all how the luck runs, Sinclair. We'd had a pretty bad time with crooks around these parts, and them that was nabbed in Sour Creek got away; about two out of three, before they was brought to me at Woodville. So the boys got together and ponied up for this little jail, and it's as neat a pile of mud and steel as ever you see. Look at them bars. Kind of rusty, they look, but inside they're toolproof. Oh, it's an up-to-date outfit, this jail. It's been a comfort to me, and it's a credit to Sour Creek. But the trouble is that since it was built they ain't been more'n one or two to put in it. Maybe you can make out here for the night. Have you over to Woodville in a couple of days, Sinclair."

He brought his prisoner into a cagelike cell, heavily guarded with bars on all sides. The adobe walls had been trusted in no direction. The steel lining was the strength of the Sour Creek jail. The sheriff himself set about shaking out the blankets. When this was done, he bade his two companions draw their guns and stand guard at the steel door to the cell.

"Not that I don't trust you a good deal, Sinclair," he said, "but I know that a gent sometimes takes big chances."

So saying, he cut the bonds of his prisoner, but instead of making a plunge at the door, Sinclair merely stretched his long arms luxuriously above his head. The sheriff slipped out of the door and closed it after him. A heavy and prolonged clangor followed, as steel jarred home against steel.

"Don't go sheriff," said Sinclair. "I need a chat with you."

"I'm in no hurry. And here's the gent we was talking about. Here's Arizona!"

The sheriff had waved his two companions out of the jail, as soon as the prisoner was securely lodged, and no sooner was this done, and they had departed through the doorway, than the heavy figure of Arizona himself appeared. He came slowly into the circle of the lantern light, an oddly changed man.

His swaggering gait, with heels that pounded heavily, was gone. He slunk forward, soft-footed. His head, usually so bouyantly erect, was now sunk lower and forward. His high color had faded to a drab olive. In fact, from a free-swinging, jovial, somewhat overbearing demeanor, Arizona had changed to a mien of malicious and rather frightened cunning. In this wise he advanced, heedless of the curious and astonished sheriff, until his face was literally pressed against the bars. He peered steadily at Sinclair.

On the face of the latter there had been at first blank surprise, then a gradually dawning recognition. Finally he walked slowly to the bars. As Sinclair approached, the fat cowpuncher drew back, with lingering catlike steps, as if he grudged every inch of his retreat and yet dared not remain to meet Sinclair.

"By the Eternal," said Sinclair, "it's Dago!"

Arizona halted, quivering with emotions which the sheriff could not identify, save for a blind, intense malice. The tall man turned to the sheriff, smiling: "Dago Lansing, eh?"

"Never heard that name," said the sheriff.

"Maybe not," replied Sinclair, "but that's the man I—"

"You lie!" cried Arizona huskily, and his fat, swift hand fluttered nervously around the butt of the revolver. "Sheriff, they ain't nothing but lies stocked up in him. Don't believe nothing he says!"

"Huh!" chuckled Sinclair. "Why, Kern, he's a man about eight years ago that I—"

Pausing, he looked into the convulsed face of Arizona, who was apparently tortured with apprehension.

"I won't go on, Dago," said Sinclair mildly. "But—so you've carried this grudge all these days, eh?"

Arizona tossed up his head. For a moment he was the Arizona the sheriff had known, but his laughter was too strident, and it was easy to see that he was at a point of hysterically high tension.

"Well, I'd have carried it eighty years as easy as eight," declared Arizona. "I been waiting all this time, and now I got you, Sinclair. You'll rot behind the bars the best part of the life that's left to you. And when you come out—I'll meet you ag'in!"

Sinclair smiled in a singular fashion. "Sorry to disappoint you, Dago. But I'm not coming out. I'm going to stay put. I'm through."

The other blinked. "How come?"

"It's something you couldn't figure," said Sinclair calmly, and he eyed the fat man as if from a great distance.

Sinclair was remembering the day, eight years ago, in a lumber camp to the north when a shivering, meager, shifty-eyed youngster had come among them asking for work. They had taken pity on him, those big lumberjacks, put him up, given him money, kept him at the bunk house.

Then articles began to disappear, watches, money. It was Sinclair who had caught the friendless stripling in the act of sleight of hand in the middle of the night when the laborers, tired out, slept as if stunned. And when the others would have let the cringing, weeping youth go with a lecture and the return of his illicit spoils, it was the stern Sinclair who had insisted on driving home the lesson. He forced them to strip Dago to the waist. Two stalwarts held his hands, and Sinclair laid on the whip. And Dago, the moment the lash fell, ceased his wailing and begging, and stood quivering, with his head bent, his teeth set and gritting, until the punishment was ended.

It was Sinclair, also, when the thing was ended, and the others would have thrust the boy out penniless, who split the contents of his wallet with Dago. He remembered the words he had spoken to the stripling that day eight years before.

"You ain't had much luck out here in the West, kid, but stay around. Go south. Learn to ride a hoss. They's nothing that puts heart and honesty in a man like a good hoss. Don't go back to your city. You'll turn into a snake there. Stay out here and practice being a man, will you? Get the feel of a Colt. Fight your way. Keep you mouth shut and work with your hands. And don't brag about what you know or what you've done. That's the way to get on. You got the makings in you, son. You got grit. I seen it when you was under the whip, and I wish I had the doing of that over again. I made a mistake with you, kid. But do what I've told you to do, and one of these days you'll meet up with me and beat me to the draw and take everything you got as a grudge out on me. But you can't do it unless you turn into a man."

Dago had listened in the most profound silence, accepted the money without thanks, and disappeared, never to be heard from again. In the sleek-faced man before him, Sinclair could hardly recognize that slender fellow of the lumber camp. Only the bright and agile eyes were the same; that, and a certain telltale nervousness of hand. The color was coming back into his face.

"I guess I've done it," Arizona was saying. "I guess we're squared up, Sinclair."

"Yep, and a balance on your side."

"Maybe, maybe not. But I've followed your advice, Long Riley. I've never forgot a word of it. It was printed into me!"

He made a significant, short gesture, as if he were snapping a whip, and a snarl of undying malice curled his lips.

"As long as you live, Sinclair," he added. "As long as you live, I'll remember."

Even the sheriff shuddered at that glimpse into the black soul of the man; Sinclair alone was unmoved.

"I reckon you've barked enough, Arizona," he suggested. "S'pose you trot along. I got to have words with my friend, the sheriff."

Arizona waved his fat hand. He was recovering his ordinary poise, and with a smiling good night to the sheriff, he turned away through the door.

"Nice, friendly sort, eh?" remarked Sinclair the moment he was alone with Kern.

"I still got the chills," said the sheriff. "Sure has got a wicked pair of eyes, that Arizona."

Kern cast an apprehensive glance at the closed door, yet, in spite of the fact that it was closed, he lowered his voice.

"What in thunder have you done to him, Sinclair?"

"About eight years ago—" began Sinclair and then stopped short.

"Let it go," he went on. "No matter what Arizona is today, he's sure improved on the gent I used to know. What's done is done. Besides, I made a mistake that time. I went too far with him, and a mistake is like borrowed money, sheriff. It lays up interest and keeps compounding. When you have to pay back what you done a long time ago, you find it's a terrible pile. That's all I got to say about Arizona."

Sheriff Kern nodded. "That's straight talk, Sinclair," he said softly. "But what was it you wanted to see me about?"

"Cold Feet," said Sinclair.

At once the sheriff brightened. "That's right," he said hurriedly. "You got the right idea now, partner. Glad to see you're using hoss sense. And if you gimme an idea of the trail that'll lead to Cold Feet, I can see to it that you get out of this mess pretty pronto. After all, you ain't done no real harm except for nicking Cartwright in the arm, and I figure that he needs a little punishment. It'll cool his temper down."

"You think I ought to tell you where Cold Feet is?" asked Sinclair without emotion.

"Why not?"

"Him and me sat around the same campfire, sheriff, and ate off'n the same deer."

At this the sheriff winced. "I know," he murmured. "It's hard—mighty hard!" He continued more smoothly: "But listen to me, partner. There's twenty-five-hundred dollars on the head of Cold Feet. Why not come in? Why not split on it? Plenty for both of us; and, speaking personal, I could use half that money, and maybe you could use the other half just as well!"

"I'll tell you what I'll do," said Sinclair, "I'll give you the layout for finding Cold Feet. Ride west out of Sour Creek and head for a flat-topped mountain. On the shoulder just under the head of the peak you'll find Cold Feet. Go get him!"

The sheriff caught his breath, then whirled on his heel. The sharp voice of Sinclair called him back.

"Wait a minute. I ain't through. When you catch Cold Feet you go after him without guns."

"How come?"

"Because you might hurt him, and he can't fight, sheriff. Even if he was to pull a gun, he couldn't hit nothing with it. He couldn't hit the ground he's standing on with a gun."

Sheriff Kern scratched his head.

"And when you get him," went on Sinclair, "tell him to go back and take up his life where he left off, because they's no harm coming to him."

"Great guns, man! No harm coming to him with a murder to his count and a price on his head?"

"I mean what I say. Break it to him real gentle."

"And who pays for the killing of Quade?"

Sinclair smiled. He was finding it far easier to do it than he had ever imagined. The moment he made the resolve, his way was smoothed for him.

"I pay for Quade," he said quietly.

"What d'you mean?"

"Because I killed him, sheriff. Now go tell Cold Feet that his score is clean!"

26

Toward that flat-topped mountain, with the feeling of his fate upon him, Bill Sandersen pushed his mustang through the late evening, while the darkness fell. He had long since stopped thinking, reasoning. There was only the strong, blind feeling that he must meet Sinclair face to face and decide his destiny in one brief struggle.

So he kept on until his shadow fell faintly on his path before him, long, shapeless, grotesque. He turned and saw the moon coming up above the eastern mountains, a wan, sickly moon hardly out of her first quarter, and even in the pure mountain air her light was dim.

But it gave thought and pause to Sandersen. First there was the outcropping of a singular superstition which he had heard long before and never remembered until this moment: that a moon seen over the left shoulder meant the worst of bad luck. It boded very ill for the end of this adventure.

Suppose he were able only partially to surprise the big cowpuncher from the north, and that there was a call for fighting. What chance would he have in the dim and bewildering light of that moon against the surety of Sinclair who shot, he knew, as other men point the finger—instinctively hitting the target? It would be a mere butchery, not a battle.

Sending his mustang into a copse of young trees, he dismounted. His mind was made up not to attempt the blow until the first light of dawn. He would try to reach the top of the flat-crested mountain well before sunup, when there would be a real light instead of this ghostly and partial illumination from the moon.

Among the trees he sat down and took up the dreadful watches of the night. Sleep never came near him. He was turning the back pages of his memory, reviewing his past with the singular clearness of a man about to die. For Sandersen had this mortal certainty resting upon his mind that he must try to strike down Sinclair, and that he would fail. And failure meant only one alternative—death. He was perfectly confident that this was the truth. He knew with prophetic surety that he would never again see the kind light of the sun, that in a half-light, in the cold of the dawn, a bullet would end his life.

What he saw in the past was not comforting. A long train of vivid memories came up in his mind. He had accomplished nothing. In the total course of his life he had not made a man his friend, or won the love of a woman. In all his attempts to succeed in life there had been nothing but disastrous failures, and wherever he moved he involved others in his fall. Certainly the prospecting trip with the three other men had been worse than all the rest, but it had been typical. It had been he who first suggested the trip, and he had rounded the party together and sustained it with enthusiasm.

It had been he who led it into the mountains and across the desert. And on the terrible return trip he knew, with an abiding sense of guilt, that he alone could have checked the murderous and cowardly impulse of Quade. He alone could have overruled Quade and Lowrie; or, failing to overrule them, he should at least have stayed with the cripple and helped him on, with the chance of death for them both.

When he thought of that noble opportunity lost, he writhed. It would have gained the deathless affection of Hal Sinclair and saved that young, strong life. It would have won him more. It would have made Riley Sinclair his ally so long as he lived. And how easy to have done it, he thought, looking back.

Instead, he had given way; and already the result had been the death of three men. The tale was not yet told, he was sure. Another death was due. A curse lay on that entire party, and it would not be ended until he, Sandersen, the soul of the enterprise, fell.

The moon grew old in the west. Then he took the saddle again and rode, brooding, up the trail, his horse stumbling over the stones as the animal grew wearier in the climb.

And then, keeping his gaze fastened above him, he saw the outline of the crests grow more and more distinct. He looked behind. In the east the light was growing. The whole horizon was rimmed with a pale glow.

Now his spirits rose. Even this gray dawn was far better than the treacherous moonlight. A daylight calm came over him. He was stronger, surer of himself. Impatiently he drew out his Colt and looked to its action. The familiar weight added to his self-belief. It became possible for him to fight, and being possible to fight, it was also possible to conquer.

Presently he reached a bald upland. The fresh wind of the morning struck his face, and he breathed deep of it. Why could he not return to Sour Creek as a hero, and why could he not collect the price on the head of Riley Sinclair?

The thought made him alert, savage. A moment later, his head pushing up to the level of the shoulder of the mountain, he saw his quarry. In the dimness of that early dawn he made out the form of a sleeper huddled in blankets, but it was enough. That must be Riley Sinclair. It could not be another, and all his premonitions were correct.

Suddenly he became aware that he could not fail. It was impossible! As gloomy as he had been before, his spirits now leaped to the heights. He swung down from the saddle, softly, slowly, and went up the hill without once drawing his eyes from that motionless form in the blankets.

Once something stirred to the right and far below him.

He flashed a glance in that direction and saw that it was a hobbled horse, though not the horse of Sinclair; but that mattered nothing. The second horse might be among the trees.

Easing his step and tightening the grip on his revolver, he drew closer. Should he shoot without warning? No, he would lean over the sleeper, call his name, and let him waken and see his death before it came to him. Otherwise the triumph would be robbed of half of its sweetness.

Now he had come sufficiently near to make out distinctly that there was only one sleeper. Had Sinclair and Cold Feet separated? If so, this must be Sinclair. The latter might have the boldness to linger so close to danger, but certainly never Cold Feet, even if he had once worked his courage to the point of killing a man. He stepped closer, leaned, and then by the half-light made out the pale, delicate features of the schoolteacher.

For the moment Sandersen was stunned with disappointment, and yet his spirits rose again almost at once. If Sinclair had fled, all the better. He would not return, at least for a long time, and in the meantime, he, Sandersen, would collect the money on the head of Cold Feet!

With the Colt close to the breast of Jig, he said: "Wake up, Cold Feet!"

The girl opened her eyes, struggled to sit up, and was thrust back by the muzzle of the gun, held with rocklike firmness in the hand of Sandersen.

"Riley—what—" she muttered sleepily, and then she made out the face of Sandersen distinctly.

Instantly she was wide awake, whiter than ever, staring. Better to take the desperado alive than dead—far better. Cold Feet would make a show in Sour Creek for the glorification of Sandersen, as he rode down through the main street, and the men would come out to see the prize which even Sheriff Kern and his posse had not yet been able to take.

"Roll over on your face."

Cold Feet obeyed without a murmur. There was a coiled rope by the cinders of the fire. Sandersen cut off a convenient length and bound the slender wrists behind the back of the schoolteacher. Then he jerked his quarry to a sitting posture.

"Where's Sinclair gone?"

To his astonishment, Cold Feet's face brightened wonderfully.

"Oh, then you haven't found him? You haven't found him? Thank goodness!"

Sandersen studied the schoolteacher closely. It was impossible to mistake the frankness of the latter's face.

"By guns," he said at last, "I see it all now. The skunk sneaked off in the middle of the night and left you alone here to face the music?"

Jig flushed, as she exclaimed: "That's not true. He's never run away in his life."

"Maybe not," muttered Sandersen apprehensively. "Maybe he'll come back ag'in. Maybe he's just rode off after something and will be back."

At once the old fear swept over him. His apprehensive glance flickered over the rocks and the trees around him—a thousand secure hiding places. He faced the schoolteacher again.

"Look here, Jig: You're charged with a murder, you see? I can take you dead or alive; and the shot that bumped you off might bring Sinclair running to find out what'd happened, and he'd go the same way. But will you promise to keep your mouth shut and give no warning when Sinclair heaves in sight? Take your pick. It don't make no difference to me, one way or the other; but I can't have the two of you on my hands."

To his surprise Jig did not answer at once.

"Ain't I made myself clear? Speak out!"

"I won't promise," said Cold Feet, raising the colorless face.

"Then, by thunder, I'll—"

In the sudden contorting of his face she saw her death, but as she closed her eyes and waited for the report and the tear of the bullet, she heard him muttering: "No, they's a better way."

A moment later her mouth was wrenched open, and a huge wadded bandanna was stuffed into it. Sandersen pushed her back to the ground and tossed the blanket over her again.

"You ain't much of a man, Jig, but as a bait for my trap you'll do tolerable well. You're right: Sinclair's coming back, and when he comes, I'll be waiting for him out of sight behind that rock. But listen to this, Jig. If you wrastle around and try to get that gag out of your mouth, I ain't going to take no chances. Whether Sinclair's in sight or not, I'm going to drill you clean. Now lie still and keep thinking on what I told you. I mean it all!"

With a final scowl he left her and hurried to the rock. It made an ideal shelter for his purposes. On three sides, the rock made a thick and effectual parapet. A thousand bullets might splash harmlessly against that stone; and through crevices he commanded the whole sweep of the mountainside beneath them. The courage which had been growing in Sandersen, now reached a climax. Below him lay the helpless body of one prize—from a distance apparently a sound and quiet sleeper, though Sandersen could see the terrified glint of Jig's eyes.

But he forgot that a moment later, when he saw the form of a horseman break out of covert from the trees farther down the mountain and immediately disappear again. Sinclair? He steadied the barrel of the revolver, but the horseman appeared no more in the brightening and misty dawn. It was only after a long pause that there issued from the trees, not Riley Sinclair, but the squat, thick form of Arizona!

27

Behind the sheriff's apprehensive glance there had been reason. True the door had closed upon Arizona, and the door was thick. But the moment Arizona had passed through the door, he clapped his ear to the keyhole and listened, holding his breath, for he was certain that the moment his back was turned the shameful story of his exploits in the lumber camp eight years before would come out for the edification of Kern. If so, it meant ruin for him. Arizona was closed to him; all this district would be closed by the story of his early light-fingeredness. He felt as if he were being driven to the wall. Consequently he listened with set teeth to the early questions of the sheriff; then he breathed easier, still incredulous, when he heard Sinclair refuse to tell the tale.

Still he lingered, dreading that the truth might out, and so heard the talk turn to a new channel—Cold Feet. Cold Feet meant many things to Sour Creek; to Arizona, the schoolteacher meant only one thing—twenty-five-hundred dollars. And Arizona was broke.

To his hungry ear came the tidings: "I'll tell you what I'll do. I'll give you the layout for finding Cold Feet. Ride west out of Sour Creek and head for a flat-topped mountain. On the shoulder just under the head you'll find Cold Feet. Go get him!"

To Arizona it seemed as if this last injunction were personal advice. He waited to hear no more; if he had paused for a moment he might have learned that the hope of twenty-five hundred was an illusion and a snare. He saw the bright vision of a small fortune placed in his hands as the result of a single gunplay. He had seen the school-teacher. He knew by instinct that there was no fighting quality in Jig. And the moment he heard the location it was as good as cash in his pocket, he was sure.

There was only one difficulty. He must beat out the sheriff. To that end he hurried to the stable behind the hotel, broke all records for speed in getting the saddle on his roan mare, and then jogged her quietly out of town so as to rouse no suspicions. But hardly was he past the outskirts, hardly crediting his good luck that the sheriff himself was not yet on the way, than he touched the flanks with his spurs and sent the mare flying west.

In the west the moon was dropping behind the upper ranges, as he rode through the foothills; when he began to climb the side of the mountain, the dawn began to grow. So much the better for Arizona. But, knowing that he had only Cold Feet to deal with, he did not adopt all the caution of Sandersen on the same trail. Instead he cut boldly straight for the shoulder of the mountain, knowing what he would find there on his arrival. In the nearest grove he left his horse and then walked swiftly up to the level. There the first thing that caught his eyes was the form wrapped in the blanket. But the next thing he saw was the pale glimmer of the dawn on the barrel of a revolver. He reached for his own gun, only to see, over the rock above him, the grinning face of Sandersen arise.

"Too late, Arizona," called the tall man. "Too late for one job, partner, but just in time for the next!"

Arizona cursed softly, steadily, through snarling lips.

"What job?"

"Sinclair! He's gone, but he'll be back any minute. And it'll need us both to down him, Arizona. We'll split on Sinclair's reward."

Disgust and wrath consumed Arizona. Without other answer he strode to the prostrate form, slashed the rope and tore the handkerchief from between the teeth of Cold

Feet. The schoolteacher sat up, gasping for breath, purple of face.

"Leave him be!" cried Sandersen, his voice shrill with anger. "Leave him be! He's the bait, Arizona, and we're the trap that'll catch Sinclair."

But Arizona cursed again bitterly. "Leave that bait lie till the sun burns it up. You'll never catch Sinclair with it."

"How come?"

From around the rock Sandersen appeared and walked down to the fat man.

"Because Sinclair's already caught."

If he had expected the tall man to groan with disappointment, there was a surprise in store for him. Sandersen exclaimed shrilly for joy.

"Sinclair took! Took dead, then!"

"Dead? Why?"

"You don't mean he was taken alive?"

"Yes, I sure do! And I done the figuring that led up to him being caught."

The slender form of Jig rose before them, trembling.

"It isn't true! It isn't true! There aren't enough of you in Sour Creek to take Riley Sinclair!"

"Ain't it true?" asked Arizona. "All right, son, you'll meet him pronto in the Sour Creek jail, unless the boys finish their party of the other day and string you up before you get inside the jail."

This brought a peculiar, low-pitched moan from Cold Feet.

"Cheer up," said Sandersen. "You ain't swinging yet awhile."

"But he's hurt! If he's alive, he's terribly wounded?"

Arizona beat down the appealing hand with a brutal gesture.

"No, he ain't particular hurt. Just his neck squashed a bit where the sheriff throttled him. He didn't fight enough to get hurt, curse him!"

Frowning, Sandersen shook his head. "He's a fighting man, Arizona, if they ever was one."

It seemed that everything infuriated the fat man.

"What d'you know about it, Lanky?" he demanded of Sandersen. "Didn't I run the affair? Wasn't it me that planted the whole trap? Wasn't it me that knowed he'd come into town for you or Cartwright?"

"Cartwright!" gasped Jig.

"Sure! We nailed him in Cartwright's room, just the way I said we would. And they laughed at me, the fools!"

He might have gathered singular inferences from the lowered head of Jig and the soft murmur: "I might have known—I might have known he'd try for me."

"And I might have had the pleasure of drilling him clean," said Arizona, harking back to it with savage pleasure, "but I shot out the light. I wanted him to die slow, and before the end I wanted to pry his eyes open and make him see my face and know that it was me that done for him! That was what I wanted. But he turned yaller and wouldn't fight."

"He wouldn't kill," said Jig coldly. "But for courage—I laugh at you, Arizona!"

"Easy," scowled the cowpuncher. "Easy, Jig. You ain't behind the bars yet. You're in reach of my fist, and I'd think nothing of busting you in the face. Shut up till I talk to you."

The misty eyes of Sandersen brightened a little and grew hard. There was a great deal of fighting spirit in the man, and his easy victory of that morning had roused him to a battling pitch.

"Looks to me like you ain't running this here party, Arizona," he said dryly. "If they's any directions to give Cold Feet, I'll give 'em. It was me that took him!"

No direct answer could Arizona find to this true statement, and, as always when a man is at a loss for words, his temper rose, and his fists clenched. For the first time he looked at Sandersen with an eye of savage calculation. He had come to the hope of a tidy little fortune. He had found it snatched out of his hand, and, as he measured Sandersen, his heart rose. Twenty-five-hundred dollars would fairly well equip him in life. The anger faded out of his eyes, and in its place came the cold gleam of the man who thinks and calculates. All at once he began to smile, a mirthless smile that was of the lips only.

"Maybe you're right, Sandersen, but I'm thinking you'd have to prove that you took Cold Feet."

"Prove it?"

"Sure! The boys wouldn't be apt to believe that sleepy Sandersen woke up and took Cold Feet alive."

Instantly the gorge of Sandersen rose, and he began to see red.

"Are you out to find trouble, Fatty?"

The adjective found no comfortable lodging place in the mind of Arizona.

"Me? Sure I ain't. I'm just stating facts the way I know 'em."

"Well, the facts you know ain't worth a damn."

"No?"

It was growing clearer and clearer to the fat man that between him and twenty-five-hundred dollars there stood only the unamiable figure of the long, lean cowpuncher. He steadied his eye till a fixed glitter came in it. He hated lean men by instinct and distrusted them.

"Sure they ain't. How you going to get around the fact that I did take Cold Feet?"

"Well, Sandersen, you see that they's twenty-five-hundred dollars hanging on the head of this Cold Feet?"

"Certainly! And I see ten ways of spending just that amount."

"So do I," said Arizona.

"You do?"

"Partner, you've heard me talk!"

"Arizona, you're talking mighty queer. What d'ye mean?"

"Now, suppose it was me that brought in Cold Feet, who'd get the money?"

"Why, you that brought him in?"

"Yep, me. And suppose I brought him in with two murders charged to him instead of one."

"I don't foller you. What's the second murder, Fatty?"

"You!"

Sandersen blinked and gave back a little. Plainly he was beginning to fear that the reason of Arizona was unbalanced.

He shook his head.

"I'll show you how it'll be charged to Cold Feet," said the fat man.

Taking the cartridge belt of Jig he shook the revolver out of the holster and pumped a shot into the ground. The sharp crack of the explosion roused no echo for a perceptible space. Then it struck back at them from a solid wall of rock, almost as loud as it had been in fact. Off among the hills the echo was repeated to a faint whisper. Arizona dropped the revolver carelessly on the ground.

"Fatty, you've gone nutty," said Sandersen.

"I'll tell you a yarn," said Arizona.

Sandersen looked past him to the east. The light was growing rapidly about the mountains. In another moment or so that sunrise which he had been looking forward to with such solemn dread, would occur. He was safe, of course, and still that sense of impending danger would not leave him. He noted Jig, erect, very pale, watching them with intense and frightened interest.

"Here's the story," went on the fat man. "I come out of Sour Creek hunting for Cold Feet. I come straight to this here mountain. Halfway up the side I hear a shot. I hurry along and soft-foot on to this shoulder. I see Cold Feet standing over the dead body of Sandersen. Then I stick up

Cold Feet and take him back to Sour Creek and get the reward. Won't that be two murders on his head?"

The thin Swede rubbed his chin. "For a grown man, Fatty, you're doing a lot of supposing."

"I'm going to turn it into fact," said Arizona.

"How?"

"With a chunk of lead! Pull your gun, you lanky fool!"

It seemed to Jig, watching with terrible interest, that Sandersen stared not at Arizona, as he went for his gun, but beyond the stubby cowpuncher—far beyond and into the east, where the dawn was growing brighter, losing its color, as sunrises do, just before the rising of the sun. His long arm jerked back, the revolver whipped into his hand, and he stiffened his forearm for the shot.

All that Jig saw, with eyes sharpened, so that each movement seemed to be taking whole seconds, was a sneering Arizona, waiting till the last second. When he moved, however, it was with an almost leisurely flip of the wrist. The heavy Colt was conjured into his hand. With graceful ease the big weapon slipped out and exploded before Sandersen's forefinger had curled around the trigger.

Out of the hand of the Swede slipped the gun and clanged unheeded on the ground at his feet. She saw a patch of red spring up on his breast, while he lurched forward with long, stiff strides, threw up his hands to the east, and pitched on his face. She turned from the dead thing at her feet.

The white rim of the sun had just slid over the top of a mountain.

28

She dropped to her knees, and with a sudden, hysterical strength she was able to turn him on his back. He was dead. The first glimpse of his face told her that. She looked up into the eyes of the murderer.

Arizona was methodically cleaning his gun. His color had not changed. There was a singular placidity about all his movements.

"I just hurried up what was coming to him," said Arizona coolly, as he finished reloading his Colt. "Sinclair was after him, and that meant he was done for."

Oddly enough, she found that she was neither very much afraid of the fat man, nor did she loathe him for his crime. He seemed outside of the jurisdiction of the laws which govern most men.

"You said Sinclair is in jail."

"Sure, and he is. But they don't make jails strong enough in these parts to hold Sinclair. He'd have come out and landed Sandersen, just as he's going to come out and land Cartwright. What has he got agin' Cartwright, d'you know?"

Oh, it was incredible that he could talk so calmly with the dead man before him.

"I don't know," she murmured and drew back.

"Well, take it all in all," pursued Arizona, "this deal of mine is pretty rotten, but you'd swing just the same for one murder as for two. They won't hang you no deader, eh? And when they come to look at it, this is pretty neat. Sandersen wasn't no good. Everybody knowed that. But he had one thing I wanted—which was you and the twenty-five hundred that goes with the gent that brings you into

Sour Creek. So, at the price of one bullet, I get the coin. Pretty neat, I say ag'in."

Dropping the revolver back into the holster he patted it with a caressing hand.

"There's your gun," went on Arizona, chuckling. "It's got a bullet fired out of it. There's Sandersen's gun with no bullet fired, showing that, while he was stalking you, you shot and drilled him. Here's my gun with no sign of a shot fired. Which proves that I just slid in here and stuck you up from behind, while you was looking over the gent you'd just killed."

He rubbed his hands together, and bracing himself firmly on his stubby legs, looked almost benevolently on Jig.

Not only did she lose her horror of him, but she gained an impersonal, detached interest in the workings of his mind. She looked on him not as a man but as a monster in the guise of a man.

"Two deaths," she said quietly, "for your money. You work cheaply, Arizona."

Jig's criticism seemed to pique him.

"How come?"

"Sandersen's death by your bullet, and mine when I die in the law. Both to your account, Arizona, because you know I'm innocent."

"I know it, but a hunch ain't proof in the eyes of the law. Besides, I don't work so cheap. Sandersen was no good. He ain't worth thinking about. And as for you, Jig, though I don't like to throw it in your face, as a schoolteacher you may be all right, but as a man you ain't worth a damn. Nope, I won't give neither of you a thought—except for Sinclair."

"Ah?"

"Him and you have been bunkies, if he ever should find out what I done, he'd go on my trail. Maybe he will anyway. And he's a bad one to have on a gent's trail."

"You fear him?" she asked curiously, for it had seemed

impossible that this cold-blooded gunman feared any living thing.

He rolled a cigarette meditatively before he answered.

"Sure," he said, "I fear him. I ain't a fool. It was him that started me, and him that gave me the first main lessons. But I ain't got the nacheral talent with a gun that Sinclair has got."

Nodding his head in confirmation, his expression softened, as with the admiration of one artist for a greater kindred spirit.

"The proof is that they's a long list of gunfights in Sinclair's past, but not more deaths than you can count on the fingers of one hand. And them that he killed was plumb no good. The rest he winged and let 'em go. That's his way, and it takes an artist with a gun to work like that. Yep, he's a great man, curse him! Only one weak thing I ever hear of him doing. He buckled to the sheriff and told him where to find you!"

Scratching a match on his trousers, the cowpuncher was amazed to hear Jig cry: "You lie!"

He gaped at her until the match singed his fingers. "That's a tolerable loud word for a kid to use!"

Apparently he meditated punishment, but then he shrugged his shoulders and lighted his cigarette.

"Wild horses couldn't have dragged it out of him!" Jig was repeating.

"Say," said the fat man, grinning, "how d'you think *I* knew where you was?"

Like a blow in the face it silenced her. She looked miserably down to the ground. Was it possible that Sinclair had betrayed her? Not for the murder of Quade. He would be more apt to confess that himself, and indeed she dreaded the confession. But if he let her be dragged back, if her identity became known, she faced what was more horrible to her than hanging, and that was life with Cartwright.

"Which reminds me," said Arizona, "that the old sheriff

may not wait for morning before he starts after you. Just slope down the hill and saddle your hoss, will you?"

Automatically she obeyed, wild thoughts running through her mind. To go back to Sour Creek meant a return to Cartwright, and then nothing could save her from him. Halfway to her saddle her foot struck metal, her own gun, which Arizona had dropped after firing the bullet. Was there not a possibility of escape? She heard Arizona humming idly behind her. Plainly he was entirely off guard.

Bending with the speed of a bird in picking up a seed, she scooped up the gun, whirling with the heavy weapon extended, her forefinger curling on the trigger. But, as she turned, the humming of Arizona changed to a low snarl. She saw him coming like a bolt. The gun exploded of its own volition, it seemed to her, but Arizona had swerved in his course, and the shot went wild.

The next instant he struck her. The gun was wrenched from her hand, and a powerful arm caught her and whirled her up, only to hurl her to the ground; Arizona's snarling, panting face bent over her. In the very midst of that fury she felt Arizona stiffen and freeze; the snarling stopped; his nerveless arm fell away, and she was allowed to stagger to her feet. She found him staring at her with a peculiar horror.

"Murdering guns!" whispered Arizona.

Now she understood that he knew. She saw him changed, humbled, disarmed before her. But even then she did not understand the profound meaning of that moment in the life of Arizona.

But to have understood, she would have had to know how that life began in a city slum. She would have had to see the career of the sneak thief which culminated in the episode of the lumber camp eight years before. She would have had to understand how the lesson from the hand of big Sinclair had begun the change which transformed the sneak into the dangerous man of action. And now the second change had come. For Arizona had made the unique discovery that he could be ashamed!

He would have laughed had another told him. Virtue was a name and no more to the fat man. But in spite of himself those eight years under free skies had altered him. He had been growing when he thought he was standing still. When the eye plunges forty miles from mountain to mountain, through crystal-clear air, the mind is enlarged. He had lived exclusively among hard-handed men, rejoicing in a strength greater than their own. He suddenly found that the feeble hand from which he had so easily torn the weapon a moment before, had in an instant acquired strength to make or break him.

All that Jig could discern of this was that her life was no longer in danger, and that her enemy had been disarmed. But she was not prepared for what followed.

Dragging off his hat, as if he acted reluctantly, his eyes sank until they rested on the ground at her feet.

"Lady," he said, "I didn't know. I didn't even dream what you was."

29

Gradually she found her breath and greater self-possession.

"You mean I'm free?" she asked him. "You won't make me go into Sour Creek?"

His face twisted as if in pain. "Make you?" he asked violently. "I'd blow the head off the first one that tried to make you take a step."

Suddenly it seemed to her that all this was ordered and arranged, that some mysterious Providence had sent this man here to save her from Sandersen and all the horror that the future promised, just as Sinclair had saved her once before from a danger which he himself had half created.

"I got this to say," went on Arizona, struggling for the words. "Looks to me like you might have need of a friend to help you along, wherever you're going." He shook his thick shoulders. "Sure gives me a jolt to think of what you must have gone through, wandering around here all by yourself! I sure don't see how you done it!"

And all this time the man whom Arizona had killed, was lying face up to the morning, hardly a pace behind him! But she dared not try to analyze this man. She could only feel vaguely that an ally had been given her, an ally of strength. He, too, must have sensed what was in her mind.

"You'll be wanting this, I reckon."

Returning the Colt to her, he slowly dragged his glance from the ground and let it cross her face for a fleeting instant. She slipped the gun back into its holster.

"And now suppose we go down the hill and get your hoss?"

Evidently he was painfully eager to get the dead man out of sight. Yet he paused while he picked up her saddle.

"They'll be along pretty pronto—the sheriff and his men. They'll take care of—him."

Leading the way down to her hobbled horse he saddled it swiftly, while she stood aside and watched. When he was done he turned to her.

"Maybe we better be starting. It wouldn't come in very handy for Kern to find us here, eh?"

Obediently she came. With one hand he held the stirrup, while the other steadied her weight by the elbow, as she raised her foot. In spite of herself she shivered at his touch. A moment later, from the saddle, she was looking down into a darkly crimsoned face. Plainly he had understood that impulse of aversion, but he said nothing.

There was a low neigh from the other side of the hill in answer to his soft whistle, and then out of the trees came a beautifully formed roan mare, with high head and pricking ears. With mincing steps she went straight to her master, and Jig saw the face of the other brighten. But he was gloomy again by the time he had swung into the saddle.

"Now," he said, "where away?"

"You're coming with me?" she asked, with a new touch of alarm. She regretted her tone the moment she had spoken. She saw Arizona wince.

"Lady," he said, "suppose I come clean to you? I been in my time about everything that's bad. I ain't done a killing except squarely. Sinclair taught me that. And you got to allow that what I done to Sandersen was after I give him all the advantage in the draw. I took even chances, and I give him better than an even break. Ain't that correct?"

She nodded, fascinated by the struggle in his face between pride and shame and anger.

"Worse'n that," he went on, forcing out the bitter truth. "I been everything down to a sharp with the cards, which is tolerable low. But I got this to say: I'm playing clean with you. I'll prove it before I'm done. If you want me to break loose and leave you alone, say the word, and I'm gone. If you want me to stay and help where I can help, say the word, and I stay and take orders. Come out with it!"

Gathering his reins, he sat very straight and looked her fairly and squarely in the eye, for the first time since he had discovered the truth about Cold Feet. In spite of herself Jig found that she was drawn to trust the fat man. She let a smile grow, let her glance become as level and as straight as his own. She reined her horse beside his and stretched out her hand.

"I know you mean what you say," said Jig. "And I don't care what you have been in the past. I *do* need a friend—

desperately. Riley Sinclair says that a friend is the most sacred thing in the world. I don't ask that much, but of all the men I know you are the only one who can help me as I need to be helped. Will you shake hands for a new start between us?"

"Lady," said the cowpuncher huskily, "this sure means a lot to me. And the—other things—you'll forget?"

"I never knew you," said the girl, smiling at him again, "until this moment."

"Oh, it's a go!" cried Arizona. "Now try me out!"

Jig saw his self-respect come back to him, saw his eye grow bright and clear. Arizona was like a man with a new "good resolution." He wanted to test his strength and astonish someone with his change.

"There is one great thing in which I need help," said she.

"Good! And what's that?"

"Riley Sinclair is in jail."

"H'm," muttered Arizona. "He ain't in on a serious charge. Let him stay a while." Stiffening in the saddle he stared at her. "Does Sinclair know?"

"What?" asked the girl, but she flushed in spite of herself.

"That you ain't a man?"

"Yes."

For a moment he considered her crimson face gloomily. "You and Sinclair was sort of pals, I guess," he said at length.

Faintly she replied in the affirmative, and her secret was written as clearly as sunlight on her face. Yet she kept her eyes raised bravely.

As for Arizona, the newborn hope died in him, and then flickered back to an evil life. If Sinclair was in his way, why give up? Why not remove this obstacle as he had removed others in his time. The hurrying voice of the girl broke in on his somber thoughts.

"He went to Sour Creek to help me as soon as he found out that I was not a man. He put himself in terrible danger there on my account."

"Did Cartwright have something to do with you and him?"

"Yes."

But Arizona made no effort to read her riddle.

She went on: "Now that he has been taken, I know what has happened. To keep me out of danger he told—"

"That you're a woman?"

"No, he wouldn't do that, because he knows that is the last thing in the world that I want revealed. But he's told them that he killed Quade, and now he's in danger of his life."

"Let's ride on," said Arizona. "I got to think a pile."

She did not speak, while the horses wound down the steep side of the mountain. Mile after mile rose behind them. The sun increased in power, flashing on the leaves of the trees and beginning to burn the face with its slanting heat. Now and then she ventured a side-glance at Arizona, and always she found him in a brown study. Vaguely she knew that he was fighting the old battle of good and evil in the silence of the morning. Finally he stopped his horse and turned to her again.

They were in the foothills by this time, and they had drawn out from the trees to a little level space on the top of a rise. The morning mist was thinning rapidly in the heart of the hollow beneath them. Far off, they heard the lowing of cows being driven into the pasture land after the morning milking, and they could make out tiny figures in the fields.

"Lady," Arizona was saying to her, "they's one gent in the world that I've got an eight-year-old grudge agin'. I've swore to get him sooner or later, and that gent is Riley Sinclair. Make it something else, and I'll work for you till the skin's off my hands. But Sinclair—" He stopped, studying her intently. "Will you tell me one thing? How much does Sinclair mean to you."

"A great deal," said the girl gently. "But if you hate him, I can't ask you."

"He's a hard man," said Arizona, "and he's got a mean name, lady. You know that. But when you say that he means a lot to you, maybe it's because he's taken a big chance for you in Sour Creek and—"

She shook her head. "It's more than that—much more."

"Well, I guess I understand," said Arizona.

Burying the last of his hopes, Arizona looked straight into the sun.

"Eight years ago he was a better man than I am," said he at length. "And he's a better man still. Lady, I'm going to get Riley Sinclair free!"

30

As Arizona had predicted, Sheriff Kern was greatly tempted not to start on the hard ride for the mountains before morning, and finally he followed his impulse. With the first break of the dawn he was up, and a few minutes later he had taken the trail alone. There was no need of numbers, for that matter, to tell a single man that he no longer need dread the law. But it was only common decency to inform him of the change, and Kern was a decent sort.

He was thoughtful on the trail. A great many things had happened to upset the sheriff. The capture of Sinclair, take it all in all, was an important event. To be sure, the chief glory was attributable to the cunning of Arizona;

nevertheless, the community was sure to pay homage to the skill of the sheriff who had led the party and managed the capture.

But now the sheriff found himself regretting the capture and all its attendant glory. Not even a personal grudge against the man who had taken his first prisoner from him, could give an edge to the sheriff's satisfaction, for, during the late hours of the preceding night he had heard from Sinclair the true story of the killing of Quade; not a murder, but a fair fight. And he had heard more—the whole unhappy tale which began with the death of Hal Sinclair in the desert, a story which now included, so far as the sheriff knew, three deaths, with a promise of another in the future.

It was little wonder that he was disturbed. His philosophy was of the kind that is built up in a country of horses, hard riding, hard work, hard fighting. According to the precepts of that philosophy, Sinclair would have shirked a vital moral duty had he failed to avenge the pitiful death of his brother.

The sheriff put himself into the boots of the man who was now his prisoner and facing a sentence of death. In that man's place he knew that he would have taken the same course. It was a matter of necessary principle; and the sheriff also knew that no jury in the country could allow Sinclair to go free. It might not be the death sentence, but it would certainly be a prison term as bad as death.

These thoughts consumed the time for the sheriff until his horse had labored up the height, and he came to the little plateau where so much had happened outside of his ken. And there he saw Bill Sandersen, with the all-seeing sun on his dead eyes.

For a moment the sheriff could not believe what he saw. Sandersen was, in the phrase of the land, "Sinclair's meat." It suddenly seemed to him that Sinclair must have broken from jail and done this killing during the night. But a moment's reflection assured him that this could not be. The mind of the sheriff whirled. Not Sinclair, certainly. The man had been dead for some hours. In the sky, far above and to the north, there were certain black specks, moving in great circles that drifted gradually south. The buzzards were already coming to the dead. He watched them for a moment, with the sinking of the heart which always comes to the man of the mountain desert when he sees those grim birds.

It was not Sinclair. But who, then?

He examined the body and the wound. It was a center shot, nicely placed. Certainly not the sort of shot that Cold Feet, according to the description which Sinclair had given of the latter's marksmanship, would be apt to make. But there was no other conclusion to come to. Cold Feet had certainly been here according to Sinclair's confession, and it was certainly reasonable to suppose that Cold Feet had committed this crime. The sheriff placed the hat of Sandersen over his face and swung back into his saddle; he must hurry back to Sour Creek and send up a burial party, for no one would have an interest in interring the body in the town.

But once in the saddle he paused again. The thought of the schoolteacher having killed so formidable a fighter as Sandersen stuck in his mind as a thing too contrary to probability. Moreover the sheriff had grown extremely cautious. He had made one great failure very recently—the escape of this same Cold Feet. He would have failed again had it not been for Arizona. He shuddered at the thought of how his reputation would have been ruined had he gone on the trail and allowed Sinclair to double back on Sour Creek and take the town by surprise.

Dismounting, he threw his reins and went back to review the scene of the killing. There were plenty of tracks around the place. The gravel obscured a great part of the marks, and still other prints were blurred by the dead grass. But there were pockets of rich, loamy soil, moist enough and firm enough to take an impression as clearly as paper takes ink. The sheriff removed the right shoe from the foot of Sandersen and made a series of fresh prints.

They were quite distinctive. The heel was turned out to such an extent that the track was always a narrow indentation, where the heel fell on the soft soil. He identified the same tracks in many places, and, dismissing the other tracks, the sheriff proceeded to make up a trail history for Sandersen.

Here he came up the hill, on foot. Here he paused beside the embers of the fire and remained standing for a long time, for the marks were worked in deeply. After a time the trail went—he followed it with difficulty over the hard-packed gravel—up the side of the hill to a semicircular arrangement of rocks, and there, distinct in the soil, was the impression of the body, where the cowpuncher had lain down. The sheriff lay down in turn, and at once he was sure why Sandersen had chosen this spot. He was defended perfectly on three sides from bullets, and in the meantime, through crevices in the rock, he maintained a clear outlook over the whole side of the hill.

Obviously Sandersen had lain down to keep watch. For what? For Cold Feet, of course, on whose head a price rested. Or, at least, so Sandersen must have believed at the time. The news had not yet been published abroad that Cold Feet had been exculpated by the confession of Sinclair to the killing of Quade.

So much was clear. But presently Sandersen had risen and gone down the hill again, leaving from the other side of the rock. Had he covered Cold Feet when the latter returned to his camp, having been absent when Sandersen first arrived? No, the tracks down the hill were leisurely, not the long strides which a man would make to get close to one whom he had covered with a revolver from a distance.

Reaching the shoulder of the mountain, Kern puzzled anew. He began a fresh study of the tracks. Those of Cold Feet were instantly known by the tiny size of the marks of the soles. The sheriff remembered that he had often wondered at the smallness of the schoolteacher's feet. Cold Feet was there, and Sandersen was dead. Again it seemed certain that Cold Feet had been guilty of the crime, but the sheriff kept on systematically hunting for new evidence. He found no third set of tracks for some time, but when he did find them, they were very clear—a short, broad foot, the imprint of a heavy man. A fat man, then, no doubt. From the length of the footprint it was very doubtful if the man were tall, and certainly by the clearness of the indentation, the man was heavy. The sheriff could tell by making a track beside that of the quarry.

A second possibility, therefore, had entered, and the sheriff felt a reasonable conviction that this must be the guilty man.

Now he combed the whole area for some means of identifying the third man who had been on the mountainside. But nothing had been dropped except a brilliant bandanna, wadded compactly together, which the sheriff recognized as belonging to Sandersen. There was only one definite means of recognizing the third man. Very faint in the center of the impression made by his sole, were two crossed arrows, the sign of the bootmaker.

The sheriff shook his head. Could he examine the soles of the boots of every man in the vicinity of Sour Creek, even if he limited his inquiry to those who were short and stocky? And might there not be many a man who wore the same type of boots?

He flung himself gloomily into his saddle again, and this time he headed straight down the trail for Sour Creek.

At the hotel he was surrounded by an excited knot of

people who wished to know how he had extracted the amazing confession from Riley Sinclair. The sheriff tore himself away from a dozen hands who wished to buttonhole him in close conversation.

"I'll tell you gents this," he said. "Quade was killed because he needed killing, and Sinclair confessed because he's straight."

With that, casting an ugly glance at the lot of them, he went back into the kitchen and demanded a cup of coffee. The Chinese cook obeyed the order in a hurry, highly flattered and not a little nervous at the presence of the great man in the kitchen.

While Kern was there, Arizona entered. The sheriff greeted him cheerfully, with his coffee cup balanced in one hand.

"Arizona," he said, "or Dago, or whatever you like to be called—"

"Cut the Dago part, will you?" demanded Arizona. "I ain't no ways wishing to be reminded of that name. Nobody calls me that."

Kern grinned covertly.

"I s'pose," said Arizona slowly, "that you and Sinclair had a long yarn about when he knew me some time back?"

The sheriff shook his head.

"Between you and me," he said frankly, "it sounded to me like Sinclair knew something you mightn't want to have noised around. Is that straight?"

"I'll tell you," answered the other. "When I was a kid I was a fool kid. That's all it amounts to."

Sheriff Kern grunted. "All right, Arizona, I ain't asking. But you can lay to it that Sinclair won't talk. He's as straight as ever I seen!"

"Maybe," said Arizona, "but he's slippery. And I got this to say: Lemme have the watch over Sinclair while he's in Sour Creek, or are you taking him back to Woodville today?"

"I'm held over," said the sheriff.

He paused. Twice the little olive-skinned man from the south had demonstrated his superiority in working out criminal puzzles. The sheriff was prone to unravel the new mystery by himself, if he might.

"By what?"

"Oh, by something I'll tell you about later on," said the sheriff. "It don't amount to much, but I want to look into it."

Purposely he had delayed sending the party to bury Sandersen. It would be simply warning the murderer if that man were in Sour Creek.

"About you and Sinclair," went on the sheriff, "there ain't much good feeling between you, eh?"

"I won't shoot him in the back if I guard him," declared Arizona. "But if you want one of the other boys to take the job, go ahead. Put Red on it."

"He's too young. Sinclair'd get him off guard by talking."

"Then try Wood."

"Wood ain't at his best off the trail. Come to think about it, I'd rather trust Sinclair to you—that is, if you make up your mind to treat him square."

"Sheriff, I'll give him a squarer deal than you think."

Kern nodded.

"More coffee, Li!" he called.

Li obeyed with such haste that he overbrimmed the cup, and some of the liquid washed out of the saucer onto the floor.

"Coming back to shop talk," went on the sheriff, as Li mopped up the spilled coffee, mumbling excuses, "I ain't had a real chance to tell you what a fine job you done for us last night, Arizona."

Arizona, with due modesty, waved the praise away and stepped to the container of matches hanging beside the stove. He came back lighting a cigarette and contentedly puffed out a great cloud.

"Forget all that, sheriff, will you?"

"Not if I live to be a hundred," answered the sheriff with frank admiration.

So saying, his eye dropped to the floor and remained there, riveted. The foot of Arizona had rested on the spot where the coffee had fallen. The print was clearly marked with dust, except that in the center, where the sole had lain, there was a sharply defined pair of crossed arrows!

A short, fat, heavy man.

The sheriff raised his glance and examined the bulky shoulders of the man. Then he hastily swallowed the rest of his coffee.

Yet there might be a dozen other short, stocky men in town, whose boots had the same impression. He looked thoughtfully out the kitchen window, striving to remember some clue. But, as far as he could make out, the only time Arizona and Sandersen had crossed had been when the latter applied for a place on the posse. Surely a small thing to make a man commit a murder!

"If you gimme the job of guarding Sinclair," said Arizona, "I'd sure—"

"Wait a minute," cut in the sheriff. "I'll be back right away. I think that was MacKenzie who went into the stable. Don't leave till I come back, Arizona."

Hurriedly he went out. There was no MacKenzie in the stable, and the sheriff did not look for one. He went straight to Arizona's horse. The roan was perfectly dry, but examining the hide, the sheriff saw that the horse had been recently groomed, and a thorough grooming would soon dry the hair and remove all traces of a long ride.

Stepping back to the peg from which the saddle hung, he raised the stirrup leather. On the inside, where the leather had chafed the side of the horse, there was a dirty gray coating, the accumulation of the dust and sweat of many a ride. But it was soft with recent sweat, and along the edges of the leather there was a barely dried line of foam that rubbed away readily under the touch of his fingertip.

Next he examined the bridle. There, also, were similar evidences of recent riding. The sheriff returned calmly to the kitchen of the hotel.

"And your mind's made up?" asked Arizona.

"Yes," said the sheriff. "You go in with Sinclair."

"Go *in* with him?" asked Arizona, baffled.

"For murder," said the sheriff. "Stick up your hands, Arizona!"

31

Even though he was taken utterly by surprise, habit made Arizona go for his own gun, as the sheriff whipped out his weapon. But under those conditions he was beaten badly to the draw. Before his weapon was half out of the holster, the sheriff had the drop.

Arizona paused, but, for a moment, his eyes fought Kern, figuring chances. It was only the hesitation of an instant. The battle was lost before it had begun, and Arizona was clever enough to know it. Swiftly he turned on a new tack. He shoved his revolver back into the holster and smiled benevolently on the sheriff.

"What's the new game, Kern?"

"It ain't new," said the sheriff joylessly. "It's about the oldest game in the world. Arizona, you sure killed Sandersen."

"Sandersen?" Arizona laughed. "Why, man, I ain't hardly seen him more than once. How come that I would kill him?"

"Get your hands up, Arizona."

"Oh, sure." He obeyed with apparent willingness. "But don't let anybody see you making this fool play, sheriff."

"Maybe not so foolish. I'll tell you why you killed him.

You're broke, Arizona. Ten days ago Mississippi Slim cleaned you out at dice. Well, when Sinclair told me where Cold Feet was, you listened through the door, but you didn't stay to find out that Jig wasn't wanted no more. You beat it up to the mountain, and there you found Sandersen was ahead of your time. You drilled Sandersen, hoping to throw the blame on Cold Feet. Then you come down, but on the way Cold Feet gives you the slip and gets away. And that's why you're here."

Arizona blinked. So much of this tale was true that it shook even his iron nerve. He managed to smile.

"That's a wild yarn, sheriff. D'you think it'll go down with a jury?"

"It'll go down with any jury around these parts. What's more, Arizona, I ain't going to rest on what I think. I'm going to find out. And, if I send down to the south inquiring about you, I got an idea that I'll find out enough to hang ten like you, eh?"

Once more Arizona received a vital blow, and he winced under the impact. Moreover, he was bewildered. His own superior intelligence had inclined him to despise the sheriff, whom he put down as a fellow of more bulldog power than mental agility. All in a moment it was being borne in upon him that he had underrated his man. He could not answer. His smooth tongue was chained.

"Not that I got any personal grudge agin' you," went on the sheriff, "but it's gents like you that I'm after, Arizona, and not one like Sinclair. You ain't clean, Arizona. You're slick, and they ain't elbowroom enough in the West for slick gents. Besides, you got a bad way with your gun. I can tell you this, speaking private and confidential, I'm going to hang you, Arizona, if there's any way possible!"

He said all this quietly, but the revolver remained poised with rocklike firmness. He drew out a pair of manacles.

"Stand up, Arizona."

Listlessly the fat man got up. He had been changing

singularly during the last speech of the sheriff. Now he dropped a hand on the edge of the table, as if to support himself. The sheriff saw that hand grip the wood until the knuckles went white. Arizona moistened his colorless lips.

"Not the irons, sheriff," he said softly. "Not them!"

If it had been any other man, Kern would have imagined that he was losing his nerve; but he knew Arizona, had seen him in action, and he was certain that his courage was above question. Consequently he was amazed. As certainly as he had ever seen them exposed, these were the horrible symptoms of cowardice that make a brave man shudder to see.

"Can't trust you," he said wonderingly. "Wouldn't trust you a minute, Arizona, without the irons on you. You're a bad actor, son, and I've seen you acting up. Don't forget that."

"Sheriff, I'll give you my word that I'll go quiet as a lamb."

A moment elapsed before Kern could answer, for the voice of Arizona had trembled as he spoke. The sheriff could not believe his ears.

"Well, I'm sorry, Arizona," he said more gently, because he was striving to banish this disgusting suspicion from his own mind. "I can't take no chances. Just turn around, will you. And keep them hands up!"

He barked the last words, for the arms of Arizona had crooked suddenly. They stiffened at the sharp command of the sheriff. Slowly, trembling, as if they possessed a volition of their own hardly controlled by the fat man, those hands fought their way back to their former position, and then Arizona gradually turned his back on the sheriff. A convulsive shudder ran through him as Kern removed his gun and then seized one of the raised hands, drew it down, and fastened one part of the iron on it. The other hand followed, and, as the sheriff snapped the lock, he saw a singular transformation in the figure of his captive. The shoulders of Arizona slouched forward, his head sank. From the erect, powerful figure of the moment before, he became, in comparison, a flabby pile of flesh, animated by no will.

"What's the matter?" asked the sheriff. "You ain't lost your nerve, have you, Fatty?"

Arizona did not answer. Kern stepped to one side and glanced at the face of his captive. It was strangely altered. The mouth had become trembling, loose, uncertain. The head had fallen, and the bright, keen eyes were dull. The man looked up with darting side-glances.

The sheriff stood back and wiped a sudden perspiration from his forehead. Under his very eyes the spirit of this gunfighter was disintegrating. The sheriff felt a cold shame pour through him. He wanted to hide this man from the eyes of the others. It was not right that he should be seen. His weakness was written too patently.

Kern was no psychologist, but he knew that some men out of their peculiar element are like fish out of water. He shook his head.

"Walk out that back door, will you?" he asked softly.

"We ain't going down the street?" demanded Arizona.

"No."

"Thanks, sheriff."

Again Kern shuddered, swallowed, and then commanded: "Start along, Arizona."

Slinking through the door, the fat man hesitated on the little porch and cast a quick glance up and down.

"No, one near!" he said. "Hurry up, sheriff."

Quickly they skirted down behind the houses—not unseen, however. A small boy playing behind his father's house raised his head to watch the hurrying pair, and when he saw the glitter of the irons, they heard him gasp. He was old enough to know the meaning of that. Irons on Arizona, who had been a town hero the night before! They saw the youngster dart around the house.

"Blast him!" groaned Arizona. "He'll spread it everywhere. Hurry!"

He was right. The sheriff hurried with a will, but, as they crossed the street for the door of the jail, voices blew down to them. Looking toward the hotel, they saw men pouring out into the street, pointing, shouting to one another. Then they swept down on the pair.

But the sheriff and his prisoner gained the door of the jail first, and Kern locked it behind him. His deputy on guard rose with a start, and at the same time there was a hurried knocking on the door and a clamor of voices without. Arizona shrank away from that sound, scowling over his shoulder, but the sheriff nodded good-humoredly.

"Take it easy, Arizona. I ain't going to make a show of you!"

"Sure, that's like you sheriff," said a hurried, half-whining voice. "You're square. I'll sure show you one of these days how I appreciate the way you treat me!"

Kern was staggered. It seemed to him that a new personality had taken possession of the body of the fat man. He led the way past his gaping deputy. The jail was not constructed for a crowd. It was merely a temporary abiding place before prisoners were taken to the larger institution at Woodville. Consequently there was only one big cell. The sheriff unlocked the door, slipped the manacles from the wrists of Arizona, and jabbed the muzzle of a revolver into his back!

The last act was decidedly necessary, for the moment his wrists were released from the grip of the steel, Arizona twitched halfway round toward the sheriff. The scrape of the gun muzzle against his ribs, however, convinced him. Over his shoulder he cast one murderous glance at the sheriff and then slouched forward into the cell.

"Company for you, Riley," said the sheriff, as the tall cowpuncher rose.

The other's back was turned, and thereby the sheriff

was enabled to pass a significant gesture and look to Sinclair. With that he left them. In the outer room he found his deputy much alarmed.

"You ain't turned them two in together?" he asked. "Why, Sinclair'll kill that gent in about a minute. Ain't it Arizona that nailed him?"

"Sinclair will play square," Kern insisted, "and Arizona won't fight!"

Leaving the other to digest these mysterious tidings, the sheriff went out to disperse the crowd.

In the meantime Sinclair had received the newcomer in perfect silence, his head raised high, his thin mouth set in an ugly line—very much as an eagle might receive an owl which floundered by mistake onto the same crag, far above his element. The eagle hesitated between scorn of the visitor and a faint desire to pounce on him and rend him to pieces. That glittering eye, however, was soon dulled with wonder, when he watched the actions of Arizona.

The fat man paused in the center of the cell, regarded Sinclair with a single flash of the eyes, and then glanced uneasily from side to side. That done, he slipped away to a corner and slouched down on a stool, his head bent down on his breast.

Apparently he had fallen into a profound reverie, but Sinclair found that the eyes of Arizona continually whipped up and across to him. Once the newcomer shifted his position a little, and Sinclair saw him test the weight of the stool beneath him with his hand. Even in the cell Arizona had found a weapon.

Gradually Sinclair understood the meaning of that glance and the gesture of the sheriff, as the latter left; he read other things in the gray pallor of Arizona, and in the fallen head. The man was unnerved. Sinclair's reaction was very much what that of the sheriff had been—a sinking of the heart and a momentary doubt of himself. But he was something more of a philosopher than Kern. He had seen more of life and men and put two and two together.

One thing stared him plainly in the face. The Arizona who skulked in the corner had relapsed eight years. He was the same sneak thief whom Sinclair had first met in the lumber camp, and he knew instinctively that this was the first time since that unpleasant episode that Arizona had been cornered. The loathing left Sinclair, and in its place came pity. He had no fondness for Arizona, but he had seen him in the role of a strong man, which made the contrast more awful. It reminded Sinclair of the wild horse which loses its spirit when it is broken. Such was Arizona. Free to come and go, he had been a danger. Shut up helplessly in a cell, he was as feeble as a child, and his only strength was a sort of cunning malice. Sinclair turned quietly to the fat man.

"Arizona," he said, "you look sort of underfed today. Bring your stool a bit nearer and let's talk. I been hungry for a chat with someone."

In reply Arizona rolled back his head and for a moment glared thoughtfully at Sinclair. He made no answer. Presently his glance fell, like that of a dog. Sinclair shivered. He tried brutality.

"Looks to me, Arizona, as though you'd lost your nerve."

The other moistened his lips, but said nothing.

"But the point is," said the tall cowpuncher, "that you've given up before you're beaten."

Riley Sinclair's words brought a flash from Arizona, a sudden lifting of the head, as if he had not before thought of hoping. Then he began to slump back into his former position, without a reply. Sinclair followed his opening advantage at once.

"What you in for?"

"Murder!"

"Great guns! Of whom?"

"Sandersen."

It brought Sinclair stiffly to his feet. Sandersen! His trail was ended; Hal was avenged at last!

"And you done it? Fatty, you took that job out of my hands. I'm thanking you. Besides, it ain't nothing to be downhearted about. Sandersen was a skunk. Can they prove it on you?"

The need to talk overwhelmed Arizona. It burst out of him, not to Sinclair, but rather at him. His shifting eyes made sure that no one was near.

"Kern is going to send south for the dope. I'm done for. They can hang me three times on what they'll learn, and—"

"Shut up," snapped Sinclair. "Don't talk foolish. The south is a tolerable big place to send to. They don't know where you come from. Take 'em a month to find out, and by that time, you won't be at hand."

"Eh?"

"Because you and me are going to bust out of this paper jail they got!"

He had not the slightest hope of escape. But he tried the experiment of that suggestion merely to see what the fat man's reaction would be. The result was more than he could have dreamed. Arizona whirled on him with eyes ablaze.

"What d'you mean, Sinclair?"

"Just what I say. D'you think they can keep two like us in here? No, not if you come to your old self."

The need to confide again fell on Arizona. He dragged his stool nearer. His voice was a whisper.

"Sinclair, something's busted in me. When them irons grabbed my arms they took everything out of me. I got no chance. They got me cornered."

"And you'll fight like a wildcat to the end of things. Sure you will! Buck up, man! You think you've turned yaller. You ain't. You're just out of place. Take a gent that's used to a forty-foot rope and a pony, give him sixty feet on a sixteen-hand hoss, and ain't he out of place? Sure! He looks like a clumsy fool. And the other way around it works the same way. A trout may be a flash of light in water, but on dry land he ain't worth a damn. Same way with you, Fatty. While you got a free foot you're all right, but when they put you behind a wall and say they're going to keep you there, you darned near bust down. Why? Because it looks to you like you ain't got a chance to fight back. So you quit altogether. But you'll come back to yourself, Arizona. You—"

Arizona raised his hand. He was sitting erect now, drinking in the words of Sinclair, as if they were air to a stifling man. His face worked.

"Why are you doing this for me, Sinclair—after I landed you here?"

"Because I made a man out of you once," answered the tall man evenly, "and I ain't going to see you backslide. Why, Arizona, you're one of the fastest-thinkin', quickest-handed gents that ever buckled on a gun, and here you are lying down like a kid that ain't never faced trouble before. Come alive, man. You and me are going to bust this ol' jail to smithereens, and when we get outside I'll blow your head off if I can!"

Riley's words had carried Arizona with him. Suddenly an olive-skinned hand shot out and clutched his own bony, strong fingers. The hand was fat and cold, but it gripped that of Riley Sinclair with a desperate energy.

"Sinclair, you mean it? You'll play in with me?"

"I will—sure!"

He had to drag the words out, but after he had spoken he was glad. New life shone in the face of Arizona.

"A man with you for a partner ain't done, Sinclair—not if he had a rope around his neck. Listen! D'you know why I come in town?"

"Well?"

"To get you out."

"I believe you, Arizona," lied Sinclair.

"Not for your sake—but hers."

Sinclair's face suddenly went white.

"Who?"

"The girl!" whispered Arizona. "I cached her away outside of town to wait for—us! Sinclair, she loves you."

Riley Sinclair sat as one stunned and dragged the hat from his head.

32

Through the branches of the copse in which she was hidden, the girl saw the sun descend in the west, a streak of slowly dropping fire. And now she became excited.

"As soon as it's dark," Arizona had promised, "I'll make my start. Have your hoss ready. Be in the saddle, and the minute you see us come down that trail out of Sour Creek, be ready to feed your hoss the spur and join us, because when we come, we'll come fast. Don't make no mistake. If you ride too slow we'll have to ride slow, too, and slow ridin' means gunplay on both sides, and gunplay means dead men, because if Sinclair is fightin' for you he'll fight to kill. Wait till the dusk comes. That's when I'll make my move, because the evenin' is a pile worse nor the dark for fooling a man's aim. You'll see me and Sinclair scoot along that there road, with the gang yellin' behind us!"

Having made this farewell speech, he waved his hand and, with a smile of confidence, jogged away from her. It was the beginning of a dull day of waiting for her, yet a day in which she dared not altogether relax her vigilance, because at any time the break might come, and Arizona might appear flying down the trail with the familiar tall form of Sinclair beside him. Wearily she waited until sundown.

With the coming of dusk she wakened suddenly and became tinglingly alert. The night spread rapidly down out of the mountains. The color faded, and the sudden chill of the high altitude settled about her. Her hands and her feet were cold with the fear of excitement.

Into the gathering gloom she strained her eyes; toward Sour Creek she strained her ears, starting at every faint sound of a man's shout or the barking of a dog, as if this might be the beginning of the uproar that would announce the escape.

Something swung on to the road out of the end of the main street. She was instantly in the saddle, but, by the time she reached the edge of the copse, she found it to be only a wagon filled with singing men going back to some nearby ranch. Then quiet dropped over the valley, and she became aware that it was the utter dark.

Arizona had failed! That knowledge grew more surely upon her with every moment. His intention must have been guessed, for she could not imagine that slippery and cold-minded fellow being thwarted, if he were left free to work as he pleased toward an object he desired. She could not stay in the grove all night. Besides, this was the critical time for Riley Sinclair. Tomorrow he would be taken to the security of the Woodville jail, and the end would be close. If anything were done for him, it must be before morning.

With this thought in mind she rode boldly out of the trees and took the road into town, where the lights of the early evening had turned from white to yellow, as the night deepened. Sour Creek was hardly a mile away when a rattling in the dark announced the approach of a buckboard. She drew rein at the side of the trail. Suddenly the wagon loomed out at her, with two down-headed horses jogging along and the loose reins swinging above their backs.

"Halloo!" called Jig.

The brakes ground against the wheels, squeaking in

protest. The horses came to a halt so willing and sudden that the collars shoved halfway up their necks, and the tongue of the wagon lurched beyond their noses.

"Whoa! Evening, there! You gimme a kind of a start, stranger."

Parodying the dialect as well as she was able, Jig said: "Sorry, stranger. Might that be Sour Creek?"

"It sure might be," said the driver, leaning through the dark to make out Jig. "New in these parts?"

"Yep, I'm over from Whiteacre way, and I'm aiming for Woodville."

"Whiteacre? Doggone me if it ain't good to meet a Whiteacre boy. I was raised there, son! Joe Lunids is my name."

"I'm Texas Lou," said the girl.

There was a subdued chuckle from the darkness.

"You sound kind of young for a name like that, kid. Leastwise, your voice is tolerable young."

"I'm old enough," said Jig aggressively.

"Sure, sure," placated the other. "Sure you are."

"Besides," she went on, "I wanted a name that I could grow up to."

It brought a hearty burst of laughter from the wagon.

"That's a good one, Texas. Have a drink?"

She set her teeth over the refusal that had come to her lips and, reining near, reached out for the flask. The driver passed over the bottle and at the same time lighted a match for the apparent purpose of starting his cigarette. But Jig nodded her head in time to obscure her face with the flopping brim of her sombrero. The other coughed his disappointment. She raised the bottle after uncorking it, firmly securing the neck with her thumb. After a moment she lowered it and sighed with satisfaction, as she had heard men do.

"Thanks," said Jig, handing back the flask. "Hot stuff, partner."

"You got a tough throat," observed the rancher. "First I ever see that didn't choke on a swig of that. But you youngsters has the advantage of a sound lining for your innards."

He helped himself from the flask, coughed heavily, and then pounded home the cork.

"How's things up Whiteacre way?"

"Fair to middlin'," said Jig. "They ain't hollering for rain so much as they was."

"I reckon not," agreed the rancher.

"And how's things down Sour Creek way?" asked Jig.

"Trouble busting every minute," said the other. "Murder, gun scrapes, brawls in the hotel—to beat anything I ever see. The town is sure going plumb to the dogs at this rate!"

"You don't say! Well, I heard something about a gent named Quade being plugged."

"Him? He was just the beginning—just the start! Since then we had a man took away from old Kern, which don't happen once in a coon's age. Then we had a fine fresh murder right this morning, and the present minute they's two in jail on murder charges, and both are sure to swing!"

Jig gasped. "Two!" she exclaimed.

"Yep. They was a skinny schoolteacher named—I forget what. Most general he was called Cold Feet, which fitted. They thought he killed Quade account of a girl. But a gent named Sinclair up and confessed, and he is waiting for the rope. And then the sheriff all by himself grabbed Arizona for the murder of Sandersen. Oh, times is picking up considerable in Sour Creek. Reminds me of twenty years back before Kern come on the job and cleaned up the gunfighters!"

"Two murders!" repeated the girl faintly. "And has Arizona confessed, too?"

"Not him! But the sheriff has enough to give him a hard run. I got to be drifting on, son. Take my advice and head straight for Woodville. You lack five years of being old enough for Sour Creek these days!" He called his farewell, threw off the brake and cursed the span of horses into their former trot.

As for Jig, she waited until the scent of alkali dust died away, and the rattle of the buckboard was faint in the distance. Then she turned her horse back toward Sour Creek and urged it to a steady gallop, bouncing in the saddle.

There seemed a fatality about her. On her account Sinclair had thrown his life in peril, and now Arizona was caught and held in the same danger. Enough of sacrifices for her; her mind was firm to repay some of these services at any cost, and she had thought of a way.

With that gloomy purpose before her, her ordinary timidity disappeared. It was strange to ride into Sour Creek, and she passed in review among the rough men of the town, constantly fearful that they might pierce her disguise. She had trained herself to a long stride and a swaggering demeanor, and by constant practice she had been able to lower the pitch of her voice and roughen its quality. Yet, in spite of the constant practice, she never had been able to gain absolute self-confidence. Tonight, however, there was no fear in her.

She went straight to the hotel, threw the reins, and walked boldly through the door into a cluster of men. They yelled at the sight of her.

"Jig, by guns! He's come in! Say, kid, the sheriff's been looking for you."

They swerved around her, grinning good-naturedly. When a person has been almost lynched for a crime another has committed, he gains a certain standing, no matter what may be the public opinion of his courage. The schoolteacher had become a personage. But Jig met their smiles with a level eye.

"If the sheriff's looking for me," she said, "tell him I have a room in the hotel. He can find me here."

Pop shook hands before he shoved the register toward her. "My kids will sure be glad to see you safe back," he said. "And I'm glad, too, Jig."

Nodding, she turned to sign her name in the bold, free hand which she had cultivated. She could feel the crowd staring behind her, and she could hear their murmurs. But she was not nervous. It seemed that all apprehension had left her.

"Where's Cartwright?" she asked.

"Sitting in a game of poker."

"Hello, buddy!" she called to a redheaded youngster. "Go in and tell Cartwright that I'm waiting for him in my room, will you?"

"Ain't no use," said Pop, staring at this new and more masculine Jig. "Cartwright is all heated up about the game. And he's lost enough to get anybody excited. He won't come. Better go in there if you want to see him."

"I'll try my luck this way," said Jig coldly. "Run along, buddy."

Buddy obeyed, and Jig went up the stairs to her room.

"What come over him?" asked the crowd, the moment Cold Feet was out of sight. "Looks like he's growed up in a day!"

"He's gone through enough to make a man of him," answered Pop. "Never can tell how a kid will turn out."

But in her room Jig had sunk into a chair, dropped her elbows on the table, and buried her face in her hands, trying to steady her thoughts. She heard the heavy pounding of feet on the stairs, a strong tread in the hall that made the flooring of the old building quiver, and then the door was flung open, slammed shut, and the key turned in the lock. Cartwright set his shoulders against the door, as though he feared she would try to rush past him. He stared at her, with a queer admixture of fear, rage, and astonishment.

"So I've got you at last, eh? I've got you, after all this?"

Curiously she stared at him. She had dreaded the interview, but now that he was before her she was surprised to find that she felt no fear. She examined him as if from a distance.

"Yes," she admitted, "you have me. Will you sit down?"

"I need room to talk," he said, swaggering to the table. He struck his fist on it. "Now, to start with, what in thunder did you mean by running away?"

"We're leaving the past to bury the past," she said. "That's the first concession you have to make."

He laughed, his laughter ending with a choked sound. "And why should *I* make concessions?"

Jig watched the veins of fury swell in his forehead, watched calmly, and then threw her sombrero on the bed and smoothed back her hair, still watching without a change of expression. It seemed as if her calm acted to sober him, and the passing of her hand across the bright, silken hair all at once softened him. He sank into the opposite chair, leaning far across the table toward her.

"Honey, take you all in all, you're prettier right here in this man's outfit than I ever see you—a pile prettier!"

For a moment she closed her eyes. The sacrifice which she intended was becoming harder, desperately hard to make.

"I'm going to take you back and forgive you," said Cartwright, apparently blind to what was going on in her mind. "I ain't one to carry malice. You keep to the line from now on, and we'll get along fine. But you step crooked just once more, and I'll learn you a pile of things you never even dreamed could happen!"

To her it seemed that he stood in a shaft of consuming light that exposed every shadowy nook and cranny of his nature, and the narrow-minded meanness that she saw, startled her.

"What you do afterward with me is your own affair," she said. "It's about the present that I've come to bargain."

"Bargain?"

"Exactly! Do what I ask, and I go back and act as your wife. If you refuse, I walk out of your life forever."

He could not speak for a moment. Then he exploded.

"It's funny. I could almost laugh hearing you chatter crazy like this. Don't you think I got a right to make my own wife come home with me, now that I've found her? Wouldn't the law stand behind me?"

"You can force me to come," she admitted quietly, "but if you do, I'll let the whole truth be known that I ran away from you. Can your pride stand that, Jude?"

He writhed. "And how'll you get around that, even if I don't make you, and you come back of your own free will?"

"Somehow I'll manage. I'll find a story of how I was carried away by half a dozen men who had come to loot the upper rooms of the house, while the wedding party was downstairs. I'll find a story that will wash."

"Yes, I think you will," said Cartwright, breathing heavily. "I sure think you will. You was always a clever little devil, I know! But a bargain! I'd ought to—" He checked himself. "But I'm through with the black talk. When I get you back on the ranch I'll show you that you can be happy up there. And when you get over your fool notions, you'll be a wife to be proud of. Now, honey, tell me what you want?"

"I want you to save the lives of two men. They're both in jail—on my account. And they're both charged with murder. You know whom I mean."

Cartwright rose out of his chair.

"Sinclair!" he groaned! "Curse him! Sinclair, ag'in, eh? What's they between you two?"

Her answer smothered his fury again. It was pain that was giving her strength.

"Jude, if you really want me to go back with you, don't ask that question. He has treated me as an honorable man always treats a woman—he tried to serve me."

"Serve you? By coming here and trying to kill me?"

"He may have thought I wished to be free. He didn't tell me what he was going to do."

"That's a lie." He stopped, watching her white face. "I don't mean that, you know. But you ain't actually asking me to get Sinclair out of jail? Besides, I couldn't do it!"

"You could easily. Moreover, it's to your interest. It will take a strong jail to hold him, and if he breaks away, you know that he's a dangerous man. He hates you, Jude, and he might try to find you. If he did—"

She waved her hand, and Cartwright followed the gesture with great, fascinated eyes, as if he saw himself dissolving into thin air.

"I know; he's a desperado, right enough, this Sinclair. Ain't I seen him work?" He shuddered at the memory.

"But get him out of the jail, Jude, and that will be ended. He'll be your friend."

"Could I trust him?"

"Don't you think Riley Sinclair is a man to be trusted?"

"I dunno." He lowered his eyes. "Maybe he is."

"As for Arizona," she went on, "the same thing holds for him."

"Yes; if I could get one out, I could get two. But how can I do it? This Sheriff Kern is a fighting idiot, and loves a gunplay. I ain't no man-killer, honey."

"But you're rich, Jude."

"Tolerable. They may be one or two has more than me, around these parts."

"And money buys men!"

"Don't it, though?" said Jude, expanding. "Why, when they found that I was a spender they started in hounding me. One gent wanted me to help him on a mortgage—only fifty bucks to meet a payment. And they's half a dozen would mortgage their souls if I'd stake 'em to enough downstairs to get them into a crap game, or something."

"Then let them have the money they need. Why, it

wouldn't be more than a hundred dollars altogether."

"A hundred is a hundred. Why should I throw it away on them bums?"

"Because after you've done it, you'll have a dozen men who'll follow you. You'll have a mob."

"Sure! But what of that? Expect me to lead an attack on a jail, eh? Throw my life away? By guns, I think you'd like that!"

"You don't have to lead. Just give them the money they need and then spread the word around that Riley Sinclair is really an honorable man who killed Quade in a fair fight. I know what they thought of Quade. He was a bully. No one liked him. Tell them it's a shame that a man like Sinclair should die because he killed a big, hulking cur such as Quade. They'll listen—particularly if they have your money. I know these men, Jude. If they think an injustice is being done, they'll risk their necks to right it! And if you work on them in the right way, you can have twenty men who'll risk everything to get Riley out. But there won't be a risk. If twenty men rush the jail, the guards will simply throw down their guns and give up."

"Well, I wonder!" muttered Cartwright.

"I'm sure of it, Jude. Do you think a deputy will let himself be killed simply to keep a prisoner safely? They won't do it!"

"You don't know this Kern!"

"I *do* know him, and I know that he's human. I've seen him beaten once already."

"By Sinclair! You keep coming back to him!"

"Jude, if you do this thing for me," she said steadily, "I'll go back with you. I don't love you, but if I go back I'll keep you from a great deal of shameful talk. I'm sorry, truly, that I left. I couldn't help it. It was an impulse that—took me by the throat. And if I go back I'll honestly try to make you a good wife."

She faltered a little before that last word, and her voice

fell. But Jude Cartwright was wholly fascinated by the color in her face, and the softness of her voice he mistook for a sudden rise of tenderness.

"They's only one thing I got to ask—you and Sinclair—have you ever—I mean—have you ever told him you're pretty fond of him—that you love him?" He blurted it out, stammering.

Certainly she knew that her answer was a lie, though it was true in the letter.

"I have never told him so," she said firmly. "But I owe him a great debt—he must not die because he's a gentleman, Jude."

All the time that she was speaking, he watched her with ferret sharpness, thinking busily. Before she ended he had reached his decision.

"I'm going to raise that mob."

"Jude!"

What a ring in her voice! If he had been in doubt he would have known then. No matter what she said, she loved Riley Sinclair. He smiled sourly down on her.

"Keep your thanks. You'll hear news of Sinclair before morning." And he stalked out of the room.

33

Cartwright went downstairs in the highest good humor. He had been convinced of two things in the interview with his wife: The first was that she could be induced to return to him; the second was that she loved Riley Sinclair. He did not hate her for such fickleness. He merely despised her for her lack of brains. No thinking woman could hesitate a moment between the ranches and the lumber tracts of Cartwright and the empty purse of Riley Sinclair.

As for hatred, that he concentrated on the head of Sinclair himself. He had already excellent reasons for hating the rangy cowpuncher. Those reasons were now intensified and given weight by what he had recently learned. He determined to raise a mob, but not to accomplish his wife's desires. What she had said about the weakness of jails, the strength of Sinclair, and the probability that once out he would take the trail of the rancher, appealed vigorously to his imagination. He did not dream that such a man as Sinclair would hesitate at a killing. And, loving the girl, the first thing Sinclair would do would be to remove the obstacle through the simple expedient of a well-placed bullet.

But the girl had not only convinced him in this direction, she had taught him where his strength lay, and she had pointed a novel use for that strength. He went to work instantly when he entered the big back room of the hotel which was used for cards and surreptitious drinking. A little, patient-faced man in a corner, who had been sucking a pipe all evening and watching the crap game hungrily, was the first object of his charity. Ten dollars slipped into the pocket of the little cowpuncher brought him out of his chair, with a grin of gratitude and bewilderment. A moment later he was on his knees calling to the dice in a cackling voice.

Crossing the room, Cartwright picked out two more obviously stalled gamblers and gave them a new start. Returning to the table, he found that the game was lagging. In the first place he had from the start supplied most of the sinews of war to that game. Also, two disgruntled members had gone broke in his absence, through trying to plunge for the spoils of the evening. They sat back, with black faces, and watched him come.

"We're getting down to a small game," said the gray-headed man who was dealing.

But Cartwright had other ideas. "A friend's a friend," he said jovially. "And a gent that's been playing beside me all evening I figure for a friend. Sit in, boys. I'll stake you to a couple of rounds, eh?"

Gladly they came, astonished and exchanging glances.

Cartwright had made a sour loser all the game. This sudden generosity took them off balance. It let in a merciful light upon the cruel criticism which they had been leveling at him in private. The pale man, with the blond eyelashes and the faded blue eyes, who had been dexterously stacking the cards all through the game, decided at that moment that he would not only stop cheating, but he would even lose some of his ill-gotten gains back into the game; only a sudden rush of unbelievable luck kept him from executing his generous and silent promise.

This pale-faced man was named Whitey, from the excessive blondness of his hair and his pallor. He was not popular in Sour Creek, but he was much respected. A proof of his ingenuity was that he had cheated at cards in that community for five years, and still he had never been caught at his work. He was not a bold-talking man. In fact he never started arguments or trouble of any kind; but he was a most dexterous and thoroughgoing fighter when he was cornered. In fact he was what is widely known as a "finisher." And it was Whitey whom Cartwright had chosen as the leader of the mob which he intended raising. He waited until the first shuffle was in progress after the hand, then he began his theme.

"Understand the sheriff is pretty strong for this Sinclair that murdered Quade," he said carelessly.

"'Murder' is a tolerable strong word," came back the unfriendly answer. "Maybe it was a fair fight."

Cartwright laughed. "Maybe it was," he said.

Whitey interrupted himself in the act of shoving the pack across to be cut. He raised his pale eyes to the face of the rancher. "What makes you laugh, Cartwright?"

"Nothing," said Jude hastily. "Nothing at all. If you gents don't know Sinclair, it ain't up to me to give you light. Let him go."

Nothing more was said during that hand which Whitey won. Jude, apparently bluffing shamelessly, bucked him up to fifty dollars, and then he allowed himself to be called with a pair of tens against a full house. Not only did he lose, but he started a laugh against himself, and he joined in cheerfully. He was aware of Whitey frowning curiously at him and smiling faintly, which was the nearest that Whitey ever came to laughter. And, indeed, the laugh cost Cartwright more than the money, but it was a price—the price he was paying for the adherence of Whitey.

"What about this Sinclair?" asked the man with the great, red, blotchy freckles across his face and the back of his neck, so that the skin between looked red and raw. "You come from up north, which is his direction, too. Know anything about him? He looks like pretty much of a man to me, and the sheriff says he's a square shooter from the word go."

"Maybe he is," said Cartwright. "But I don't want to go around digging the ground away from nobody's reputation."

"Whatever he's got, he won't last long," said Whitey definitely. "He'll swing sure."

It was Cartwright's opening. He took advantage of it dexterously, without too much haste. He even yawned to show his lack of interest.

"Well, I got a hundred that says he don't hang," he observed quietly and looked full at Whitey across the table. It was a challenge which the gambling spirit of the latter could not afford to overlook.

"Money talks," began Whitey, then he checked himself. "Do you *know* anything, Cartwright?"

"Sure I don't," said Jude in the manner of one who has abundant knowledge in reserve. "But they say that the sheriff and Sinclair have become regular bunkies. Don't do nothing hardly but sit and chin with each other over in the jail. Ever know Kern to do that before?"

They shook their heads.

"Which is a sign that Sinclair may be all right," said the sober Whitey.

"Which is a sign that he might have something on the sheriff," said Jude Cartwright. "I don't say that he *has*, mind you, but it looks kind of queer. He yanked a prisoner away from the sheriff one day, and the next day he's took for murder. Did the sheriff have much to do with his taking? No, he didn't. By all accounts it was Arizona that done the taking, planning and everything. And after Sinclair is took, what does the sheriff do? He gets on the trail of Arizona and has him checked in for murder of another gent. Maybe Arizona is guilty, maybe he ain't. But it kind of looks as if they was something between Sinclair and Kern, don't it?"

At this bold exposition of possibilities they paused.

"Kern is figured tolerable straight," declared Whitey.

"Sure he is. That's because he don't talk none and does his work. Besides, he's a killer. That's his job. So is Sinclair a killer. Maybe he did fight Quade square, but Quade ain't the only one. Why, boys, this Sinclair has got a record as long as my arm."

In silence they sat around the table, each man thinking hard. The professional gunman gets scant sympathy from ordinary cowpunchers.

"Now I dropped in at the jail," said the man of the great freckles, "and come to think about it, I heard Sinclair singing, and I seen him polishing his spurs."

"Sure, he's getting ready for a ride," put in Cartwright.

There was a growl from the others. They were slowly turning their interest from the game to Cartwright.

"What d'you mean a ride?"

"Got another hundred," said Cartwright calmly, "that

when the morning comes it won't find Sinclair in the jail."

At once they were absolutely silenced, for money talks in an eloquent voice. Deliberately Cartwright counted out the two stacks of shimmering twenty-dollar gold pieces, five to a stack.

"One hundred that he don't hang; another hundred that he ain't in the jail when the morning comes. Any takers, boys? It had ought to be easy money—if everything's square."

Whitey made a move, but finally merely raised his hand and rubbed his chin. He was watching that gold on the table with catlike interest. A man *must* know something to be so sure.

"I'd like to know," murmured the man of the freckles disconnectedly.

"Well," said Cartwright, "they ain't much of a mystery about it. For one thing, if the sheriff was plumb set on keeping them two, why didn't he take 'em over to Woodville today, where they's a jail they couldn't bust out of, eh?"

Again they were silenced, and in an argument, when a man falls silent, it simply means that he is thinking hard on the other side.

"But as far as I'm concerned," went on Cartwright, yawning again, "it don't make no difference one way or another. Sour Creek ain't my town, and I don't care if it gets the ha-ha for having its jail busted open. Of course, after the birds have flown, the sheriff will ride hard after 'em—on the wrong trail!"

Whitey raised his slender, agile, efficient hand.

"Gents," he said, "something has got to be done. This man Cartwright is giving us the truth! He's got his hunch, and hunches is mostly always right."

"Speak out, Whitey," said the man with the freckles encouragingly. "I like your style of thinking."

Nodding his acknowledgments, Whitey said:

"The main thing seems to be that Sinclair and Arizona is old hands at killing. And they had ought to be hung. Well, if the sheriff ain't got the rope, maybe we could help him out, eh?"

34

The moment her husband was gone, Jig dropped back in her chair and buried her face in her arms, weeping. But there is a sort of sad happiness in making sacrifices for those we love, and presently Jig was laughing through her tears and trembling as she wiped the tears away. After a time she was able to make herself ready for another appearance in the street of Sour Creek. She practiced back and forth in her room that exaggerated swagger, jerked her sombrero rakishly over one eye, cocked up her cartridge belt at one side, and swung down the stairs.

She went straight to the jail and met the sheriff at the door, where he sat, smoking a stub of a pipe. He gaped widely at the sight of her, smoke streaming up past his eyes. Then he rose and shook hands violently.

"All I got to say, Jig," he remarked, "is that the others was the ones that made the big mistake. When I went and arrested you, I was just following in line. But I'm sorry, and I'm mighty glad that you been found to be O.K."

Wanly she smiled and thanked him for his good wishes.

"I'd like to see Sinclair," she said.

Kern's amiability increased.

"The best thing I know about you, Jig, is that you ain't turning Sinclair down, now that he's in trouble. Go right back in the jail. Him and Arizona is chinning. Wait a minute. I guess I got to keep an eye on you to see you don't pass nothing through the bars. Keep clean back from them bars, Jig, and then you can talk all you want. I'll stay here where I can watch you but can't hear. Is that square?"

"Nothing squarer in the world," said Jig and went in.

She left the sheriff grinning vacantly into the dark. There was a peculiar something in Jig's smile that softened men.

But when she stepped into the sphere of the lantern light that spread faintly through the cell, she was astonished to see Arizona and Sinclair kneeling opposite each other, shooting dice with abandon and snapping of the fingers. They rose, laughing at the sight of her, and came to the bars.

"But you aren't worried?" asked Jig. "You aren't upset by all this?"

It was Arizona who answered, a strangely changed Arizona since his entrance into the jail.

"Look here," he said gaily, "why should we be worryin'? Ain't we got a good sound roof over our heads, with a set of blankets to sleep in?"

He smiled at tall Sinclair, then changed his voice.

"Things fell through," he said softly, glancing at the far-off, shadowy figure of the sheriff. "Sorry, but we'll work this out yet."

"I know," she answered. She lowered her voice to caution. "I'm only going to stay a moment to keep away suspicions. Listen! Something is going to happen tonight that will set you both free. Don't ask me what is is. But, among those cottonwoods behind the blacksmith shop, I'm going to have two good horses saddled and ready for you. One will be your roan, Arizona. And I'll have a good horse for you, Riley. And when you're free start for those horses."

Sinclair laid hold on the bars with his big hands and pressed his face close to the iron, staring at her.

"You ain't coming along with us?" he asked.

"I—no."

"Are you going to stay here?"

"Perhaps! I don't know—I haven't made up my mind."

"Has Cartwright—"

She broke away from those entangling questions. "I must go."

"But you'll be at the place with the horses?"

"Yes."

"Then so long till the time comes. And—you're a brick, Jig!"

Once outside the jail, she set to work at once. As for getting the roan, it was the simplest thing in the world. There was no one in the stable behind the hotel, and no one to ask questions. She calmly saddled the roan, mounted him, and rode by a wider detour to the cottonwoods behind the blacksmith shop.

Her own horse was to be for Sinclair. But before she took him, she went into the hotel, and the first man she found on the veranda was Cartwright. He came to her at once, shifting away from the others.

"How are things?"

"Good," said Cartwright. "Ain't you heard 'em talking?"

Here and there about the hotel, men stood in knots of three and four, talking in low voices.

"Are they talking about *that?*"

"Sure they are," said Cartwright, relieved. "You ain't heard nothing?"

"Not a word."

"Then the thing for you to do is to keep under cover. You don't want to get mixed up in this thing, eh?"

"I suppose not."

"Keep out of sight, honey. The crowd will start pretty soon and tear things loose." He could not resist one savage thrust. "A rope, or a pair of ropes, will do the work."

"Ropes?"

"One to tie Kern, and one to tie his deputy," he explained smoothly. "Where you going now?"

"Getting their retreat ready," she whispered excitedly. "I've already warned them where to go to get the horses."

She waved to him and stepped back into the night, convinced that all was well. As for Cartwright, he hesitated, staring after her. After all, if his plan developed, it would be wise for him to allow the others to do the work of mischief. He had no wish to be actively mixed up with a lynching party. Sometimes there were after results. And if he had done no more than talk, there would be small hold upon him by the law.

Moreover, things were going smoothly under the guidance of Whitey. The pale-faced man had thrown himself body and soul into the movement. It was a rare thing to see Whitey excited. Other men were readily impressed. After a time, when anger had reached a certain point where men melt into hot action, these fixed figures of men would sweep into fluid action. And then the fates of Arizona and Sinclair would be determined.

It pleased Cartwright more than any action of his life to feel that he had stirred up this movement. It pleased him still more to know that he could now step back and watch the work of ruin go on. It was like disturbing the one small stone which starts the avalanche, which eventually smashes the far-off forest.

So much was done, then. And now why not make sure that the very last means of retreat for the pair was blocked? The girl went to get horses. And if, by the one chance in twenty, the two should actually break out of the jail, it would remain to Cartwright to kill the horses or the men. He did not care which.

He slipped behind the hotel and presently saw the girl come out of the stable with her horse. He followed, skulking softly behind her until he reached the appointed place among the cottonwoods. The trees grew tall and thick of trunk, and about their bases was a growth of dense shrubbery. It was a simple thing to conceal two saddled horses in a hollow which sank into the edge of the shrubbery.

Cartwright's first desire was to couch himself in shooting distance. Then he remembered that shooting with a revolver by moonlight was uncertain work. He slipped away to the hotel and got a rifle readily enough. Men were milling through the lower rooms of the hotel. The point of discussion had long since been passed. The ringleaders had made up their minds. They went about with faces so black that those who were asked to join, hardly had the courage to question. There was broad-voiced rumor growing swiftly. Something was wrong—something was very wrong. It was like that mysterious whisper which goes through the forest before the heavy storm strikes. Something was terribly wrong and must be righted.

How the ringleaders had reasoned, nobody paused to ask. It was sufficient that a score of men were saying: "The sheriff figures on letting Sinclair and Arizona go."

A typical scene between two men. They meet casually, one man whistling, the other thoughtful.

"What's the bad luck?" asks the whistler.

"No time for whistling," says the other.

"Say, what you mean?"

"I ask you just this," said the gloomy man, with a mystery of much knowledge in his face: "Are gents around here going to be murdered, and the murderers go free?"

"Well?"

"Sinclair and Arizona—that's what's up! They're going to bust loose."

"I dunno about Arizona, but Sinclair, they say, is a square shooter."

"Who told you that? Sinclair himself? He's got a rep as long as my arm. He's a bad one, son!"

"You don't say!"

"I do say. And something has got to be done, or Sour Creek won't be a decent man's town no more."

"Let me in." Off they went arm in arm.

Cartwright saw half a dozen little interviews of this nature, as he entered the hotel. Men were excited, they hardly knew why. There is no need for reason in a mob. One has only to cry, "Kill!" and the mob will start of its own volition to find something that may be slain. Also, a mob has no conscience and no remorse. It is the nearest thing to a devil that exists, and it is also the nearest thing to the divine mercy and courage. It is braver than the bravest man; it is more timorous than the most fearful; it is fiercer than a lion, gentler than a lamb. All these things by turns, and each one to the exclusion of all the others.

Now the thunderclouds were piling on the horizon, and Cartwright could feel the electricity in the air. He went to Pop.

"I got to have a rifle."

"What for?"

"You know," said Cartwright significantly.

The hotelkeeper nodded. He brought out an old Winchester, still mobile of action and deadly. With that weapon under his arm, Cartwright started back, but then he remembered that there were excellent chances of missing even with a rifle, when he was shooting through the shadows and by the treacherous moonlight. It would be better, far better, to have his horse with him. Then, if he actually succeeded in wounding one or both of them, he could run his victim down, or, perhaps, keep up a steady fire of rifle shots from the rear, that would bring half the town pouring out to join in the chase.

So he swung back to the stables, saddled his horse, trotted it around in a comfortably wide detour, and, coming within sound distance of the cottonwoods behind the blacksmith shop, he dismounted and led his horse into a dense growth of shrubbery. That close approach would have been impossible without alarming the girl, had it not been for a stiff wind blowing across into his face, completely muffling the noise of his coming. In the bushes he ensconced himself safely. Only a few yards away he kept his eye on the opening among the cottonwoods, behind which the girl and the two horses moved from time to time, growing more and more visible, as the moon climbed above the horizon mist.

He tightened his grip on the rifle and amused himself with drawing beads on stumps and bright bits of foliage, from time to time. He must be ready for any sort of action if the two should ever appear.

While he waited, sounds reached his ear from the town, sounds eloquent of purpose. He listened to them as to beautiful music. It was a low, distinct, and continuous humming sound. Voices of men went into it, low as the growl of an angered dog, and there was a background of slamming doors, and footsteps on verandas. Sour Creek was mustering for the assault.

35

Now that sound had entered the jail, and it had a peculiar effect. It was like that distant murmuring of the storm which walks over the treetops far away. It made the sheriff and his two prisoners lift their heads and look at one another in silence, for the sheriff was most unprofessionally tilted back in a chair, with his feet braced against the bars of the cell, while he chatted with his bad men about men, women, and events. The sheriff had a distinct curiosity to learn how Arizona had recovered so suddenly from his "blue funk."

Unquestionably the fat man had recovered. His voice was as steady now as any man's, and the old, insolent glitter was in his eyes. He squared his shoulders and blew his smoke straight at the face of the sheriff, as he talked. What caused it, the sheriff could not tell, this rehabilitation of a fighting man, but he connected the influence of Sinclair with the change.

By this time Sinclair himself was the more restless of the two. While Arizona sat at ease on the bunk, the tall man ranged up and down the cell, with long, noiseless steps, turning quickly back and forth beside the bars. He had spent his nervous energy cheering up Arizona, until the latter was filled with a reckless, careless courage. What would happen Arizona could not guess, but Sinclair had assured him that something *would* happen, and he trusted implicitly to the word of his tall companion. Sooner or later he would learn that they were hopeless, and Sinclair dreaded the breakdown which he knew would follow that discovery.

In his heart Sinclair knew that there would be no hope, no chance. The girl, he felt, has been swept off her feet with some absurd dream of freeing them. For his own part he had implicit faith in the strength of the toolproof steel of the bars on the one hand, and the gun of the sheriff on the other. As long as they held, they would keep their prisoners. The key to freedom was the key to the sheriff's heart, and Sinclair was too much of a man to whine.

He had come to the end of his trail, and that was evident in the restlessness of his walking to and fro. The love of the one thing on earth that he cared for was his, according to Arizona, and there was nothing to make the fat man lie. It seemed to Riley Sinclair that, at the very moment he had set his hands upon priceless gold, the treasure was crumbling to dead sand. He had lost her by the very thing that won her.

In the midst of his pacing he stopped and lifted his head, just as the sheriff and Arizona did the same thing. The far-off murmur hummed and moaned toward them, gathering strength. Then the sheriff pushed back his chair and went to the front of the jail. They heard him give directions to his deputy to find out what the murmuring meant. When Kern returned he was patently worried.

"Gents," he said, "I've heard that same sort of a sound twice before, and it means business."

None of the three spoke again until the door of the jail was burst open, and the deputy came on them, running.

"Kern," he gasped, as he reached the sheriff, "they're coming."

"Who?"

"Every man in Sour Creek. They tried to get me with 'em. I told 'em I'd stay and then slipped off. They want both of these. They want 'em bad. They're going to fight to get 'em!"

"Do they want to grab Arizona and Sinclair?" asked the sheriff, with surprising lack of emotion. "Don't think they're guilty?"

"You're wrong. They think they're sure guilty, and they're going to lynch 'em."

He whispered this, but his panting made the words louder than he thought. Sinclair heard; and by the shudder of Arizona, he knew that his companion had heard as well.

Now came the low-pitched voice of the sheriff: "Are you with me, Pat?"

The deputy receded. "Why, man, you ain't going to fight the whole town?"

"I'd fight the whole town," said the sheriff smoothly, "but I don't need you with me. You're through, partner. Close the door soft when you go out!"

Pat made no argument, offered no sentimental protest of devotion. He was glad of any excuse, and he retreated at once. After him went the sheriff, and Sinclair heard the heavy door of the jail locked. Kern came back, carrying a bundle. Outside, the murmuring had increased at a single leap to a roar. The rush for the jail was beginning.

Arizona shrank back against the wall, his little eyes glaring desperately at Sinclair, his last hope in the emergency. But Sinclair looked to the sheriff. The bundle in the arms of the latter unrolled and showed two cartridge belts, with guns appended. Next, still in silence, the sheriff unlocked the door to the cell.

"Sinclair!"

The tall cowpuncher leaped beside him. Arizona skirted away to one side stealthily.

"None of that!" commanded Kern. "No crooked work, Arizona. I'm giving you a fighting chance for your lives."

Here he tossed a gun and belt to Sinclair. The latter without a word buckled it on.

"Now, quick work, boys," said the sheriff. "It's going to be the second time in my life that prisoners have got away and tied me up. Understand? They ain't going to be no massacre if I can help it. Gents like Sinclair don't come in pairs, and he's going to have a fighting chance. Boys, tie me up fast and throw me in the corner. I'll tell 'em that you slugged me through the bars and got the keys away. You hear?"

As he spoke he threw Arizona a gun and belt, and the latter imitated Sinclair in buckling it on. But the fat man then made for the door of the cell. Outside the rush reached the entrance to the jail and split on it. The voices leaped into a tumult.

"By thunder," demanded Arizona, "are you going to wait for *that?*"

"You want Kern to get into trouble?" asked Sinclair. "Grab this end and tie his ankles, while I fix his hands."

Frantically they worked together.

"Are you comfortable, sheriff?"

He lay securely trussed in a corner of the passageway.

"Dead easy, boys. Now what's your plan?"

"Is there a back way out?"

"No way in or out but the front door. You got to wait till they smash it. There they start now! Then dive out, as they rush. They won't be expecting nothing like that. But gag me first."

Hastily Sinclair obeyed. The door of the jail was shaking and groaning under the attack from without, and the shouts were a steady roar. Then he hurried to the front of the little building. Arizona was already there, gun in hand, watching the door bulge under the impact. Evidently they had caught up a heavy timber, and a dozen men were pounding it against the massive door. Sinclair caught the gun arm of his companion.

"Fatty," he said hastily, "gunplay will spoil everything. We got to take 'em by surprise. Fast running will save us, maybe. Fast shooting ain't any good when it's one man agin' fifty, and these boys mean business."

Arizona reluctantly let his gun drop back in its holster. He nodded to Sinclair. The latter gave his directions swiftly, speaking loudly to make his voice carry over the roar of the crowd.

"When the door goes down, which it'll do pretty pronto, I'll dive out from this side, and you run from the other side, straight into the crowd. I'll turn to the right, and you turn to the left. The minute you're around the corner of the building shoot back over your shoulder, or straight into the air. It'll make 'em think that you've stopped and are going to fight 'em off from the corner. They'll take it slow, you can bet. Then beat it straight on for the cottonwoods behind the blacksmith shop."

"They'll drop us the minute we show."

"Sure, we got the long chance, and nothing more. Is that good enough for you?"

He was rewarded in the dimness by a glint in the eyes of Arizona, and then the fat man gripped his hand.

"You and me agin' the world."

In the meantime the door was bulging in the center under blows of increasing weight. A second battering ram was now brought into play, and the rain of blows was unceasing. Still between shocks, the door sprang back, but there was a telltale rattle at every blow. Finally, as a yell sprang up from the crowd at the sight, the upper hinge snapped loudly, and the door sagged in. Both timbers were now apparently swung at the same moment. Under the joint impact the door was literally lifted from its last hinge and hurled inward. And with it lunged the two battering rams and the men who had wielded them. They tumbled headlong, carried away by the very weight of their successful blow.

"Now!" called Sinclair, and he sprang with an Indian yell over the heads of the sprawling men in the doorway and into the thick of the crowd.

Half a dozen of the drawn guns whipped up at that sight, but no one could make sure in the half-light of the identity of the man who had dashed out. Their imaginations placed the two prisoners safely behind the bars inside. Before they could think twice, a second figure leaped through the doorway and passed them in the opposite direction.

Then they awakened to the fact, but they awakened in confusion. A dozen shots blazed in either direction, but they were wild, snapshots of men taken off balance.

Two leaps took Sinclair through the thick of the astonished men before him. He came to the scattering edges and saw a man dive at him. The cowpuncher beat the butt of his gun into the latter's face and sped on, whipping around the corner of the little jail, with bullets whistling after him.

His own gun, as he leaped out of sight, he fired into the ground, and he heard a similar shot from the far side of the building. Those two shots, as he had predicted, checked the pursuers one vital second and kept them milling in front of the jail. Then they spilled out around the corners, each man running low, his gun ready.

But Sinclair, deep in the darkness of the tree shadows behind the jail, was already out of sight. He caught a glimpse of Arizona sprinting ahead of him for dear life. They reached the cottonwoods together and were greeted by a low shout from the girl; she was running out from the shelter, dragging the horses after her.

Arizona went into his saddle with a single leap. Sinclair paused to take the jump, with his hand on the pommel, and as he lifted himself up with a jump, a gun blazed in point-blank range from the nearest shrubbery.

There was a yell from Arizona, not of pain, but of rage. They saw his gun glisten in his hand, and, swerving his horse to disturb the aim of the marksman, his weapon's first report blended with the second shot from the bushes, a tongue of darting flame. Straight at the flash of a target Arizona had fired, and there was an answering yell. Out of the dark of the shrubbery a great form leaped, with a grotesque shadow beneath it on the moon-whitened ground.

"Cartwright!" cried Sinclair, as the big man collapsed and became a shapeless, inanimate black heap.

Straight ahead Arizona was already spurring, and Sinclair waved once to the white face of Jig, then shot after his companion, while the trees and shrubbery to their left emitted a sudden swarm of men and barking guns.

But to strike a rapidly moving object with a revolver is never easy, and to strike by the moonlight is difficult indeed. A dangerous flight of slugs bored the air around the fugitives for the first hundred yards of their flight, but after that the firing ceased, as the men of Sour Creek ran for their horses.

Straight on into the night rode the pair.

* * *

One year had made Arizona a little plumper, and one year had drawn Riley Sinclair more lean and somber, when they rode out on the shoulder of a flat-topped mountain and looked down into the hollow, where the late afternoon sun was already sending broad shadows out from every rise of ground. Sour Creek was a blur and a twinkle of glass in the distance.

"Come to think of it," said Arizona, "it's just one year today. Riley, was it that that brung you back here, and me, unknowing?"

The tall man made no answer, but shaded his eyes to peer down into the valley, and Arizona made no attempt to pursue the conversation. He was long since accustomed to the silences of his traveling mate. Seeing that Sinclair showed no disposition either to speak or move, he left the big cowpuncher to himself and started off through the trees in search of game. The sign of a deer caught his eye and hurried him on into a futile chase, from which he returned in the early dark of the evening. He was guided by the fire which Sinclair had kindled on the shoulder, but to his surprise, as he drew nearer, the fire dwindled, very much as if Riley had entirely forgotten to replenish it with dry wood.

A year of wild life had sharpened the caution of Arizona. That neglect of his fire was by no means in keeping with the usual methods of Sinclair. Before he came to the last spur of the hill, Arizona dismounted and stole up on foot. He listened intently. There was not a sound of anyone moving about. There was only an occasional crackle of the dying fire. When he came to the edge of the shoulder, Arizona raised his head cautiously to peer over.

He saw a faintly illumined picture of Riley Sinclair, sitting with his hat off, his face raised, and such a light in his face that there needed no play of the fire to tell its meaning. Beside him sat a girl, more distinct, for she was dressed in white, and the fire gleamed and curled and modeled her hair and cast a highlight on her chin, her throat, and her hand in the brown hand of Sinclair.

Arizona winced down out of sight and stole back under the trees.

"Doggone me," he said to his horse, "they both remembered the day."